Winner's Loss

Winner's Loss

Mel Bradshaw

Mel Bradshaw

IGUANA

Publisher: Mary Ann J. Blair
Editor: Jen R. Albert
Front cover image: National Gallery
Front cover design: Daniella Postavsky

Library and Archives Canada Cataloguing in Publication

Bradshaw, Mel, 1947-, author
        Winner's loss / Mel Bradshaw.

Issued in print and electronic formats.
ISBN 978-1-77180-219-2 (softcover)
ISBN 978-1-77180-221-5 (EPUB)
ISBN 978-1-77180-220-8 (Kindle)

        I. Title.

PS8603.R332W56 2017   C813'.6   C2017-904659-4
                                    C2017-904660-8

This is an original print edition of *Winner's Loss*.

For Carol Jackson, my love

I cannot hold to home life being the incentive to creative work —
the quiet home lover is not an artist.

— *Frederick Varley*

Chapter 1

"Who's winning?" said Ruth after Round 1.

Our seats were good and close, just out of spitting range, and I didn't think there was anything wrong with her startling green eyes, but it was her first boxing match.

Not her first time in the CNE Coliseum. Built five years earlier, in 1922, this palatial shed had hosted concerts, religious meetings, horse shows, and bazaars; Ruth Stone had written up a goodly portion of such female-welcoming events for the back pages of the *Daily Dispatch*. Tonight, the arena, set up for prizefighting, was maybe two-thirds full, and of those eight thousand spectators a small minority were women — women not allergic to the smell of cigars and the sound of men screaming for blood to be spilled. Here tonight at my invitation and not on assignment, Ruth was on the edge of her chair.

"Paul?" Patience wasn't her long suit.

"Lucan, in the black shorts there, has the more powerful punch. 'Lights-out' Lucan, they call him."

"But I haven't seen him land a punch."

"Exactly — because Wellington has faster reflexes."

"Go on."

"Every move Lucan makes looks slower to Jack. Danny also tends to cock his fist — pull it back before he punches. It's as bad as a roundhouse swing for sending your opponent a telegram."

"So," said Ruth, "even though Mr. Blue Shorts only seems to be patting Black Shorts with his gloves, nothing heavy at all, he's making contact — and making points?" She squinted her emeralds as she worked this out and with a freckled hand held back off her forehead a wad of frizzy red hair.

Quick *and* cute. I'd never thought a police detective could have this sweet an evening in the company of a newspaper woman.

"The odds were already in Jack's favour, but they'll be longer against Lucan now."

"You betting, Paul?"

I shook my head. The bell for the start of Round 2 rang before she could ask me why not. The truth was I had no quarrel with someone making a buck, albeit an illegal buck, on a clean fight. I just preferred to save my slender pay for rye and, for example, redheads.

By Round 9, the second last, Jack Wellington had extended his lead on points and appeared to have a lock on the Ontario middleweight championship. Without breaking a sweat, he was still dancing away from every punch Lucan threw. The crowd was growing restive. More than a few, both office workers in suits and labourers in overalls, were already making for the exits. Many that remained raised to the naked steel girders overhead cries of "Nuts to this sissy stuff!" and "Paste him, Jack. Knock him cold!"

Ruth's attention too had started to wander. When I'd first suggested an evening of boxing to her, she'd curled a neatly rouged lip and cleared her throat. To get her here, I'd had to make a deal I expected to regret. But then, once the title bout had started, she seemed caught up in it. After her initial fear of being forced to witness maiming and butchery, I wondered if she was now disappointed not to see so much as a split lip.

The referee seemed to be having trouble keeping his attention on the match. He was Roly Hardcastle, a former boxer himself, rumoured to have lost the sight in his left eye to a thumb gouge. Not a fatal handicap if he'd kept his agility, but he was paunchy and stiffer in the joints than a man his age should have been. Physically he resembled Dave Barry, famous as the ref of the recent Tunney–Dempsey rematch.

Then in the ring something changed. It happened fast; distracted spectators could well have missed it. For no apparent reason, Wellington's right foot slid forward when it should have stepped back. I touched Ruth's arm and directed her attention back to the two fighters in time for her to see the consequence of this — frankly unconvincing — stumble. Lucan landed a left square in the middle of Jack's chest. Not with full force: Jack pulled back too far for that. But Lucan at last had something to show for nearly nine scoreless rounds.

I couldn't yet see what Jack was playing at. In the one remaining round, he couldn't walk into enough punches to hand the match to Lucan and make it look real. Perhaps someone had a side bet as to whether Danny would get a glove on Jack, and Jack would get his share if he let it happen. But more drama was in store.

An exaggerated frown settled on Jack's handsome face. He rushed in on Lucan as if that tap on the chest had been a mortal insult. Punches rained down on Danny, above and below the belt. Lucan could take the punishment, blow after blow, but was too slow to retaliate. There was new energy in the Coliseum, and the fans got it now all right. Those on their way out the doors stopped dead in their tracks, mostly to cheer Jack on.

Roly surprised me too. Habitually permissive, he now lost no time moving in to warn Jack about the kidney punches. When the round-ending bell rang, Jack retired scowling to his corner.

"What a temper!" said Ruth. "You'd think Blue Shorts would have himself in hand. He's not a kid, after all."

"Done any theatre reviews?" I asked her.

"Garden *fêtes* and charity balls — that's all they think girl reporters are good for. Are you saying that his anger's all ham acting?"

"Someone's convinced him he can do better throwing this fight than winning it." If I sounded like I knew the score, that it was all old hat for me, I can tell you that was far from true. I'd never have picked nimble Jack Wellington for a cheat.

"Throw it how?"

"Jack's not going to let himself be kayoed. He doesn't have time in one more round to get hit enough to lose it on points, so watch him lose it on fouls."

Round 10 was anticlimax. Wellington had had his warning about not hitting south of Lucan's navel. He did it again and again and Roly disqualified him. To resounding boos, Hardcastle held a grinning Danny "Lights-out" Lucan's hand aloft. Many spectators pelted Roly with apple cores and cigar butts. Someone even threw a chair at him as he was climbing out of the ring.

Jack Wellington meanwhile was spared the crowd's anger. No boos were hurled his way. I watched him slip out flanked by broad-shouldered men with suit jackets buttoned up to hide, I presumed, pistols in shoulder holsters.

Ruth wanted to know if the referee had done anything wrong.

"Nothing," I said. "He was just enforcing the rules. The thing is, that referee usually doesn't. At least, not that quick."

"He's been bought," said Ruth. It wasn't a question, for her or me.

I'd never seen or heard of Ruth Stone before she'd buttonholed me on the steps of City Hall last Friday evening. I noticed a particularly well-shaped pair of legs below her navy pea jacket, but October showers were blowing up from the lake, and I was already late for a dinner invitation to Ned Cruickshank's. I hadn't felt like stopping. Even less so when I saw the notepad in her hand. I don't begrudge journalists a living, but anything I say to one of them always seems to result in nuisance of one sort or another. Here was a case in point: I'd confirmed to a man from the *Toronto Examiner* that I'd won a pistol shoot at the 1927 edition of the Police Games in August. As a result, this girl reporter had clearly settled on me to be the cop that would give her inside guff on the Toronto crime scene. I was to be her ticket up out of the women's columns — columns buried under opaque layers of sports, finance, and political news. She'd been toiling in those inky depths seven long years, she'd have me know. It was time, and then some, to burst into the sunlight of the front page.

I rarely glanced at the *Daily Dispatch*, a rag that couldn't stop crabbing about "undesirable aliens," labour agitators, and the eight-hour day. If I had two cents to throw away on a paper, it was usually the *Toronto Examiner*. Not because of its politics — it favoured restricting the sale of alcohol and lowering the taxes on cigarettes — but because the publisher was related to the detective inspector's wife. In consequence, this was the daily that Sanderson most needed his sleuths to look good in.

I didn't want a nosy newshound underfoot at the crowded detective office in City Hall and had been glad to be able to tell Ruth I had at present no big investigation underway. I found my work boring and was sure she would too. I lifted my hand in something between a salute and a wave and took my leave.

But then I turned and asked her to wait. What had I been thinking? I must have forgotten how fed up I was with the small change of corner-store shoplifters and schoolboy arsonists. It must have slipped my routine-numbed mind that my evenings just now were nothing to look forward to either. And here was a pretty girl offering me some of her time.

She did wait. Pressing her hat down on her head when a gust tried to lift it off, she asked what the ham sandwich I wanted. I asked for her office phone number. She said it was in the book. Instead of looking, I called on her in person the next Monday.

When I told her about the Lucan–Wellington fight, she said that was the worst idea for a date she'd ever heard, but that she'd go if I would subsequently visit an art gallery with her. I gave her credit for finding an equivalent torment.

I'd intended to show her that boxing wasn't all butchery — that, as practised by nimble Jack Wellington, it could be elegant as dance. Now all I could do was make sure she learned as much as possible from this rigged match. She said she wanted to write about crooks, after all.

"Roly's been bought," I said, "but so has Jack."

"You sound disappointed. Jeepers creepers, Paul, you didn't think boxing was pure and perfect, did you? Poor baby." She gave my sleeve a pat.

"I don't know everything about boxing, Miss Stone, but up till now if you wanted to rig a fight, you just bribed the ref. Payoffs to boxers never happen — not in the seven years that fights have been legal in this province. Sure I thought Jack Wellington was straight; that's why I wanted you to see him. He wins his matches without murder and without fouls. So I'm sore enough now to want a word with him. The referee? Forget him. I never had any illusions about Roly; he has no big purses to look forward to and I'm guessing nothing saved for retirement. It'll be hard to pin anything on him anyway. He only did what he should have been doing ever since he traded the gloves for a bow tie. But Jack will have to explain moves both illegal and out of character."

I could hear I was pretty wound up; I didn't mind when a gruff voice broke in.

"I'm with you, Paul. This house of chumps can't see it."

The tall man standing in the aisle beside our seats had a neck as wide as his head. His black eyebrows and moustache bristled fiercely, but curling dark hair and sad, hazel eyes domesticated his looks somewhat. I knew him only as a boxing fan named Oscar. We'd been to a dozen or more of the same fights, and we both liked to sit near the action, so we'd got to trading gossip. He seemed to have no trouble appealing to women. I'd never seen him with the same one twice. This evening, for the first time, he appeared to be alone.

"Who do you think pieced the two of them off?" I named a couple of notorious gamblers. "Pork Chops Lariviere? Duke Abernathy?"

"More Lariviere's style. Complicated, innovative. How you doing, Ruthie?"

"Quite well thank you, Mr. Craig," Ruth drawled. "Broadening my horizons, improving my mind. Close your mouth, Paul. Oscar Craig knows all the females in this town."

"All quarter million of them," I said pleasantly, "not counting pets and insects — and yet he doesn't appear to have a date tonight."

"Tonight I came to paint." Oscar hefted a worn wooden box smudged with traces of various colours.

"And did you?" I was surprised to hear about Oscar's painting. He fit my image of the underfed, tubercular artist so little that I was curious to see his work.

"Nothing on show tonight worth setting up for."

"Put money on Wellington?" I asked.

From Oscar's pained expression, I gathered he had — quite a bit. "Actually," he said, "the picture I wanted was of Lucan knocking that lily out of the ring. Some washout!"

"Not my evening," Ruth bragged. "Mr. Shenstone's going to make an arrest. I've never seen one before."

"And you won't be seeing one tonight," I said.

All humanity went out of Oscar's eyes. His cheek muscles tightened. I was used to bad reactions to the news I'm a cop. Maybe Craig's was more extreme because he'd been unlawfully gambling on a fight. To do him credit, he recovered his balance quicker than most people do.

"I could drive Ruth home if you want to chase after the bad guys," he said.

I told him that wouldn't be necessary. Minutes later we saw Oscar speed out of the parking lot behind the wheel of a battle-scarred black roadster while we stood in line outside the Coliseum waiting for a taxi. I was torn between, on the one hand, taking Ruth straight back to her parents' house in Forest Hill so I could go looking for Wellington and Lariviere and, on the other, inviting her to a speak. Sale of alcohol for home consumption had been legal since the end of March, but there were still no licensed bars or restaurants.

Sticking with Ruth had the edge. I was still thinking of the mocking yet familiar way she'd caressed my arm — my jacket at least — after the fight; I wanted to see what next.

"Would you like to go — "

"My Blue Heaven," she blurted out.

"Somewhere quiet, for a drink."

"I don't drink," she said, "but I'm sure Pork Chops Lariviere would serve you."

"I'm not taking you to his club."

"Phooey to that. I can look after myself."

"Odds are you can — but I'm not going to risk it."

I could almost hear her teeth grinding.

"Then take me to the *Dispatch* building, King and Bay."

I hadn't got her to change her tune by the time all the people ahead of us had left and a big, square-backed cab was waiting for us to climb in. She gave the address even before we were settled onto the cracked leather back seat. I debated with her a bit more, but couldn't shake her. She was determined to get back to her typewriter.

"Won't your sports reporter be filing the story of the fight?" I asked at last.

"My story will be better. Buy tomorrow's paper and see whose they publish."

"I like your spunk, Ruth. Just don't go making accusations you can't prove — and whatever you do, keep me out of it."

I was sure I was going to regret telling her anything about boxing.

"You'll be 'a source who asked not to be identified.'"

This didn't sound like the cue for a good-night kiss. I took one anyway. She didn't fight it, but kept it brief. I asked when I could see her again.

"As soon as you have a juicy murder case to tell me about. Or when you're ready to keep your end of our bargain."

"I'd rather look at you than a flat bunch of pictures."

"That's because you can't look without tasting."

The cab jolted to a stop with a squeak from the brakes. I got out and opened her door. Then I held open one of the brass-bound glass doors of her building. Ruth brushed my cheek with the back of her hand as she went through. I watched the swaying back of her knee-length navy skirt all the way across the lobby until it and she disappeared into an elevator.

Lariviere had built his joint just out of town, beyond a Toronto detective's jurisdiction. He'd picked a lot on the east bank of the Don River, near a street that happened to be called Gamble Avenue. Public transportation was sparse. I kept the taxi, even though it would mean living on stale bread and Klim powdered milk the rest of the week. At least it wasn't one of those clubs that charged a membership fee.

As it turned out, all I got for my money and time was support for Oscar's hunch that Pork Chops was behind the rigged fight. In the large brick house, I found neither club owner nor crooked boxer, but I did see Roly Hardcastle gambling away a wad of money I fancied could only be his share of the payoff. Inquiries after Wellington got me nowhere. I borrowed a phone book. He wasn't in there either.

I had the cab drop me at City Hall. I could get a Queen streetcar home from here. And I wanted to poke my nose into police headquarters to see if one of the other detective sergeants could spot me five dollars till payday. Howarth was the softest touch, but Parsons or Nichol would likely also oblige. Unluckily, Rudy Crate was the only one on duty — a tall, well-fed, rosy-complexioned Englishman, who in his four decades on earth had absorbed the wrong half of "neither a borrower nor a lender be."

"Desolate, old man. I haven't a sixpence. Say, you know the woman that fell off a scaffold while painting a mural at Christ Church Grange Park?"

A lame diversion if I ever heard one. "Sure," I said. "The coroner has ruled it an accident."

"The parish priest phoned our inspector to report that the dead woman had been the object of threats."

"Oh?" With a missed breakfast staring me in the face, I hadn't much appetite for office gossip.

"Sanderson means to have you look into them as soon as you show up for work tomorrow morning."

"I'd better be on time then."

Rudy grinned, but I meant it. What started as gossip had turned into a job.

The threats could be the work of a crackpot, perhaps a poor loser. I seemed to recall that the deceased's mural design had won a competition with a sizable purse. As I rode the streetcar home that evening — Thursday, October 13 — I was ready for the assignment to lead nowhere. But it was a life and death matter, and it reminded me of why I'd wanted this work in the first place.

At the same time, the feeling was growing on me that — whether I liked it or not — my art education was about to begin.

Chapter 2

Next morning, I found Inspector Sanderson no more convinced than I was that the rumour of threats against the life of the painter Nora Britton would lead anywhere. Nonetheless, the source of the report — rector of the church where the mural was being painted — was owed the courtesy of a face-to-face interview with a detective. Was social status the ace of trumps for the inspector? You never heard that from me, but he was always aware of a citizen's place in the pecking order and tried to accommodate it. For my part, I'd have been just as happy to speak to a street sweeper. Anything to get out of the office on my own.

Christ Church Grange Park lay a half-dozen blocks or so west of City Hall along Queen Street, not many minutes at a brisk walk. A morning temperature hovering around fifty degrees meant I wasn't going to work up a sweat.

As I walked, I took note of the people I was sharing the streets and sidewalks with. It was a habit formed at the start of my police career when I pounded a beat. Today, though, there was something more. I was still sore about the rigged fight I'd paid to see last night. And had taken a girl to, a new date I'd wanted to impress. Jack Wellington had no reason I knew of to be afoot on Queen Street this morning, but I didn't want to miss him on the off chance he was. I scrutinized every face.

To my left, south towards Union Station, lay the many office towers and sites where more towers — but taller — were scheduled to be built. Stenographer-typists and clerks of various descriptions went scurrying across my path in that direction to arrive ahead of their overlords — men sauntering along after them in morning coats and starched shirts with detachable stiff collars. One of the few benefits of the Great War was the coming into vogue of soft shirts with sewn-on soft collars. These were what we soldiers had been issued, and if they were smart enough for the city's military heroes, they would without question do nicely in peacetime for those of us that didn't have the misfortune to be chairman of the board.

The people I passed, those walking east towards Queen and Yonge while I walked west, likely included sales clerks, their pace quickened by the necessity to arrive at the shops in time to open the doors to the public.

The magnets drawing pedestrians north, to my right, were more varied. Lawyers were hastening into Osgoode Hall to argue their cases in one of the handsome courtrooms; well-dressed students were pressing into the lecture rooms of the Hall's law school. Just behind the pillared and porticoed Osgoode Hall, however, and behind the stone towers and turrets of City Hall, all the way up to the hospitals on College Street stretched a neighbourhood known as the Ward, the city's most notorious slum. Not a tenement-house slum typical of many a metropolis. Instead, in the Ward you'd find streets full of once respectable, now disintegrating, single-storey frame or roughcast houses with the addition of shacks inexpertly cobbled together from scraps and shoehorned into the miniature back yards. For fifty years, these had been the first dwellings of immigrants, impoverished refugees who paid low rents and got nothing back by way of maintenance or repairs. The land was valuable and becoming more so every year as the city grew, but few of the residents owned the premises they occupied. The landlords lived in Rosedale or Forest Hill.

Comfortably remote from the smell and squalour, they were simply waiting for the chance to sell dear to some institution or company that required a site in the heart of town.

Men heading in or out of the Ward were, if lucky, factory or construction workers in denim overalls. Those denied salaried employment because they were unskilled or spoke or worshipped strangely might be ragpickers, bootleggers, or bookies' touts. The women would sew or take in laundry, which they hung out to dry in sooty alleys. Some sold scrawny chickens or rabbits raised in spaces already crowded with children that just kept coming. More surprising than the seediness of many of the Ward's residents was the carefully brushed and scrubbed appearance of others. Their clothes might be ill-fitting castoffs, but they took pride in looking clean and decent when they stepped out onto Queen Street.

Someone had told me that the Ward was where Jack Wellington had grown up. Jack Kaplinsky he was then. Unlikely, though, that he still had family here. As the old sheds got bulldozed, the evicted Jews and Italians had been moving west, into the Kensington Market area on the far side of University Avenue. Now that block was in turn becoming the sardine can of the least well off.

It was in this "New Ward," not far from the art gallery, that I found Christ Church Grange Park. I made the mistake of referring to the detached house behind it as the manse, but the Reverend Eric Hutchinson put me straight on his doorstep, before I'd even been shown into his study.

"You're betraying your Presbyterian background there, Mr. Shenstone. The Church of England in Canada calls this the rectory. We need not get into the difference between a rectory and a vicarage. That distinction has meaning only in the Church of England proper."

Inspector Sanderson had warned me that Hutchinson was known for his precision of mind and could also be long-winded, but that I should hear him out. I'd also been told not to infer that the man lacked drive or ability from the fact that at age seventy plus he was still a priest and not a bishop.

A black-and-white photograph of the rector behind a radio microphone bearing the letters CFRB hung prominently on one study wall, while another was decorated with one of him pouring a glass of milk for a girl in a torn dress under a sign reading "Downtown Children's Clinic."

He seated me at the dining room table that served him as a desk and took a place opposite. Before either of us spoke, there was a moment of mutual summing up. He would have seen in me a clean-shaven, brown-haired, brown-eyed man of thirty-five years, a bit short for a cop perhaps, but someone otherwise meeting popular expectations in terms of physique. Someone you might put on a tug-of-war team, though not heavy enough for the anchor. My wardrobe was far from dapper. Some policemen wore plain clothes as if they were a uniform — made-to-measure if they could stretch their pay that far. The elderly Detective Sergeant Parsons came to mind. My grey ready-to-wear suit needed a pressing; the four-in-hand knot in my tie was never chokingly tight. From what he could see, Eric Hutchinson might have concluded that my shoes under his table needed polishing. He wouldn't have been wrong.

Meanwhile, looking across the table, I noted that the rector had white hair, large ears, and creases bracketing his firm mouth. The flesh of his face was lined with experience, but taut. His neck appeared to fit neatly within his starched clerical collar. Neither stout nor emaciated, he sat erect and still except for his pale hands, which restlessly nudged about the table before him two or three hand-written pages of notes. What I'd noticed first about his appearance, though, before any of this, was his silver-rimmed pince-nez spectacles, a style which had been common enough towards the end of the last century. On an older face today, they could look like a stale holdover. Not on him. Perhaps it was the sharply focused copper-brown eyes behind the lenses.

I kicked off the interview on a formal note. The public expected it.

"Mr. Hutchinson, I'm advised you have information relevant to the death of Nora Britton. Something you didn't mention when you telephoned the police to report finding her body, or afterwards when Constable Nanos came to the scene."

"Just so. Why didn't I speak up? At first, I was too shocked at seeing her lying crumpled on the floor of the chancel. In life, she didn't give the impression of being a small woman. She had a quiet radiance that seemed to fill the space around her. But in death she looked no bigger than a child. A dead child — there is no more pitiful sight. And then, later, when I had my wits more about me..." The rector's resonant voice trailed off, but he quickly adjusted his pince-nez and resumed his professorial air. "Mr. Shenstone, I've always disliked being the retailer of tittle-tattling gossip, and what I heard may be no more than that. So I said nothing. Only when I saw Nora's death written up in the papers as unequivocally an accident did I experience a change of heart. I felt angry on her behalf. It was as if she wasn't getting her due from any of us, and who was I to put my aversion to telling tales out of school above her need for justice?"

"I understand that this gossip so-called took the form of threats. Who made them?"

"Detective, how much do you know about Nora Britton and the mural commission?"

Questions were mounting up into a log jam. I added one more: "Do you plan on answering me eventually, Mr. Hutchinson?"

"Indeed, yes."

"Swell," I said. I was prepared to give the rector all morning as long as we were getting to the bottom of this death. I was in no rush to get back to the office. "You haven't had another change of heart?"

"Nothing like that, Mr. Shenstone."

"All I've read is the constable's report. It doesn't give the background."

"Allow me to supply it. The previous church on this site, the old St. Pancras, burned down forty-three years ago." Hutchinson shifted his notes and looked to confirm that the number he'd mentioned was accurate. A small smile told me it was. "The present structure is a late Victorian replacement, a third larger than its predecessor. But there was a price to be paid for the enlargement. As this area was already built up, the new east wall had to be constructed flush against the glove factory next door. The customary east window behind the altar was out of the question. Instead, it was suggested that a mural be painted on that wall. In 1910, the Art Gallery of Toronto — at the time called the Art Museum of Toronto — moved into the old Boulton house, known as the Grange. Art-loving members of our congregation, wishing to celebrate our proximity to this cultural institution, moved to have the new St. Pancras renamed Christ Church Grange Park. In this atmosphere, the mural idea gained in popularity, but still with no agreement on a subject or how such an ambitious painting was to be paid for. Meanwhile, the change of name proceeded with little expenditure and, not coincidentally, little debate. Then came the war — among the many consequences of which was to give the mural project an urgency and a theme. Almost from the moment of the Armistice, there was talk of a suitable memorial for the twenty-eight men of the congregation who fell in France and Belgium. Last year, one of our more affluent parishioners — yes, we do have them, as well as the poor — moved beyond talk. Sir Joseph Deane undertook to sponsor a competition to see who could come up with the best design for an east-wall painting that would honour our war dead."

"And Nora Britton won," I said, to nudge the narrative along.

"Not the first competition." Hutchinson seemed to take a grim satisfaction in the complexity of his tale. "Not Nora Britton — her husband. I should make it clear that the judges were instructors from the most respected academies — the

Ontario College of Art, the Slade School, the Art Institute of Chicago. And the judging was blind. The judges knew nothing whatever about the entrants, nothing outside the submissions themselves. Their choice of the best design was unanimous. I can see you have a question, detective. Go on."

"Why did Mr. Britton not get the commission?"

"Exactly. And the answer is: because his name is not Britton, but Koch."

Hutchinson pronounced it *koc*. "Spell that please," I said.

The rector did so. "And his birthplace is Hanover, Germany. When the winner was announced, the protests began. We had a mural committee consisting of myself, Sir Joseph Deane, and two other parishioners — who, truth to tell, left everything to us. Members of the congregation told the committee that the verdict of the judges must be set aside. Our boys had been killed by Germans, and it would be a travesty and an insult to let a German paint their memorial. May I ask if you served overseas?"

"Four years, infantry," I said. "It's no secret."

Still, not many people asked anymore. It wasn't often that I thought of those four years as one continuous stretch of time, the hours of waiting in barracks or a trench, the shelling and the poison gas, the named battles and the lightning raids, all strung together. All that time our enemies had been Germans, all right, but I never could feel one with the German-haters. If I harboured any distaste for the people and their names, it rarely came to my attention.

"I was too old to offer my services as a chaplain," Hutchinson continued. "There was work to do on the home front, of course, but I'm uncomfortable criticizing the attitudes of men like you, who faced the foe directly. One of the loudest voices raised in opposition to letting Koch paint the mural was that of a young man who'd served in the merchant marine. Every moment he was on the water, he lived with the fear of being torpedoed, aware that if he survived the sinking of his ship there would be no room on the attacking U-boat for prisoners and that none would be taken. I told Sir Joseph that I didn't think a sermon from me on turning the other cheek would be enough to allow the winning design to be executed and received in the proper spirit of solemn remembrance. I could see that such a sermon was needed, right enough, but judged it best delivered once the dust had settled and passions cooled."

"And what did Joe Deane think?"

I had just managed to place the sponsor of the mural competition. Joseph Deane, the pulp and paper man, president of Chapleau Forest Industries. It was said that Joe wouldn't know a forest if he were lost in one, and had certainly never made the five-hundred-mile trip to the town of Chapleau. He may never have been farther north than the cottage country of Lake Simcoe. His days were spent cultivating world markets, acquiring smaller or ailing concerns, and generally making deals on the stock exchanges of Bay Street and Wall Street. He'd done well enough at it to donate miles of paper for recruiting and bond posters during the war. He'd even paid for the advertising talent that made those posters so persuasive, and for these contributions had been awarded a baronetcy in 1916 or '17. Soldiers' jokes about city-slicker Joe were generally good-natured; he could have been one of the war profiteers and wasn't.

"*Sir* Joseph," Hutchinson insisted with some severity, "asked me to call a meeting of the congregation. He knew it would be contentious. Even his own sister, Mary-Maud Deane, was against the Koch design."

Before the rector could get farther, the study door was knocked on and immediately opened by a full-figured, fiftyish woman in a pink apron smudged with flour.

"Mr. Leavitt is here again about the Children's Clinic, Eric. He said you were expecting him."

Hutchinson got up and went to speak to her in an undertone. "Very well, my dear," he concluded before she left the room and he returned to his chair. To me, he said, "This man is a lay representative of the Goel Tzedec synagogue. I was not expecting him specifically this morning, but his visits at any hour no longer surprise me. His congregation can't seem to abide the health and nutritional aid Christ Church is providing to his poorer co-religionists, even though they need it desperately."

"The mural meeting, Mr. Hutchinson," I reminded him. "I assume it was decided to hold a second competition."

"Not then and there. Before we got that far, the gathering broke up in rancour. Oh, it started pleasantly enough. Sir Joseph Deane arrived in a jovial mood — confident that a man like himself, accustomed to subduing to his will the money men of New York, would find little challenge in guiding a parish meeting out of error. He started his remarks with evidence that Herman Koch is an artist of the first rank. Paintings of his have been bought by the National Gallery. Paintings of his were chosen to represent Canada at the British Empire Exhibition at Wembley — where they attracted favourable notice from *The Times*. The Christ Church mural design was thoroughly up to this standard, impressing the three judges with its beauty and power. But, Sir Joseph said, the congregation didn't have to take his word for the quality of Herman Koch's work: he had brought with him a magic lantern projector and slides of Koch's paintings together with those of two leading contemporaries for comparison. That's when a grandfather in the front row called out, 'Never mind the slides; the man's German.' Sir Joseph affably challenged the gathering to look carefully and see if they could distinguish the works of the Canadian-born Lawren Harris or the British-born Frederick Varley from those of the German-born Herman Koch. He pointed out that Koch had come to Canada with his parents in 1896, at age nine."

"Did Herman Koch ever apply for naturalization?" I asked.

"I was just coming to that," said the rector. "He became a British subject and Canadian citizen when he turned twenty-one, the earliest he could legally do so."

"Go on."

"Well! At this point in the meeting, a leading member of the congregation, son of the Methuselah in the front row and father of that merchant sailor I mentioned earlier, said — here, I've written down his exact words — 'Naturalization of an individual does not make him a Canadian in the true sense of the word. He may be naturalized, but he does not come in on an equal footing in any sense.' This gentleman went on to say that asking Koch to paint the memorial mural was 'like asking the relatives of a murdered man to accept a memorial or tomb constructed by the cousin of the man who committed the murder.'

"Our church wardens both agreed. One, an art collector in a minor way, claimed the style of Koch's design was Germanic, not British in the least. Sir Joseph knew his brief and wasn't about to yield a single point. He replied that Lawren Harris had studied art for four years in Berlin and that it was much more likely that his work showed German influences than that they should be found in the work of a painter who had received his artistic education exclusively in North America. Chicago, Montreal, and New York.

"In the end, however, evidence and reason stood no chance. A war amputee, who before 1914 had been a telephone lineman and keen amateur football player, said that a mural designed by a German-born artist would dishonour our war dead, and that he'd sooner spit on it than look at it. Plainly the tone of the assembly had become too intemperate to allow for the viewing of Sir Joseph's slides. Herman Koch's design, however admirable, was now a lost cause. As a way out, I suggested we award the mural commission to the runner-up in the competition. Sir Joseph wouldn't hear of it; he didn't want to sit in his pew week after week confronted with artwork that the most perceptive judges of painting had certified second rate. When he'd delivered that ultimatum, my only course was to calm passions with a moment of prayer and adjourn the meeting. Do you smoke, Mr. Shenstone?"

Hutchinson opened a silver cigarette box and tilted it in my direction. I shook my head.

"Bad lungs," I said. "Don't let me stop you, though. I can see your flock's a handful."

"I wouldn't put it quite that way. But, as I'm sure you've found for yourself, every group — however well-conducted in general — has its unstable elements."

"What happened next?"

The rector adjusted his pince-nez and continued with his lighted cigarette in one hand and his notes in the other.

"The turmoil in our parish reached the bishop's ears, and he telephoned to ask me how I intended to calm the waters. I told him and told our committee I could not permit Mr. Koch's design to be executed, even if turning it down meant the loss for Christ Church Grange Park of a very valuable gift. I was prepared to hear Sir Joseph say he would be taking his largesse to another church. St. Simon-the-Apostle is actually closer to his home. My suspicions were misplaced: Sir Joseph Deane is a bigger man than that. Disappointed as he was, his first concern was that Herman Koch receive the promised prize money of $500. I agreed that was only just, at the same time pointing out that we still had to make some provision for memorializing our war dead, even if only by attaching a bronze plaque to a wall of the chancel. Sir Joseph then offered to sponsor a second competition, the conditions of which would stipulate that entrants must have been born in this country or in one of the countries with whom we were allied in the war."

"I understand that Nora Britton was born in Aurora, Ontario. Is that correct?"

"A village thirty miles north of here. Yes, that's what I told the constable that came to the church on Tuesday morning."

"And she won that second competition?"

"Once we had screened candidates for eligibility, the judgement of artistic merit was again blind. An altogether different trio of experts agreed that the best design was that of Nora Britton."

"Do you have a copy of the design here?"

"Sir Joseph Deane has a copy. You'd have to see him about it. I couldn't even give you a description, but he'll enthuse about it and point out its many excellences. He's just as keen on this idea for the memorial mural as he was on the one before. Perhaps more so: he recognized Miss Britton as an artist that had painted sympathetic streetscapes and portraits in the poverty-stricken neighbourhoods of our own parish. The mural committee breathed a sigh of relief."

A happy ending, I thought, if you didn't take later events into account. I understood that a long road remained to get us up to the winner's death three days ago.

"Pin down some dates if you have them," I said. "The announcement of the results of the two competitions for a start."

Hutchinson put out his cigarette and re-sorted his notes. "April 1, 1926 for the first and for the second February 2, 1927."

"Eight months ago. And when did Miss Britton actually start work in your church?"

"This past August. Not incidentally a time when church attendance falls off and some of what I've called our unstable elements are out of town."

"These elements objected to Nora Britton's getting the mural commission?"

"Not immediately. Well, there were murmurs that such a large and important job should have been given to a man. And the murmurs gained currency when members of the congregation met Miss Britton for the first time. As I say, she was small even for a woman. Doubts were raised as to whether she'd have the strength to execute a painting of over four hundred square feet. But our Women's Auxiliary raised their voices for her loudly enough to drown out the early naysayers. No, the real trouble started later. In May of this year, someone brought it to the congregation's attention that Nora Britton was married to Herman Koch. Neither artist had made any secret about the marriage, and it was mentioned in passing from time to time in various periodicals. But the objectors among us are not the sort to follow art news closely. The fact that Miss Britton was indeed the wife of Mr. Koch was exclaimed upon as if it had taken industrious sleuthing to break through a conspiracy of silence and bring this scandalous connection to light."

"Was the marriage taken as a disqualification?"

"It seemed to license the know-nothings to pronounce Miss Britton's design 'Teutonic in conception.' It was even suggested that the design was not Nora Britton's at all, but rather her husband's. In any event, it was totally out of accord with how 'we British people' think of our dead."

Hutchinson raised an ironic eyebrow and looked for a reaction. I nodded him on.

"A fact conveniently overlooked is that many of our parishioners are not British at all but hail from a variety of European countries. Some are from the Far East. Not a few are former Catholics or Jews." The rector waved a hand to one side. "Well, we handled the mural dissenters differently this second time around. No meeting was called. Sir Joseph Deane was adamant that we stick to our guns. I myself advised the church wardens that I should not want to continue as rector of Christ Church Grange Park if Nora Britton were deprived of the commission. In two or three weeks, the clamour died down. I heard no more complaints through the spring and summer. Which brings us to September."

"What happened last month?" I asked. Having done without breakfast as an economy measure, my stomach was starting to think of lunch.

"When the people that had taken a vacation from church in August returned after Labour Day, they were disturbed to find a scaffold erected at the east end of the chancel. The mural became less theoretical and, for the few anti-German zealots, more threatening. This was when I heard language that, in the light of Nora Britton's death, I now think it my duty to report."

"Did these threats come from the family you alluded to — the sailor, his father, and grandfather?"

"Principally."

"It's time to tell me their names, Mr. Hutchinson."

"Stillwater. Archie Stillwater is the sailor."

"And what did you hear him say?"

"That women are no good with heights. Most likely 'Frau Koch' would fall off her scaffold and break her neck, and Christ Church would be rid of her. He'd even be happy to climb up there with her and show her the dangers."

"And did he seem in earnest?"

"He might claim now he was making a joke, but I didn't take it as one. Mind you, I don't imagine he actually pushed her to her death. She was alone when we broke into the sanctuary and found her. All the doors had been locked from the inside."

I got the rector to look up Archie Stillwater's address for me. He didn't make a fuss about it. Then I asked what else he'd heard of a similar nature.

"Archie's grandfather, Jordan Stillwater, is a retired pharmacist. He lives at the same address. Some think he's getting senile; others say he's just outspoken. He said, not to me but in my hearing, that his work had taught him how to prepare poisons the police had no way of detecting, and that if he wanted to he could rid Christ Church of this German-loving ... woman. He used another word I won't repeat. He was addressing one of the church wardens, a man Mr. Stillwater thought opposed to Miss Britton's being granted the commission."

"How about the amputee, the man that talked of spitting on Mr. Koch's mural? Was he equally opposed to letting Nora Britton do the job?"

"His name is Carl Moretti. I didn't hear anything from him one way or the other. All the same, I'll jot down his address for you too."

"Any nastiness from anyone else?"

"A few grumblings, no explicit threats. I should assure you that hostility to Miss Britton was by no means universal. I'd say rather that most people, when they actually met her, took to her right away. Some became ardent admirers."

"Including you," I said.

"Including me," Eric Hutchinson replied simply. "I have a photo here I've been meaning to frame and hang with the others in this room."

The rector went to a bookshelf and between a Bible and a hymnal found a manila envelope. From it he drew an eight-by-ten-inch photo and looked at it a moment with a softened expression on his face before handing it to me. It was of the rector and a woman, both in profile, standing in a church. The picture showed him pointing up to the left at what I thought must be the wall to be decorated, the east wall of the chancel. At his side, a half step back and nearer the camera, Nora Britton was looking where he pointed. She was indeed small and striking. Dark, straight hair was pulled tightly back from a centre part into a chignon low on the nape of her neck. If a face appeals to you, as hers did strongly to me, it's usually a waste of breath to try to break it down into the constituents of beauty. Other people may have no use for a straight nose, full lips, a clean jaw line, and pale, unblemished skin. All I can say is they looked good on her. She wore a loose white smock with wide lapels and cuffs, wore it unbuttoned and secured around the waist by a man's wide leather belt. Under her right arm she held a portfolio case.

"What you can't see in the photo," Hutchinson said, "is that she was kind and soft-spoken, quietly courageous, and immensely talented. I want to do what I can for her. I wish it were more."

Chapter 3

I got Hutchinson to show me the church. On the outside, like the rectory, it was red brick for the most part, with yellow brick at the corners, over the windows, and wherever else the Victorians thought it would look good. The windows and door frames of the church, but not the rectory, were pointy. So were the belfry and the gables. Hutchinson said the style was Gothic; I didn't argue. I thought the steep slope of the roof would come in handy in two or three months for shedding snow.

Up against the east wall, I spotted Swagger Handwear — a plain, grey-brick cube — through the open windows of which sang out a chorus of sewing machines. Across the east–west street that paralleled the south walls of factory and church stood a shabby-looking row of shops with one floor of flats above them. The west door of Christ Church faced a side street at the north end of which lay a patch of grass I recognized as Grange Park and beyond the grass, the gallery. A mixed neighbourhood in sum, with industry, culture, and commerce cheek by jowl.

While I was taking in the geography, Hutchinson was finding his key among several on a metal ring. The west door had been fitted with a lock well-regarded in police circles. That the installation was recent I inferred from the rector's apparent unfamiliarity with what the key looked like and which way it turned.

Once we got inside, I was impressed by the amount of natural light. Each one of the windows in the side walls was nine-tenths plain glass with just a few coloured pieces depicting a flower. Roughly a dozen rows of pews faced something like a very large alcove at the east end. This alcove area I took to be what Hutchinson had referred to as the chancel, for a scaffold made of wooden sticks stood up against its rear wall. The chancel, two steps up from the body of the church, had no windows, so I had to get the rector to turn on some electric lamps. By their light, I saw that the raised floor was made up of broad boards of bare polished wood. No possibility of a soft landing there. Hutchinson walked me across them to the base of the bamboo frame and pointed up to its top.

"That's where she was last working."

"Do you know what time she arrived at the church?"

"She had a key, so as a rule she came and went as she pleased without notification. But last Monday evening, just after seven, she stopped by to let me know she intended to paint all night. She came straight here from the rectory. I've kept the sanctuary locked since Tuesday morning. I didn't think the scaffold should be touched in case the authorities wanted to look at it."

I looked. I hadn't encountered anything like it before. There was a building boom on in Toronto, so you saw lots of construction scaffolding, but all of it was metal tubes with metal couplers. Wood was used only for the deck elements men stood on to do their work. This scaffold in the church was apparently bamboo poles lashed together not with rope or wire but with fibre strips. The poles formed squares of a little less than a yard each side, with the occasional reinforcement of poles lashed on diagonally.

I didn't know what artists customarily stood on for mural painting. Perhaps bamboo scaffolding was standard. Indoors there would be no worry about weather rot. But still it seemed a remarkable structure. I tugged at it experimentally and chinned myself on one of the cross members just above my head. Nothing budged. Still I hesitated before climbing the ladder incorporated into one end. It was possible that Nora Britton's death had resulted from some accidental defect or deliberate sabotage of this jumble of matchsticks. In neither case could the surviving portion be counted on as sound.

What the hell, I thought, and went up.

Because of the slope of the chancel roof, the scaffold was higher in the centre, where Hutchinson had pointed. To get to this highest level, I had to leave the first ladder and proceed along some deck planking to the centre, where a shorter ladder took me the rest of the way. Looking down, I judged the artist must have fallen a distance of between twenty-two and twenty-five feet.

On the deck at this point sat what I presumed were Nora Britton's art supplies and knapsack. The portion of the plaster wall adjacent to where she had been working was painted green. I hadn't seen her design, so had no idea what this represented — whether sky or foliage — or whether it was a foundation layer of colour meant to be painted over later. None of this set off any alarm bells. It did seem as if Miss Britton had spilled a lot of something on her canvas knapsack. It was so stained and encrusted that in places its original khaki colour disappeared entirely. It smelled bad too: after one sniff, I kept it as far from my nose as possible. But what did I know about a muralist's materials? An expert could have told me that paint only binds to plaster with a mixture of rotten eggs and skunk's urine and I wouldn't have raised an eyebrow.

If there was anything at all screwy about the set-up, it was the railing that ran between the deck and the drop. Nothing was broken or loose, but the horizontal bamboo poles had been lashed on too low, I thought, to provide any measure of safety. It might not have been hard for Nora Britton to topple over. On the other hand, Hutchinson had said she was an uncommonly small woman. I left the paints and brushes and took the knapsack back down with me.

"What did Miss Britton normally carry in here?" I asked Hutchinson when I got back to floor level.

"Food and drink, I suppose." The rector drew a gold watch from his waistcoat pocket and gave it a quick glance. "She worked through mealtimes, and sometimes through the night. Mr. Shenstone, I'm afraid I have a meeting with the local branch of the CETS at twelve. So if you have more questions, you'd better telephone me later in the afternoon."

Waiting while I clambered about the scaffolding had made Hutchinson impatient. I tried to hide my satisfaction. Now he would have no time to listen to himself talk; his answers to my questions stood a much better chance of being brief and to the point. And if they were incomplete, I could, as he said, always come at him again later.

"Working through the night can make you woozy. Was she under pressure to meet a deadline?"

"No pressure from me," said Hutchinson. "I may have asked her what she thought the chances were of having the mural completed for Armistice Day."

"But neither you nor Joe Deane nor anyone associated with the project held a gun to her head?"

"Emphatically not. She knew we'd never have wanted her to endanger her health."

"November 11 is less than a month away. Given how little colour is on the wall now, it looks like she hadn't a prayer of finishing by then. Not on her own. Did she have anyone to help her with the painting?"

"There was talk, but nothing definite. She told me frankly we should be thinking of a dedication closer to Christmas."

"The former pharmacist mentioned poison." I jiggled the knapsack I had hooked over my arm. "Would Jordan Stillwater have had access to Miss Britton's food?"

"Not in a regular way."

"Irregularly?" I persisted.

"I've told you she won admirers in the congregation. Women knew how hard she worked and quite often prepared treats or snacks for her — cake, sandwiches, fruit baskets, salads."

"Where would Jordan Stillwater come in?"

"He has time on his hands now that he's retired. Sometimes he fills it with visits to parishioners' homes. It's possible he delivered some of those food parcels to the church when Miss Britton was there."

"But surely any admirer would have avoided entrusting food for Nora Britton to a man who had talked of killing her."

"Not everyone would have heard that talk."

"And if they had?"

"And if they had they mightn't have set any store by it whatever. People were used to hearing Jordan spout any sort of foolishness."

"But you did set store by it, or I wouldn't be here. Why was your attitude to the man different?"

"I knew he'd been in trouble with the law. You can look that up. Now I really should — "

"Just a few more questions, Mr. Hutchinson," I said pleasantly. "I know you want to help Miss Britton. You can talk while I walk you back to the rectory. The floor here looks clean: did Nora Britton spill any blood on it?"

"There was none, thank God." The rector shivered. "As I've said, I was upset enough as it was. I think the sight of that poor girl's blood would have broken me completely. Ah, my voice is shaking. I'm sorry, detective."

"Don't worry about that," I said. I believed his distress was real. "I see there are two doors to this sanctuary besides the one we used. You say Miss Britton couldn't have been pushed to her death because all the doors were locked Tuesday morning. Does that mean that even with your keys you couldn't get in?"

"Strangely, yes." The rector's voice strengthened. I'd given him a subject on which to hold forth. "The west door we came in and the south door both lead directly outside, and both were fitted with inside bolts when the church was built, or at least before the beginning of my tenure."

"Simple barrel lock bolts with no key and no way of opening from outside?"

"Exactly. The north door, by contrast, the door leading to the vestry, had no such fastening until Nora Britton started working here."

"Did she ask to have one installed?"

"She did not. She must have known I never would have allowed a lock with the potential to exclude me from my own church."

"So she bought and installed one herself?"

"Apparently so, because on Tuesday morning the caretaker had to break open the door to the church from the vestry. This was not difficult because the barrel bolt that had been added was smaller than those on the other doors."

"And in your comings and goings before Tuesday you never noticed the new bolt?"

"I'm embarrassed to admit I did not. If I had, I'd have had it removed."

"Any idea why she might have felt the need for such a lock?"

"None," said the rector. "I gave her a key to the church so she could work here whenever she pleased, whether I was around or not. I can only assume she had an unusually strong aversion to being disturbed or even observed while she painted."

I had a look at the door in question. The bolt was indeed better suited to a kitchen cupboard than to a door this size. The hasp was dangling by one screw from the door frame; the wood in which the other screw had been embedded had been torn away. I concluded that if anyone had pushed Nora Britton to her death, that person would have had to be concealed somewhere in the sanctuary when the rector and the caretaker broke in: the murderer could not have fled leaving all three doors bolted from inside, however insecurely.

I accompanied Hutchinson through the vestry and out into the cool, clear day. My thoughts turned again to food — and drink. I decided to let the rector get to his meeting.

"Just curious: what does CETS stand for?"

"Church of England Temperance Society. Are you an abstainer, Mr. Shenstone?"

"During interviews," I assured him. Little as I wanted to prolong this one, it occurred to me to ask if Hutchinson had ever met Herman Koch.

"No," he said. "Why do you ask?"

"Just wondering if he was jealous of his wife's success, the success that should have been his. He won the contest, then lost the commission. That could make a guy sore. Doubly so when he lost it to a wife that wouldn't take his German name."

"Oh no," said Hutchinson. "The only reason she kept the name Britton was that she already had an artistic reputation when she married. She and Herman Koch were very close and loving."

I was walking back east towards City Hall when a middle-aged man in a white jacket popped out of one of the shops opposite the church.

"Excuse me, mister. Have you just been talking to the Reverend? Simon Leavitt's the name. He won't see me. He had his good wife tell me he wasn't home, but I don't believe it. Do you think I'd find him in now?"

I said I believed the rector was meeting with foes of the demon rum.

"There's always some excuse. I know he's upset about the artist that died in his church this week. That was terrible — such a fine woman too. Still, I've been trying to get his attention for over a year."

"You knew her?"

"Yes, of course. She came into my place a lot last August." Simon Leavitt pointed to an ice cream parlour in the row of shops. "September too, on warm days. Fresh fruit sundae, that was her cup of tea. And I have to say we make them just as good as Eaton's. Are you a friend of hers?"

It was strange how this question made me feel, as if she were still capable of having friends. I wanted to say, *Not yet.*

"Did you ever see her with anyone," I asked, "or did she always come in alone?"

"I don't remember things like that, but she was a sweet woman. That's how you should think of her. Are you her husband?"

"Would you remember more if I told you I was a detective sergeant?" I showed him my badge.

A look of unwilling submission settled on Leavitt's face. "She came alone sometimes, sometimes with a man. Once or twice with a Chinaman."

"Catch any names?"

"None, I swear."

I figured Simon Leavitt or his family — back in Europe perhaps — had had reason to distrust the police. I could always come back to him later if I wanted to pursue the question of Nora Britton's associates. At the moment, I suspected he thought talking to me could do him no good.

I was wrong, though. He wasn't quite as despairing as all that.

"Say, mister detective, do you think you could do something about the Children's Downtown Clinic that Christ Church is running? They hand out free milk, and the nurses are helpful as anything when little Hymie or little Hudel has a cough or a rash, but it's all to get Jewish families to convert to the Church of England. Can you stop that?"

"I can't think of any law that's being broken."

"We never try to get anyone to give up their religion and convert to ours, let alone use the infirmities of children to do it." Leavitt shook his head at the lack of scruple. "Do you think Reverend Hutchinson would speak to our rabbi?"

"Religion is clean out of my line, and I've only ever had one talk with the rector. You have good questions, Mr. Leavitt, but you also have the rotten luck to be putting them to the wrong person. Now let me ask you one: do you know where I could find Jack Wellington?"

"The Jewish kid that lost the fight last night because of a no-good referee? You don't see him down here anymore. Once a person owns three or more suits, he buys a house in Forest Hill to hang them in."

"Thanks," I said. "Maybe I'll come back for a sundae some time."

Hungry as I was, the first order of business was a sardine salad on brown as assembled by my favourite sandwich shop. Settled on a stool at the counter of Uneeda Lunch on Queen Street, with the first two big bites inside me, I reviewed my morning. Plainly, Christ Church Grange Park was far from one happy and harmonious family. Threatening language that in isolation sounded like banana oil took on a darker colour given the whole history of the mural project.

Overall, I was inclined to believe Eric Hutchinson's version of that history. Quite possibly he had pushed Nora Britton to finish her painting by Armistice Day harder than he now wanted to admit. If anything depended on his truthfulness, however, I could easily seek confirmation from other sources for most of what he'd told me. He plainly didn't suffer from excessive modesty, but I couldn't see that he'd shaped his answers to make himself look wiser than he was. He hadn't pretended to any knowledge of art. What did he think of the merits of the first and second mural designs? I'd heard no whisper of that. In contrast, he'd practically bellowed his attraction to the artist behind the second. Being sweet on her in a fatherly way perhaps made him perceive threats where there were none. Still, I saw no reason why we shouldn't have the body of the deceased checked for poison.

Chapter 4

As soon as I set foot back in the detective office, I was told Inspector Sanderson was waiting for my report. I stormed into his glass-walled office, and before he could get out his first question, I said I wanted to see an autopsy report on Nora Britton.

Sanderson lit one of his filthy pipes and to make matters worse told me to shut the door. I didn't quite.

"The coroner didn't think any autopsy necessary," he said. "Clearly an accidental fall. Asked what I could expect when a woman was allowed to swan around up on a scaffold. Blithering fool."

"Has he released the remains to the family, sir?"

"If he has, he'll have to get them back. I've told his chief we need a post-mortem on this lady. And if she's already been buried, he'll have to issue a warrant to disinter. So you believe Mr. Hutchinson?"

"I believe there was nasty talk about the deceased, but that's a long way from murder. The church sanctuary was locked from the inside at the time of death, and no one else was found inside when the rector and the caretaker broke in. So it's unlikely she was pushed off that scaffold. If the autopsy results rule out poison, I don't see any reason to investigate further."

Inspector Sanderson pinched his lower lip and looked at me from under his black eyebrows. I was afraid I was now going to be reassigned while we waited for those results. None of the cases Sanderson was likely to put me on held the promise of useful work. At one end of the class spectrum, an Atlantic-hopping baroness claimed to have had jewellery stolen from her suite at the King Edward Hotel, an investigation much better suited to Detective Sergeant Rudy Crate with his authentically plummy English drawl. At the other end, our department had for the past week been watching a suspected bawdy house on Chestnut Street, an assignment already boring Detective Sergeants Nichol and Lazenby to twitching distraction.

"While we're waiting, though," I said, "I could just check up on the source of the poison threats, a man the rector thinks has some sort of police record."

"All right, Paul. That shouldn't take long. Then see if Rudy needs a hand."

I shut the inspector in with his pipe smoke on the way out.

"You may like the smell of rotting fish," said the detective at the desk next to mine, "but for the sake of the rest of us do you think you could find somewhere else to store your picnic?"

Parsons was pointing at Nora Britton's knapsack, which I'd left on the floor by my chair. In the stuffy detective office, the stink was pretty bad.

I hoisted it up onto my desk and undid the metal catches. Inside I found a Thermos half full of what smelled like coffee and two wax paper packages. One contained a sandwich, with a couple of bites taken out of it. The contents were some sort of grey paste. Perhaps tuna salad. In the other I found three hermit cookies and enough crumbs to suggest Nora Britton had eaten the fourth. If the autopsy showed the painter had been poisoned, we'd want coffee, sandwich, and cookies all tested. I considered sending them immediately to the province's one-man crime lab, Professor Dalton Linacre at the University of Toronto. But he was cruelly overworked by police departments around Ontario and had as well responsibilities to the chemistry department he headed. We detectives had been warned not to make him do tests on spec. To oblige my neighbour, I took the repacked knapsack down to the evidence lockers.

Back upstairs the department files smelled of nothing worse than dust. I quickly found that Jordan Stillwater's record of contacts with the police didn't amount to much — charges dating back to the Prohibition years just ended. It seemed that as a pharmacist Stillwater had sold some customers alcohol without the requisite doctor's prescription or had sold more than prescribed. That period had made criminals of a lot of us; if I personally had never got my rye from a drugstore, it was only because it would have spoiled the taste for me to think of it as medicine.

While I was at it, I checked police records to see if Jordan's grandson had ever come to the attention of the law, and here I found something more serious. In 1924 the ex-sailor had participated in a brawl at a dance and had been fined for the crime of common assault. Then in 1926 he was suspected of beating up a Chinese restaurant owner who was employing a Caucasian girl in his kitchen. Archie admitted removing the woman from the premises. He had evidently removed her with some force as she was subsequently treated for a broken arm. No charges were laid in either case because of the two victims' refusal to testify. The investigating officer was of the opinion that the woman's silence was due to the influence of her parents, who were appalled to find out where she'd been working and overjoyed to have her out.

Archie sounded like a nasty piece of work. I'll admit I couldn't see this brawler as a poisoner, even though he might have had access to restricted substances through his pharmacist grandfather. No, from what I'd read and seen, men that used poison to murder tended to be schemers rather than scrappers, scholarly types — often doctors like Cream or Crippen. I wondered if there might be another way Archie could have killed Nora Britton and left her body inside a church locked from the inside. It seemed impossible — unless he'd been hiding inside the church Tuesday morning when the rector broke in and managed to escape unnoticed. I hoped a post-mortem on Nora Britton could be performed this afternoon. I might pursue the Archie Stillwater angle if no trace of poison was found.

I looked up from my desk to see Inspector Sanderson striding towards me. From the furrows in his high forehead I surmised I wasn't going to be seeing an autopsy report any time soon.

"Paul, I've just been on the phone to the coroner. He says Nora Britton's remains were released to the next of kin Wednesday morning. He's in the process of issuing a warrant to get them back, but it's Friday afternoon and I've no faith in his sense of urgency. You'd better get in touch with Herman Koch and warn him not to have his wife buried in the meantime. He doesn't appear to have a phone, so you'll have to go round."

Constable Nanos's report was still on my desk. I scanned it for the address of the deceased. "Would that be Elizabeth Street?" I asked.

"No, Strachan Avenue south of King. As near as I can make out, it's between the Mercer Reformatory and the Provincial Lunatic Asylum, on the site of the old Central Prison. His residence and studio appear to be in the former prison chapel. I haven't been able to discover an actual street number, but you'll find it."

"By taxi, sir?"

"Streetcar," said the impatient but thrifty inspector.

Friday was payday, so I was able to pick up my slim packet of banknotes on the way out to buy a paper and catch the King car.

The long ride out gave me an opportunity to see how the *Daily Dispatch* had reported last night's fight. There was no article, just a record of the result with no suggestion that either Wellington or Hardcastle was bent. That didn't mean Lariviere had some hold over the publisher, but you had to wonder. Meanwhile, Ruth's big breakthrough onto the front page would have to wait. I hoped I'd live long enough to see it.

It was past four o'clock by the time I found the prison chapel, the weather still clear, sunny, and just about cool enough for mid-October. Isolated in the middle of an assortment of newer sheds and factories, the soot-stained red brick structure looked about fifty years old. The plain hipped roof carried no spire or cross. Only the tall, round-topped windows on the second of two storeys suggested a hall suited to a gathering of worshippers. The rectangular footprint of the building was broken here and there by the stumps of projecting walls, walls that would have connected the chapel to the now-demolished remainder of the Central Prison.

I walked all the way round the building and found three doors. My knocking at two of these went unanswered. The third was opened by a woman with curling, dark hair, held off her face by a man's cloth cap of indeterminate colour. Her face was lined, her arms muscular. She looked me over while resting her hands in the pockets of a clay-spattered, blue-checked house dress. She told me that Herman Koch's door was on the opposite side of the building. I told her Mr. Koch didn't appear to be home.

"Was it about having your portrait painted?" she asked in a deep, husky voice.

"Do I look as if I could afford it?" I admit I was entertained by the thought.

"I don't judge people by their clothes," said the woman. "But if you don't have the cash for a three-quarter length in oils, you might still consider a charcoal head for a hundred dollars."

"Or a terra cotta bust?"

She wiped the back of her right hand across her upper lip. "Even if you were serious, I haven't the time. Are you a bill collector?"

"Does Mr. Koch get many visits from them?"

The woman shrugged, her lips pressed tight. Time I came clean.

"Detective Sergeant Paul Shenstone," I said. "Mr. Koch is not in any trouble with the police, but it's urgent I see him."

"Ernestine Lopez. Herman likes to paint by natural light, so if he isn't home now he soon will be. He's only got an hour and a half till sundown. If you want to wait in my studio, you can. The partition wall between his space and mine isn't up to much. We'll hear when he comes in."

Detective Sergeant Parsons liked to say that a Mr. Lopez out on Woodbine made Toronto's best cigars, but Ernestine denied having any kin north of the Rio Grande.

I followed her through a ground floor storage area. By the light a few dirty windows let in, we picked our way among life-size and larger sculptures in plaster and stone. Some were of animals. Those of men and women were for the most part either nude or in uniform. We mounted a set of concrete stairs to the former sanctuary. This space was divided in half by a transverse plank wall that stopped well below the high ceiling. On the near side of the partition, Ernestine Lopez had organized her studio and living space. She pointed me to a wooden kitchen chair and went promptly back to work on a yard-high model of an infantryman bowed in sorrow over a grave marker. Rather than grieving bare-headed, the soldier wore his metal helmet. I understood that his position was meant to be still vulnerable to enemy fire and that he would be returning to his battle station. To pay tribute to his comrade, he had snatched from the struggle the briefest moment. The image was wrong in some ways, the cross too official-looking, too precisely engraved. Still, I felt — across the gap of gender and situation — the compassion that guided Miss Lopez's hand.

"For a war memorial?" I asked.

"No guff!" She was using a tool to deepen a crease in the sleeve of the soldier's tunic.

"Where?"

"Buckland Lake, Ontario. You won't have heard of it — so small you could drive through and miss it. But still eight names to list on the pedestal."

I said nothing. I was thinking of the cost to such a small community of those eight deaths, with the cost of a statue on top. Marking their loss, but also their pride.

Ernestine filled in the silence. "Their loss, my gain. Painters could be war artists, recording the action and the wreckage. Then, a year after the Armistice, not needed anymore. The appetite for sculpture is just getting started and won't run its course for years yet."

And a painter with a German name, it occurred to me, might not even have found work as a Canadian war artist. Sales to the National Gallery in Ottawa, while good for the reputation, couldn't be frequent. Ernestine Lopez made it sound as if Herman Koch, unlike herself, had not enough work. He wasn't too busy, at least, to take on new portrait commissions. I wondered if he had been financially dependent on Nora Britton.

"Did Mr. Koch's wife live here with him?" I asked.

"He'll answer that if he feels like it." Ernestine Lopez nodded at the plank wall, on the other side of which someone had just started to pick out a tune on the piano. "There's no way through. You'll have to go downstairs, out, and around to the other door. I'll tell him to let you in."

I thanked her. The music stuck in my head on my way around. It sounded familiar, but I couldn't place it.

A stocky man, five or six years my senior, met me at the door. Herman Koch's eyes were bloodshot and showed a lot of white below the pupils. He wore a green knitted tie and a brown corduroy suit, one that looked like he'd had it on for many months. Although his brown hair was receding around a widow's peak, he retained a shabby, bohemian glamour.

"Mr. Koch," I said, "I'm sorry for your loss."

"Did you know Nora?"

"No — I'm investigating her death. Can we go up to your studio?"

Koch stepped outside and locked his door. "You can say what you have to say out here."

His voice was firm and calm with no trace of a foreign accent. I went straight to the point.

"Have Nora Britton's remains been buried?"

"No."

I was glad to hear it. Next of kin, however composed they appeared once their loved ones were in the ground, almost invariably got upset at the prospect of disinterment.

"Where are they?"

"Buffalo."

"Buffalo, New York?"

"Yes."

"Is she being buried there?" I couldn't make this out. Her birth family was supposedly in Aurora.

"No."

He was playing with me, but I'd rather this than have him walk back inside his studio and slam the door in my face. While I was thinking how to get him to open up, I took my flask out from an inside jacket pocket. I sipped some whisky and handed the flask to Koch. He put it to his lips and drained it, returning it to me neck down to rub it in that he'd left me dry. I saw him smile for the first time.

I smiled back. "When did you send Nora's remains to Buffalo?"

"Tuesday afternoon."

"What for?"

"To have her cremated."

I felt a hole open in my stomach. I took Koch at his word about the cremation. I'd read of cadavers sent to Buffalo just because no crematorium was yet operating in Ontario. The one slight ray of hope arose from my certainty that he was lying about how soon Nora's remains had gone. The coroner hadn't released them, according to Inspector Sanderson, until Wednesday morning. Perhaps when I arrived outside his studio, Koch was returning from making the shipping arrangements.

"The cremation has to be prevented," I said. "The coroner is ordering an autopsy."

"Too late," said Koch. "It's already happened. An autopsy wouldn't serve any purpose anyway."

"Give me the phone number or at least the name of the crematorium."

"I don't know anything about it. Bates Burial Company here in Toronto handled all the arrangements."

I left him without a word, making my way at something between a walk and a run to the nearest business on Strachan Avenue. The John Inglis Company boiler factory granted me extensive use of one of their phones. My first call was to police HQ at City Hall. I got one of the detective sergeants there to phone every crematorium in Buffalo with a view to preventing Nora Britton's remains from being destroyed. It was my good fortune to pass this task to Harry O'Brian, one of my younger and more reliable colleagues. I figured he had as good a chance as anyone of getting Inspector Sanderson to authorize the long-distance charges. Next, I called Bates Burial Company, who unsurprisingly had never heard of Nora Britton or Herman Koch. Then with the help of the *City Directory*, I started in on all the other undertakers in the city, working from Koch's neighbourhood outward. Telford Squires acknowledged having Nora Britton's remains picked up from the morgue at Grace Hospital on Wednesday and held at their Dufferin Street funeral parlour while arrangements were made to send them out of the country. The late Miss Britton's casket had been put on a Buffalo train this morning and picked up in that city by a hearse from the Buffalo Cremation Company for transfer to their facility on Delavan Avenue. I had hopes that the cremation might have been held over from Friday to Monday.

Perhaps there was a backlog of bodies to be burned. Perhaps the staff of the Buffalo Cremation Company had wanted to start the weekend early. I was about to phone them when an Inglis clerk informed me there was a call for me from Detective Sergeant O'Brian on another line. We were, Harry reported, an hour too late. Nora Britton had been the oven's last client of the day and the week.

Chapter 5

While I still had Harry on the line, I asked if he'd let me rope him into another job. He laughed and pointed out that it was quitting time on payday, and a Friday to boot. What did I have in mind? I said I wanted help interviewing a murder suspect and that he should make sure to bring his service revolver.

"I'm never without it," said O'Brian, "unlike some slackers I could name. But I don't get to use it much. Where do I report?"

"The former chapel of the Central Prison — quick as you can."

I gave him directions, and while I was waiting for him to arrive asked around the Inglis plant whether anyone had had any encounters with the two tenants of the old chapel, either the sculptress or the painter. No one reported having had any conversation with them. One manager thought from seeing them walking together that they were a couple. An accountant told me that the pair of them would have to move in the new year as John Inglis owned the building they occupied and would be requiring it to expand their operations. The artists were at present getting a bargain and were unlikely to find comparable accommodation for the same price. It was the woman, he said, who came by the Inglis offices each month to pay the rent for both of them.

I thought I'd got everything I could from the office personnel by the time Harry found me. While he had been a detective sergeant a shorter time, he was a man I looked up to, having two or three inches on me in height. A little sparring with him had convinced me that he was able to use his long arms to deliver quick punches from a safe distance. Indeed, he'd distinguished himself as a better than decent amateur boxer in the most recent police games. None of the detective sergeants were under thirty, but Harry's round face and broad grin made him look a good deal younger. Like a jack-o'-lantern with a full set of teeth.

The sun was not yet down, but sinking. If Ernestine Lopez was correct, Koch would be at his easel. His haste to make an autopsy impossible was enough in my books to earn him a more thorough grilling. I'd asked Harry along to impress Koch with our seriousness and also to keep an eye out for any tricky attempts to evade us.

"This place has three doors," I said, "all metal. Two go to artists' studios. I don't know about the third. I'm going to knock on Herman Koch's. Stand where you can see if anyone leaves through either of the others."

Harry asked if there was anything he needed to know about the background. I told him he'd pick it up as we went along.

"Okay, Paul," he said, "as long as you don't mind if I let you do the talking. I don't want to put my foot in it."

"Yeah, fine. But speak up if I'm missing something."

After three minutes of intermittent knocking, first with my knuckles and then with a fragment of brick left lying around the demolition site, I heard Harry raise the alarm. It seemed Koch had left by Ernestine Lopez's door. He tried to run towards King Street, but Harry and I were both faster. Harry closed in on him first. I was afraid O'Brian would bring the painter down with a football tackle, which might have been construed as excessive force. But he simply blocked the way, whichever way Koch turned, until I came up.

"Mr. Koch," I said, "We have to talk. You are not under arrest, but we believe you can help us with an investigation.

Now, shall we go up to your studio? You don't want us to take you to police headquarters: there's a pretty bad odour of rotting fish down there just now. Besides, the coffee's cold."

Koch didn't react to mention of the fish or the coffee.

"I don't see that Nora's death is any of your business."

"Perhaps we can explain, inside. It seems to me you owe me a drink."

"My studio is for my friends and my patrons."

"There you never can tell. Perhaps Detective Sergeant O'Brian will want a charcoal head — *if* he can bargain you down to under sixty dollars."

O'Brian shot me a mocking glance as we, one on each side, steered Koch back towards the chapel.

His half of the ground floor, unlike Ernestine Lopez's, was swept and empty. Upstairs, a few canvases had been framed and hung. Dozens upon dozens more stood in stacks leaning against the outside walls while an Ennis upright piano had been pushed against the plank partition. Koch perhaps wanted Ernestine Lopez to hear every note he played. Whereas she had screened off her sleeping area, Koch's extra wide bed stood in full view. It sported a number of Turkish-looking cushions and a satiny emerald coverlet. His own clothes, mostly checked shirts and corduroy, were strewn over a couple of easy chairs. There was no sign that Nora or any woman lived here or had done so recently.

On the easel under the east windows sat a landscape of pine trees clinging to rock and assailed by a wind that was doing its utmost to pull them out by the roots. Behind this drama, another involved whitecaps foaming up and being driven by the same gale across a wide body of water. The rushing clouds above showed brown and grey and, fleetingly, golden. Patches of calm blue even broke through from the distant sky, promising that the storm itself was on the point of being blown away.

I looked more closely and saw only thick patches of paint bearing the marks of the brush. There was no precision or detail; the landscape simply vanished. And yet when I pulled back no more than eighteen inches every element was realized to perfection. It was all there.

I had, as I'd admitted to Ruth Stone, almost no experience of oil painting, but I believed I had a nose for honesty and a not much below average eye for beauty. This picture, for my money, had both. This was the Canadian Shield territory as I'd passed through it and as I'd dreamed it. It was heart-stirring. Plainly Herman Koch knew his onions. I could see why Joe Deane loved his art. It was much richer, but had the direct patriotic impact of the recruiting posters Deane had sponsored.

"Okay if we sit?" I asked. "Just shift the clothes off one of those chairs, detective."

Harry took the piano bench instead. I noticed without thinking about it much that it was pushed against a side wall, a long way from the piano. Koch sat down in a wicker chair on top of a pair of his pyjamas, crossed his legs, and proceeded to roll himself a cigarette. I took the stool in front of the easel, as much as anything to see if it made me feel talented. At the Canadian National Exhibition once, I had been allowed to sit behind the wheel of an eight-cylinder supercharged race car capable of more than 120 miles per hour and had fancied I looked like an ace driver. I wasn't so sure about my present perch, but all the same … I had another squint at the work I would have been proud to put my name to.

"You haven't signed it, Mr. Koch," I said.

I expected him to tell me the picture wasn't finished, although it looked to me as if one more brushstroke anywhere would subtract from rather than add to its effect.

"I no longer sign any of my work," he said. "Let it stand on its merits."

"Why give people that dislike a German name an excuse to dismiss it?"

"Something like that."

"Mr. Koch lost a commission on account of his name," I explained to Harry, "lost it to his late wife."

"Am I supposed to have killed her out of jealousy?"

"The rector of Christ Church Grange Park doesn't think so. But then there are some things he doesn't know about your marriage. For instance, that you lived apart."

Koch threw away his cigarette without lighting it and leaned forward, clearly rattled. "I *loved* her — more than you can understand!"

I gave him a minute. Meanwhile the tune he'd been picking out earlier on the piano came back to me, this time with a name — "The Saint Louis Blues." Most of the words as I remembered them didn't fit Herman's situation, but there was stuff about the grief resulting from the singer's lovin' baby having left town.

"Why did you have her cremated?" I asked.

"She had a horror of people just rotting slowly away in the ground."

"Cremation takes a lot of arranging, though. Sending the remains across an international border and all that."

"It was what Nora wanted. She told me often."

"How are you paying for it?"

"You think I'm broke?" Koch shouted.

Nobody answered.

After a moment, Koch said, "She gave me money especially for that and nothing else. She wasn't expecting to die, but if she did she wanted her wishes respected."

"Why were you so secretive about it? You lied to me about when you got Miss Britton's remains. And you lied to me about which undertaker was handling the arrangements from this end."

"I thought her parents had put you on to me. They're small-town Christians, totally against cremation. They believe if her body isn't intact, they won't be reunited with their daughter in heaven. I didn't know what they might do to prevent Nora's wishes from being carried out, so I tried to throw you off the track."

I exchanged glances with Harry. If I was reading his mind correctly, we both thought this story somewhat plausible.

"Why are the police making this fuss anyway?" Koch asked. "Do you have the same stupid prejudice as my in-laws?"

"Were you aware that threatening language was used about your wife in the weeks leading up to her death?"

"Threats? Hell no." Koch stabbed an accusatory index finger at Harry and me in turn. "Why didn't you policemen do something about them?"

"They didn't come to our attention until after your wife's death." Not wanting to inflame Koch further, I didn't add that we as yet had no evidence that Nora Britton had actually received any threatening letters or been the object of any direct verbal intimidation, and that in the absence of either no Crown attorney would have prosecuted.

"Some slander — yes, I knew about that," said the painter. "Just because she was my wife. I was supposed to have been the true author of her design. Quite unnecessary. After me, she was the best artist in the country." He let that sink in, then asked, "What were these threats?"

"One involved poison," I said.

"But her death was an accident. That's what we were told. She lost her footing and fell from the scaffold where she had been working."

"All we know for certain at this point is that she was found dead at the foot of the scaffold. If she fell, it may have been because she was poisoned first."

"So she was already dead when she fell?"

"Possibly. Or the poison might have made her lose her balance and caused her to fall. Once the subject of poison came up, the coroner's verdict of accidental death was called in question. An autopsy — previously thought unnecessary — was ordered. By your actions, Mr. Koch, you have made this autopsy impossible. We don't know if your wife was murdered, but your haste to cremate her remains has raised suspicions. Suspicions, I might add, not calmed by your attempt to run away from us just now."

"But of course I didn't want to speak to you!" Koch exclaimed. "Is grief allowed no privileges?"

"It's Friday evening," I said. "Detective Sergeant O'Brian and I can both think of things we'd rather be doing. So let's get this over with. When was the last time you saw Nora Britton?"

"Two weeks ago, more or less. It wasn't a bourgeois marriage."

"All the same, might you have seen her as recently as Monday?"

"No."

"Did you ever prepare food or drink for her to take to the church when she was working on the mural?"

"Never."

"You didn't send her anything to eat or drink last Monday?"

"No."

I asked in various ways if he knew either the retired pharmacist Jordan Stillwater or his grandson Archie. Koch said and kept saying no and no.

"You mentioned that your wife had set aside money for her cremation. Did she have much money of her own?"

"Enough to support her between commissions. She did all right."

"Now that she's dead, will whatever she had come to you?"

"You louse," Koch said with feeling.

"Had she made a will?"

No answer.

I walked over and put a hand on the back of his chair. "Look at me, Herman."

Koch stared out the window, giving me a great view of the top of his scurf-ridden head.

Harry got up from the piano bench and stepped forward. Neither he nor I intended to do more than crowd Koch, but Koch wasn't hero enough to call our bluff. He looked up.

"Did Nora Britton have a will, Herman?" I asked.

"I don't know."

"No need to shout," I said. Then, pointing to the landscape on the easel, "You won't set any store by my opinion, but I admire your painting."

Koch forced himself to nod.

"Would you show me your design for Christ Church Grange Park?"

"I don't have it," Koch said.

"It hasn't been destroyed, I hope."

"Nora asked for it and I gave it to her. I don't know what she did with it."

"Can you let me into her studio?"

Koch said he didn't have a key.

"Please don't leave town until further notice, Mr. Koch. We may want to speak again." I caught Harry's eye. "Shall we go?"

"Sure," my colleague said. "I'm just curious about these marks."

He pointed to tracks in the floor leading from the wheels beneath the left side of the piano out in an arc into the room. When we swung the piano out along this arc, the trap door in the partition was revealed. So much for Ernestine Lopez's assertion that there was no access from her studio to Koch's.

Harry couldn't wait to get home to his young wife and infant daughter in Riverdale. When we parted company on the eastbound King streetcar, I told him I'd report for both of us to Sanderson. At six on a Friday evening, the inspector was still filling his glass-walled office with pipe smoke and cleaning up correspondence. My news didn't upset him as much as I'd have liked. He did hold forth on how police work would be harder if cremation became general, but in this case he seemed grateful that his department was spared the work of a murder investigation. He reckoned that the case was now closed, that the coroner's finding of accidental death would have to stand, and that I should start my weekend and come back Monday morning ready to immerse myself in the apprehension of such devastators of public order as prostitutes and pickpockets.

Drudgery in my future, but for now, free time.

I'd told Koch I had better things to do than talk to him. I didn't. With my pay in my pocket, I thought of taking Ruth Stone out to dinner, but when I called the *Dispatch*, someone told me she'd left for the day. I started to look up her home number, but let the directory fall closed. I didn't have the juicy murder case she wanted to hear about. And at the same time I felt there were still angles of inquiry to pursue before I could put the death of Nora Britton out of my mind.

Two women — two modern working women, engagingly energetic carvers of their own paths. I felt the pull of each. But Ruth was alive: she could wait. Nora needed me more right now. If she'd been killed, her killer's trail was cooling.

Instead of Ruth I phoned Dalton Linacre. In view of his dual responsibilities as professor of chemistry at the University of Toronto and as forensic scientist for all of Ontario, I had a hunch he'd still be at work at six thirty on a Friday evening, but I wanted to be sure. When he answered on the third ring, I asked if I could bring him some food samples for toxicological analysis. I was one of the few detectives for whom he'd do work without a formal requisition from the inspector. I think that he was shy as well as conscientious and that he appreciated my never wasting his time or energies with small talk. On this occasion I did ask if I could bring him something to eat along with the samples for analysis, but he said he never ate in the lab: the smells killed appetite.

I could appreciate his point of view when I picked up Nora Britton's stinky knapsack from the evidence locker and made myself unpopular by transporting it on the northbound Bay streetcar. Linacre's lab was in the basement of the University Mining Building at 170 College Street. I entered his dimly lit lair without knocking and found the middle-aged professor bent over his comparison microscope. His dark cowlick stood up from the crown of his head like a bird's crest while his threadbare lab coat hung over the shoulders of his three-piece suit like a cape. His green bow tie was easily the brightest spot of colour in the room.

"I need to know if a woman was poisoned," I said, setting the knapsack down on the table by the door. "These are the remains of what we think was her last meal."

Linacre turned towards me and slipped on a pair of wire-rimmed spectacles. His half-smile of recognition was as effusive a greeting as I ever got from him.

"Are you talking about something fast like cyanide or strychnine? Or do we check for slow poisons such as hemlock, botulinum, castor beans, or ergot?"

"Possibly something found in a pharmacy." I didn't know which of the substances mentioned this covered. "We're dealing with a woman found at the foot of a scaffold twenty-something feet high. What we want to know is whether she ingested anything that within eight to ten hours could have caused her death — either because it killed her outright or because it caused her to lose her balance and fall from the scaffold."

"Fall while still alive to her death?" said Linacre.

"Uh-huh. The substance we're looking for need not be one that kills in itself, merely one that makes a person dizzy."

"Dizziness can arise from allergies, low blood pressure, anemia, a heart condition, or other conditions a doctor would know more about than I. But I'm by no means convinced that dizziness alone could account for this death. A fall of twenty feet wouldn't necessarily be fatal to a normally healthy person. Can you tell me anything of your lady's medical history?"

"No, but I'll try to find out."

"I take it the pathologist has not found any noxious substance in her stomach. You might ask him also about any signs of infection or temporary illness."

I told the professor that no autopsy had been performed and that the body had been destroyed. While taking that in, he had another look through his microscope at whatever he'd been working on when I came in. I knew he was losing patience with me, and I wasn't happy about it. I shuffled my feet. But, having already lost Nora to the cremation company's flames, I didn't want to lose the chance of finding something in that picnic supper. I stood my ground until Linacre spoke again.

"I'll give your big haystack a once-over. Come back in twenty-four hours. You're welcome to whatever needles I've been able to find by then."

I apologized for the stench coming from Nora's knapsack; he said he'd rather deal with poisons than bombs. I'd heard him say on other occasions that he'd rather deal with firearms than bombs. I hoped I never had to bring him a bomb.

When I left Linacre, I found a student cafeteria with a special on spaghetti and meatballs. I had a plate of that, then another, before walking on to Oxford Street in the Kensington Market area. I entered a yellow brick factory building, climbed unswept wooden stairs to the third floor, and sauntered through the exercise and assembly areas of an athletic club. A handful of sweat-drenched youngsters were lifting weights or laying into punching bags when I passed, but most of the activity at this hour was confined to the illegal bar in-behind. The jumbo-sized windows in that back room — as much as sixty-four square feet of glass each — were closed and covered with blackout curtains. Photos of local boxing heroes decorated the walls. Warm male bodies filled the room. From a radio turned low, Whispering Jack Smith was consoling the dateless men with his rendition of "Me and My Shadow." I took the last empty table and a seat at it with a view of the door. Over a double rye, I tried to work out what I would do with myself until I got the results of Linacre's tests.

I thought I'd like to speak to Nora Britton's family and judge for myself whether their beliefs regarding cremation adequately explained Herman Koch's behaviour. The radial, an out-of-town streetcar, would after many stops get me to the village of Aurora. But it might be more instructive to have a look at Nora's studio on Elizabeth Street first.

I finished my drink and ordered a bigger one, keeping an eye all the while on the booze can's curtained doorway. Even though it was far more likely that Jack Wellington would patronize one of the suburban clubs or perhaps the uptown Casa Loma Hotel, he was the party I hoped to see walk in. Instead, I witnessed the entrance of Oscar Craig. What made it an entrance was that the fight fan and artist had on his arm a theatrical blonde wrapped in a black ostrich boa so substantial that it was difficult to see whether she was wearing anything else.

These two were a breath of fresh air. I caught Oscar's eye and beckoned him over to my table. The couple arrived at the same time as the waiter with my tumblerful of whisky. He set it down and promptly yanked from Craig's hand the chair Craig had pulled out from the table for his feathered friend.

I got to my feet. "Why not let the lady sit down?" I suggested.

The muted radio was now massaging our ears with the peppy little ditty "Ain't She Sweet?" The waiter wasn't prepared to agree.

"No women in the bar," he said.

I didn't recognize him or know how much trouble the man was likely to be. He plainly did some work in the gym. There was no extra fat on him that I could see.

Taller by a foot at least, Oscar looked down on him with amusement in his hazel eyes. "Is that the law?" he said.

"Club rule."

"I think we'll set it aside for tonight in honour of this very special guest from New York City." Oscar pulled another chair from the table. "Have a seat, Gussie, and try to overlook the boorishness."

"You're leaving now." The waiter's raised voice attracted looks from many tables. One larger man wearing service station coveralls with an oil company name stitched on came over and grabbed Craig's right arm.

"You take the other side, Roy," he told the waiter. "We're throwing this bum out."

"Steady," I said. I disliked the sight of two against one.

The big auto mechanic turned on me a contemptuous glance and with the back of his right hand swept my drink off the table. Not to be distracted, I kept my eye on his left, which was winding up for a punch to my jaw. His mistake — for a punch to work it has to come out of nowhere. I had time to duck sideways and twist the big man's right wrist behind his back. His wrist was thick and strong: it took some prolonged effort to force him down to the floor. Out of the corner of my eye, I saw Oscar was having no trouble defending himself against Roy. Finally, I got what I wanted, my adversary pinned securely to the planks, his face in the puddle of spilled rye.

"Drink up," I said. "Shame to let good whisky go to waste."

"Get off," he gasped.

"Promise to sit quietly?"

No answer. I gave his head a twist.

"Say something while you can, Supertest."

He gasped something I charitably interpreted as assent.

When I got up, Oscar had Roy against the wall and was punching him repeatedly in the gut. The waiter was putting up no fight; his hands hung limp at his sides.

"He's finished, Oscar," I said. "Easy does it."

"Mind your own potatoes," Oscar grunted, but then stopped. "You have a point at that."

Clutching his stomach, Roy slumped down to a sitting position on the floor.

"You do know how to put on a show for a tourist," Gussie remarked in a friendly way. "Up till now, the biggest thrill Oscar thought up for me in Toronto was a visit to a fish market. This is more like it!"

"All the same," I said, still with an eye on the mechanic, "we'd best go somewhere else for refreshment."

Oscar, watchful also, was uncurling and rubbing the fingers of his right hand. "You know any other blind pigs around here, Paul?"

"Dozens."

I led the way, followed by Gussie, with Oscar as our grumbling rearguard.

"Kensington Market offers a slice of immigrant life, unvarnished, as it's lived by real people. I thought as a thespian you'd be interested."

"We have fish in New York," Gussie shot back. "It's on the ocean, snooks — remember?"

We went to a private dwelling on Augusta Street where the householder was a disabled construction worker and his wife was supporting the family by illegally selling whisky legally purchased from the newly created Liquor Control Board. Mrs. Solomon invited us to sit around an enamel table in her spotless kitchen, but Oscar suggested I buy a bottle to take to his studio where we'd enjoy more privacy. It was just a short walk north, he said, no more than half a dozen blocks.

We walked until a long, dark, castle-like building loomed up behind the streetlamps. Oscar pulled out a key. His studio turned out to be an art room in Central Technical School, where he was employed to give classes.

We climbed several flights of marble stairs to a top floor much smaller than the levels below. Oscar showed us into one of six classrooms, then went back out into the short corridor to rinse out in the communal sink three discoloured Mason jars for us to drink from. He also brought back a flower vase full of water to mix with the rye.

"It's a racket, of course," he said, gesturing at the student sketches that sat on easels grouped around a plate of fruit. "Art can't be taught."

"Yeah?" Gussie said. "Then why'd you come to New York to take lessons at the Art Students League?"

"Not for lessons — where'd you get that guff? Just to make whoopee with the more or less talented crowd slumming in Greenwich Village."

"If that's how you're playing it, Shakespeare, fine by me. You can count on Gus not to muff her lines."

It turned out Gussie was an actress, still living in the Village, who had met Oscar there before the war.

"We had an affair," she told me in a gossipy undertone. "Maybe more of a fling. I'm actually bisexual. Does that shock you, Paul?"

She pushed a wave of golden hair off her forehead and fixed me with her dramatically made-up eyes. For all her flapper glamour, I could see under the harsh schoolroom lights the wrinkles beneath her powder. I revised my estimate of her age upward to something close to my own. Girl or woman, though, she was an exotic bird, who made the Toronto she was gracing with a visit feel small and conventional.

"The last time I got shocked," I said, "I was trying to fix the wiring in my apartment."

"Paul has his own scandalous secret," said Oscar with a touch of malice. "He's a cop."

"Intriguing!" Gussie leaned towards me, her chin on her fist. "Do you get payoffs from all the speaks in town?"

"Heck no. I don't even accept free drinks anymore. Unless Oscar's treating."

Oscar pretended not to hear. He had picked up paper and pencil from the teacher's desk and was sketching Gussie, perhaps to see if his fisticuffs had done any damage to his hand.

"These days I find I prefer women to men," said Gussie, playing with her jar. She had added a lot of water to her rye, but still didn't seem to care much for the taste. "Between the two of us, I had a liaison with Edna St. Vincent Millay. You know, the poetess?"

I said I didn't.

"The Village is so progressive sexually. You can find some of everything there, every kind of experiment — free love, companionate marriage, you name it."

"Did you happen to know a painter named Herman Koch?" I asked on a whim. The rector of Christ Church had mentioned that Koch had studied art in New York.

"Koch, yes. How could I forget a name that sounds like that in a place like Greenwich Village. He was there after Oscar left, during the war. I think he came down — to study art, sure — but also because he didn't want to be drafted up here."

"Because he didn't want to fight Germans?" I asked.

"Not the way he told it. I guess with a name like that he had Germans in his family tree all right. He looked a bit like the young Emil Jannings. But he claimed to be a pacifist altogether. Didn't want to fight anyone. Now did I sleep with him or not? Wait ... yes, I did. Koch had a wife, but he bragged that they had a modern marriage, that it didn't keep either of them from 'forming other connections.' It sure didn't stop him, but I never heard of her hopping into anyone else's bed, or letting anyone but Koch hop into hers. Do you know him?"

"Slightly," I said. "Was his wife another painter?"

"Uh-huh. Very quiet and studious. Too pretty to be called mousy, but unobtrusive. Now what was her name?"

"Nora Britton," I suggested.

"That's the one!" Gussie exclaimed, then asked archly, "Do you know her 'slightly'?"

"Not even." I could hear the regret in my voice. "She died this week."

"What rotten luck!" Gussie raised her glass. "Rest in Peace, Nora."

Oscar looked up. "Did Koch use snow when he was down there, Gussie?"

"Not that I remember. Why?"

"Funny," said Oscar, although there was no mirth in his hazel eyes. "I was at a party once here in Toronto where people were shoving cocaine up their noses, but Herman said no, he never inhaled it for a lark — only when he needed extra pep to finish a painting. That was when he had portrait commissions. Then he got a reputation for insulting his sitters. I'm guessing he no longer has deadlines to meet. I haven't seen him for years. Wonder if he still snorts."

"Would his wife have had the same use for cocaine?" I asked. I wondered if the drug could have affected her balance up there on her scaffold.

"I haven't the foggiest," said Oscar, returning to his drawing.

"How well did you know her, Oscar?"

"I didn't. As Gussie says, she wasn't really in circulation. No more here than in New York."

"Suppose her work was in demand and Koch's was snubbed," I persisted. "From what you know of Koch, would he have been jealous?"

"Sure. He has an exalted opinion of his own art. Justified too. A little antiseptic for my taste — still, top drawer. You can count on genius not to be too kind."

The sky showed black outside the classroom's tall, uncurtained windows and through the skylights overhead. Feeling a chill the Seagram's didn't reach, I got up and walked around. I wondered what Oscar's own work looked like. There were signed watercolours of sand and palm trees pinned to a corkboard, but it was a large canvas on an easel beside the teacher's desk that drew most of my attention. It was perhaps six feet by four, a sombre oil painting of soldiers in muddy greatcoats standing at attention in what looked like a twilit farmyard in northeastern France.

"I'm new to the world of art and artists," I said. "Maybe you two can help me. In your experience is it common for a genius, so-called, to consider himself outside — or above — the law?"

"Not Herman," Gussie said, her face softening as some memory of Koch came back to her.

"No," said Oscar, "not Herman, but he does have a mean temper — mostly repressed, as the Freudians would say."

I asked what that meant.

"It's like this, Paul. Good as his art is, those rural landscapes of his, even the stormy ones, are too clean and bloodless. He doesn't express the dark side of his soul in his painting, so I wouldn't be surprised if it came out somewhere else."

"You don't seem to have that problem." I gestured to the picture on the easel. "A firing squad, isn't it?"

Oscar gave me a sharp look. "What makes you say that? I just call it *Dawn Muster*."

I shrugged and smiled. "Goes to show — I know nothing about art."

Everything in the picture was distorted. Colour had been applied in lurid swirls so that even the roof lines of the farm buildings were curved and out of perspective. The soldiers' feet were disproportionately large and not in contact with the ground. Nothing looked quite like anything. And yet I could make out an even dozen men with rifles. Although there was no prisoner present, the look on the faces of the soldiers didn't fit any assignment but an execution. Eleven, their faces greyish green, wore expressions of sickness and disgust rather than the fear felt in anticipation of a trench raid or an assault. The man nearest the viewer, his face red and contorted with anger, appeared to have mastered his revulsion. On his sleeve, he wore the single chevron of a lance corporal. His role would have been to assemble the squad and have them wait for the officer to lead them opposite the post or chair to which the condemned man was bound.

"That's what New Yorkers call the Ashcan style, Paul," Gussie said. "They think art is truer when it's ugly. It doesn't have to be a firing squad."

"True or not," said Oscar, "if Herman could paint like that, he wouldn't have to keep his rage bottled up and festering inside." He held up his finished sketch for us to admire. "What do you think, Pierrot? Ugly enough for you."

Oscar had shaved fifteen years off Gussie's age — taken her back, I guessed, to the age she'd been when he knew her in Greenwich Village before the war — and dressed her, in place of her feather boa, in a stage costume, a loose white blouse with a frilly collar and large pompoms for buttons. In her pencilled face I read ambition and readiness for life.

Gussie gasped. "Huh! For an Ashcan man, you're full of surprises. It's sweet."

"Ah, I think I'll throw it out."

Gussie leapt at him. After a pretend wrestling match, Oscar let her take the paper from him. By now all three of us were laughing.

"Say, Paul, you going to watch Bruno Ferrari box at the Coliseum next Thursday? That boy's an artist in his own way, in the application of pain."

I told Oscar I wasn't planning that far ahead. By Thursday, I might be at a gallery.

Chapter 6

Saturday morning, I had a large choice of seats on the streetcar in from my Queen Street West apartment to City Hall. The conductor rubbed sleep out of his eyes and yawned before taking my fare. When I greeted him by name, he asked if I were another soul damned to weekend duty. No, I said, just looking for an address.

Before I could get started on that task, I found a phone message waiting on my desk. At eight fifteen Friday evening, the note said, Eric Hutchinson had called to tell me Herman Koch was asking for the painting supplies Nora Britton had left at Christ Church Grange Park. Hutchinson wanted to know whether Koch should be allowed to take them.

I'd forgotten about the items I'd left on the scaffold in the church, but I remained suspicious of Koch and decided to err on the side of caution. I told the rector I'd send a constable to take possession of these supplies on behalf of the police and that Koch could be told they would be released to him in due course if they weren't needed as evidence.

The address I wanted was that of Nora Britton's studio on Elizabeth Street. The *City Directory* told me she shared a building with an antiquarian by the name of C. Moretti. I looked for inspiration at the ceiling of the detective room. I wondered idly if its original colour had been obscured by decades of tobacco smoke or whether it had been painted that colour to begin with. Moretti? Not a typical Church of England name, and yet I had a sneaking idea it appeared somewhere in my record of Friday morning's conversation with Eric Hutchinson. I flipped through my notebook. Sure enough, the parishioner that had threatened to spit on Koch's mural. The rector had given me the address of his residence, not his place of business. Elizabeth Street was only a block west from City Hall. How many C. Morettis could there be in the neighbourhood? I thought I'd walk over and have a word with the antique dealer. I would have bid farewell to the two detective sergeants officially on duty, but Howarth and Parsons both appeared to have stepped out for a moment, and the full force of my cordiality had to be spent on a startled secretary. It was cool enough in the shade that I'd worn a trench coat, but the strengthening sun made it almost superfluous. I carried it over my arm.

Limiting my cheerfulness somewhat was the problem of getting into Nora's studio. I couldn't get a search warrant because I didn't know what I was looking for or how it might relate to a crime. I'd just have to trust to my powers of improvisation.

Few of the structures on Nora's street posted street numbers, but by knocking on a door too far north and counting backwards I found the address. The two-storey plank building had a conventional shop front on the ground floor and a loft above with double doors opening onto the street. Inside these doors I assumed there would at one time have been a hoist for loading merchandise. The roof sloped down from right to left, so that the north side wall of the building was at least three feet higher than the south.

The shop window, mostly empty, displayed in one corner a jumble of tools, toys, appliances, dishes, cutlery, and other household items. A broken window in the shop door had been boarded over with unfinished plywood. The shop door was locked; it was opened in response to my knock by a man with one leg and ginger hair. Carl Moretti wore the trousers of a dark green suit, thick suspenders, no jacket, a dun-coloured shirt, and an expression on his clean-shaven face between anger and panic. He was upset and needed to talk.

He said his premises had been broken into the night before. He didn't think any of his wares had been taken, but Miss Britton's studio upstairs had been vandalized. I identified myself as a detective and asked him to show me.

I saw in the break-in both good luck and bad: my problem of access was solved, but evidence relevant to Nora Britton's death could have been destroyed or removed.

The staircase lay behind a second door, the Yale lock of which had been jimmied off. Leading me through, Moretti said the sight of that damage had prompted him to look upstairs this morning as soon as he'd arrived, between eight and ten past.

He managed his crutch nimbly on the stairs and we soon reached the loft, which was lit at the far end by large windows overlooking a back lane and by a couple of smaller ones let into the higher north wall. I thought it possible the latter had been added when the room was converted from a storage area to an artist's studio. A wood-burning stove in the centre of the loft might also have been a late addition. Still, I couldn't see that it would have added much to the comfort of the studio in winter, as any cold wind would blow through the cracks in the plank walls where daylight now showed. The furnishings were modest — a flimsy wardrobe, a chest of drawers, two bookcases, a kitchen table, a dry sink, three ladder-back chairs, one Windsor chair, and one wicker rocker. All unremarkable, except that all had been knocked over. The standard-width bed remained on all four feet, but the pillows and covers appeared to have been stabbed and torn with a knife. Books, dishes, and food staples littered one area of the plank floor. The rest was covered with paintings on canvas as well as sketches and watercolours on paper. Some of the papers were torn in half or into smaller bits. A few of the canvases had been stabbed. When I looked more closely, I saw that the cuts had excised or at least shredded the faces of certain persons represented in the pictures.

All this disorder spoke of the hostility that Nora Britton had aroused in certain quarters. The idea that she had enemies wasn't new. So should I have been as surprised as I was standing in her studio with the October sun pouring in on this scene of devastation? What had me catching my breath, I guess, was the passion expressed in this attack. Such fury was so at variance with the calm calculation that would have been required to kill Nora inside the locked sanctuary of the church. So I had to keep in mind that evidence of hostility was not necessarily evidence of murder.

Carl Moretti was starting to right the furniture and pick up the papers. I had to ask him to leave everything as it was.

"Have you already told the police about this break-in?" I asked.

"How the heck would you expect me to do that? I can't afford a phone, even though I did work for the company for five years." The man seemed less scared with a policeman present, but remained irritable. "I've been watching the street all morning for a constable to come by, but you people don't bother patrolling the poorer neighbourhoods."

"It looks as if Miss Britton's only access to her studio was through your shop. You must have seen a good deal of her."

"Not so much. I don't live here, you know, so how she spent her evenings I couldn't say. She had her own key to the shop."

"Was she friendly?"

"Friendly?" snapped Moretti, as if this were a quality he had no use for. "Friendly enough — but she knew I liked to be left alone, so she didn't try to make talk every time she came in or went out. I'm sorry she's dead. If the landlord can't find someone else to pay as good a rent for this space, he'll sell, and where will that leave me?"

"What did you think of her art?"

"It's all right. She gave me a picture of some soccer players. You can see it downstairs if you think you might buy it."

"Did you object to her being commissioned to paint a mural in your church?"

"What do you know about my church?" Moretti snapped.

"Christ Church Grange Park, Mr. Moretti. The rector spoke to me about you."

"The rector's a fool where this mural is concerned. It was no job for a woman. Have you seen how big that wall is? And then she got some Chinaman to build a scaffold for her. More foolishness. Something was bound to go wrong."

"Did it matter to you that she was married to Herman Koch, the winner of the first design competition?"

"I didn't give a darn about that."

"You threatened to spit on a mural painted by Koch. Would you have done that to one painted by his wife?"

"She wasn't German — and besides, she and Koch were separated. I never saw him here. Or in church."

I wondered what else I could ask Moretti. "Did you ever give Miss Britton anything to eat?"

"What? Does this look to you like a restaurant?"

"Did you at any time give or sell her food?"

"Definitely not. I don't keep food in the shop. It would attract rats."

"Did you ever give or sell her anything to drink?"

"Are you calling me a bootlegger? I don't drink alcohol; I don't sell it; and, if I had any, I certainly couldn't afford to give it away."

I explained to Mr. Moretti that I didn't just mean alcoholic drink. He assured me, in a self-congratulatory tone, that he had never offered Nora Britton so much as a sip of water. The man was making me thirsty. I told him he could go back to his shop. I wanted to take a closer look at the art.

"Ah, you'll never catch whoever made this mess."

I listened till the alternating thumps of his boot and crutch on the steps died away. My pocket flask had been refilled before breakfast from the bottle of Seagrams I kept in my kitchen. I took a belt while starting to look around. Beside a knocked over easel, I found an oil on canvas painting about three feet tall by two wide. The coloured area was rounded at the top. Within the semi-circle, the sky was a shade of green I recognized from the church. This painting I thought might be Nora's mural design.

I spent several minutes looking at it. In the church, apart from the patch of green sky, no colour had as yet been applied to the wall. I remembered seeing some charcoal marks; indeed, Nora might have sketched in all the main elements, but to anyone standing far enough back to take in the whole these lines would have been too faint to make out, as well as being largely obscured by the scaffolding.

In the centre of the painting I held in my hands stood a slender wooden cross, dividing the composition into two halves. The background of each half was a city. On the right, buildings shaped like ones I'd seen in Belgium were on fire. In the distance, people with small packages of belongings could be seen fleeing the flames. On the left, a streetscape characteristic of Toronto's Ward neighbourhood was discernible. Elizabeth Street itself was recognizable with its plank sheds and houses sheathed in crumbling roughcast. Here the background figures were rag and bone collectors and children playing in a mud puddle.

Before each cityscape stood a pair of large figures, an armed serviceman shielding a woman in each case.

On the left, in front of the Toronto slum, I believed the artist had painted herself — although I'd only seen a photo of Nora Britton in profile and this woman was depicted face on. The eyes of the woman in the picture were apprehensive, her cheeks sunken. And yet her mouth was the same shape as Nora's; her straight, dark hair was pulled back flat from a centre part in the same way. Despite her poverty and sense of danger, the woman embodied a proud beauty. The artist had given her likeness a long, plain, mud-coloured dress that nevertheless allowed to be seen an erect and well-proportioned figure beneath. Her protector wore a khaki battle tunic and a kilt in the tartan of my own regiment, the 48th Highlanders of Canada. His left arm was stretched in front of the woman, as if to keep her from falling out of the picture. His rifle was in the order arms position, with the butt resting on the ground near his right foot and his right hand around the barrel. I noted that this was no generic weapon. The artist had taken the trouble to portray exactly the Short Magazine Lee-Enfield Mk. III — standard issue to Canadian troops in 1916 after the failure of the Ross Rifle. This meticulous attention to detail I saw was characteristic of her style throughout the painting and a clear contrast to Herman Koch's approach. The Koch landscape on his easel in the chapel made you believe in detail that wasn't there. Nora Britton made you believe she was showing you a photograph, except that no photograph was this sharply focused, this pure in its colours, this well-lit. Both husband and wife were illusionists of the first order.

On the right side of the cross, Koch himself figured in Nora's painting. The pacifist's face had been given to a sturdy sergeant with the insignia of the Canadian Machine Gun Corps embroidered above the chevrons on his sleeve. Across his body he held in both hands a Lewis gun, easily recognizable for its distinctive circular pan magazine and its large-diameter aluminum pipe around the barrel, a device meant to assist with the air cooling. Sheltering in the lee of this warrior stood a woman in folk costume with a high lacey headdress. The face of this representative of Belgian womanhood had been cut away by the intruder as had that of the infantryman on the left side — the Toronto side — of the cross. Beneath the scenes depicted, a panel inside a decorative border of laurel leaves and poppy blossoms had been left blank, presumably for the inscription of names of the parishioners killed in the war.

I admired the painting as a whole. I didn't know whether it was good art, but the clean style was refreshing, and the content gave me lots to think about. At the same time, it didn't strike me as a war memorial. The painted soldiers, despite their accurately portrayed uniforms and weaponry, failed to evoke my own war dead, the fellow officers and men that our battalion had lost between 1914 and 1918. There was something of the recruiting poster about it, a celebration of heroism from a naive civvy point of view. I thought I'd like to sit Nora down and talk to her about all that. That's when, standing in her violated nest, I felt a pang of loss.

I went through all the other mutilated pictures. In all of them it was a woman's face that was shredded or cut out, usually from a scene set in the Ward. These women were poor in dress, but dignified, not dragged down by their social situation. Although in the Christ Church design it was her own face Nora had given such a woman, I didn't think it was her face that had been the intruder's target. There were plenty more self-portraits left intact, including ones that showed her impoverished. Nora had tended to use the same faces repeatedly, not just her own but Koch's as well. I thought I also recognized Ernestine Lopez depicted in a few sketches and canvases as a gypsy woman. It therefore seemed possible that every missing female face belonged to the same human subject.

Sometimes Nora drew or painted the same scene several times, varying only details of composition or colour. It occurred to me that if I could find one overlooked intact version of a scene the intruder had defaced I would get an idea of what the missing woman looked like. I looked for art in corners of the studio the intruder mightn't have thought to search. I looked under the bed, where there was nothing. While I was on my hands and knees, I looked under the mattress as well. There I found what appeared to be a sketchbook.

When I opened it, I found the first third indeed full of sketches, the second third blank, and the last third used for some sort of journal. There was no sign the intruder had discovered this book. Among the sketches figured several of a woman in the same poses as the women whose faces had been hacked away from the scattered loose pictures. She appeared stockier and older than Nora, with wavy hair of a colour neither dark nor blonde. The most distinctive feature of her face was a break in the middle of her left eyebrow. There appeared to be a short, diagonal scar where the hair had not grown back.

I was hoping the journal portion of the book would tell me who this woman was or why Nora had drawn and painted her so often, but when I flipped pages to get to the back of the book I was disappointed to see only sales records — names, addresses, prices, notes of changes to their portraits requested by clients, notes on whether these were made or refused.

I turned my attention to the handwriting itself. Nora wrote on a slight back-slant. She made her letters small and with very few loops, but she spaced them out well as they marched across the page from narrow margin to narrow margin. The writing at times looked hurried, but was never indecipherable. I doubt if there's much more to graphology than to spiritualism or psychoanalysis, but Nora Britton's hand gave me the impression of an independent and slightly reserved individual.

In the journal, I read that she had painted the portraits of various university chancellors, businessmen, and diplomats. She had sold canvases for as much as five hundred dollars each, including most recently — a week before her death — a cityscape and a nude to Sir Joseph Deane.

I looked carefully through the rest of the loft. Wood and paper had been left ready for lighting in the stove. I took all of the fuel out and examined it in case Nora had left any documents there, either for safekeeping or for destruction. There were none. I tested floor boards to see if any were loose and concealed a hidden compartment. None was; none did. I checked the scattered books as well for papers stored between their pages and likewise the pockets and seams of the clothes from the overturned wardrobe. I inspected the food that had been tipped onto the floor when the intruder upset the dry sink. There was a loaf of brown bread, stale now, of the same sort as Nora had used to make her last sandwich. There were unopened tins of a variety of foods — fish, vegetables, soup, fruit in syrup. Also three fresh but bruised apples. To none of these could I attach any significance.

I took the sketchbook when I went back downstairs. There I found Carl Moretti sorting military medals.

"There were over four hundred thousand of these issued to Canadians." He held a silver disc suspended from its blue, black, white, and orange ribbon. "Practically worthless. And yet men will come in and expect me to give them as much as twenty dollars for one."

I recognized the British War Medal, which every Canadian that had served overseas or in a theatre of war was given.

"Now this one was given to just over seventy thousand Canadians. It's the 1914–1915 Star." Moretti produced from his right trouser pocket a bronze medal in the shape of a four-pointed star with crossed swords superimposed. The ribbon was red, white, and blue. "This one is my own, but I'm willing to let you have it for $150."

"I have one with my own name on it, thanks, Mr. Moretti." This medal, like the other, was for service rather than for any act of heroism. In the case of the star, service in a theatre of war before December 31, 1915. "Did you lose your leg in the first two years of the war?"

"I didn't lose it," said Moretti. "The German war took it. Here's that picture I mentioned."

On a wall crowded with cheap coloured prints hung a pastel original of three soccer players in identical striped jerseys, dark shorts, high socks, and cleated boots. Their legs were powerfully muscled. Two appeared to be in conversation: these were a more-athletic-than-life Herman Koch and a Carl Moretti with both legs. The third, an unknown, had his head turned to face the viewer. He was clean-shaven and balding with what dark hair remained above his ears slicked back flat to his head. He had a long upper lip and a mole on his left cheek. His coldly staring blue eyes, the compression of his thin lips, his left hand on his hip, his right foot raised and pinning the soccer ball beneath it — all conveyed a determination to seize and hold the initiative in any match. I wondered if in him I was seeing the man that had removed himself from Nora's mural, as well as removing the woman with the scarred eyebrow.

"You can have it for two hundred," said Moretti.

"That's not how the police work," I said. "I'll take it along as evidence and give you a receipt. When the picture is no longer needed, it will be returned to you. Who's this man?"

Moretti squinted at the balding man. "No one I've seen play soccer in this city. Or doing anything else for that matter."

I wrote on a page torn from my notebook, "Received from Mr. Carl Moretti a picture of three soccer players." I added my name and the date and handed the document over.

"That doesn't look very official. I'll have to collect a deposit of fifty dollars."

"Really?" I opened my eyes a little wider. "I can't see why you'd be so attached to a picture of you in conversation with Herman Koch."

"Koch?" Moretti made a face as if an insect had flown into his mouth.

"A little trimmer than when I saw him yesterday, but otherwise Koch to the life."

"Get it out of here," said Moretti, adding perversely, "Don't forget it's a Nora Britton: I expect top dollar if you decide to keep it."

Chapter 7

Uneeda Lunch — if you were walking fast down Queen West, you'd overshoot it. It wasn't my job to enforce municipal bylaws, but I doubt if any narrower a shop would have been legal. A counter seating six ran parallel to the west wall and just far enough from it to leave room for a range, a frig, a sink, a few shelves, and a skinny cook to move between them. I'm told there were two small tables at the very back of the room, but I never got in that far. Harry O'Brian once asked Al why he didn't replace the counter stools with chairs; the tall detective would have appreciated some support for his back. As if Al would have wanted us to linger with customers waiting out the door. For my part, the stools were fine. They were upholstered and an improvement on my desk chair at City Hall.

On Saturday there was no trouble getting a seat. While waiting for my order, I considered whether the wrecker of Nora's studio might be Archie Stillwater. Archie had used against Nora threatening language that the rector of Christ Church had found worth reporting. Archie had a record of violence against men and was suspected of violence against a woman. I didn't know what Archie looked like, but conceivably he was the model for the soccer player I was coming to think of as Baldy.

When I'd finished my salmon and horseradish sandwich, I poured a little rye into my coffee and speculated some more.

I wanted to see if I could convince myself that Archie Stillwater had killed Nora Britton. I didn't see him as a poisoner, but I was prepared to keep an open mind. I had already entertained the possibility that Archie had been inside that locked church with Nora until morning. And yet all this waiting for the rector to break in didn't seem to suit the hot-blooded sailor either. Now I started to work on a new theory.

Suppose Archie had seen the woman he called "Frau Koch" leave the church last Monday evening for a breath of air or an ice cream sundae. The sun would already have set, so he had the cover of darkness. Suppose he'd hustled her around a corner and beaten her savagely, leaving her on the ground nearly dead. Might not Nora then have just managed to drag herself inside the church and bolt the door before falling lifeless at the foot of the scaffold, on the highest level of which she'd left her paints and knapsack? The coroner had barely looked at Nora's body. He'd hastily concluded that her death had resulted from trauma and assumed that trauma had been caused by a fall from the top of the scaffold to the chancel floor. The possibility that she had been assaulted at ground level had clearly never entered his head.

I carried my three soccer players back to City Hall. The detective office, cramped and noisy on a weekday morning, was depopulated this Saturday afternoon, and I was able to hear myself talk on the telephone. The book had no listing for Stillwater, A. or J., but Stillwater, F. matched the address the rector had given me. A man identifying himself as Fred Stillwater answered and informed me that his son Archie was a crew member on the lake freighter *Lemoyne*, currently loading over fifteen thousand tons of coal at the port of Sandusky, Ohio. When I asked to speak to Jordan Stillwater, the man told me his father was at the family store until five o'clock. Stillwater Jewellers in Yorkville. Could he have Jordan return my call? I said no thanks. And why, the man asked, did I want to speak with his father anyway? I said I'd let Jordan himself explain after our interview.

I still hadn't made arrangements to have Nora's painting supplies picked up from the church. My first thought was to send a constable or two, but I decided to go myself. I phoned the Court Street Police Station, first of the dozen neighbourhood stations that served the city of Toronto. I had the good luck of finding Acting Detective Ned Cruickshank on duty and underemployed. I invited him to join me, which he sounded happy to do.

Fair-haired, rosy-cheeked Ned Cruickshank might still look like a new boy on the force, but I'd worked and chummed with him enough to believe that at the tender age of twenty-four he already deserved promotion to the band of detective sergeants at City Hall and was only being held back by the prejudice of old men.

I gave him the soccer players and Nora's journal to carry and filled him in on the case as we walked over to Christ Church Grange Park. On what I called the case.

"So properly speaking, it's not a case at all," he said in that earnest tone of voice he never seemed able to shake. "The inspector hasn't assigned you to investigate, and your unauthorized inquiries have turned up no evidence that Miss Britton didn't die accidentally."

"Sorry you came?"

"Not at all."

"You think I need supervision."

The acting detective got red in the face. I grinned, knowing I'd read him right.

Our knock at the rectory door was answered by Mrs. Hutchinson. I recognized her from her brief interruption of my Friday morning interview with her husband. Seeing her again today, in a proper but close-fitting powder blue cardigan, confirmed my impression that she was as much as two decades younger than her husband. Her chestnut hair was just starting to go grey. Her two most characteristic facial expressions appeared to be impersonal cheerfulness and thoughtful responsibility.

She said the rector was at the radio station, but that she could let us into the church. She would just tell the ladies of the knitting circle assembled in her living room to carry on without her for a few minutes. With colder weather coming, they were making scarves to distribute to the poorer children of the parish.

Standing inside the sanctuary, I took her name — Myrtle — and showed her the picture I'd got from Moretti.

"Nora's work," she said immediately. "I haven't seen it before, but it's her all over. Beautiful faces, so clear and shining. She made all of us look better than we are — I mean, better than we appear. I'd have loved for her to do my portrait. Such a shame she's gone."

"Is this Archie Stillwater?" I asked, pointing to Baldy.

"No, his name is Lou Sweet. Not a member of this church. He helped build the scaffold, I believe. Nora had a good deal of trouble with him and tried to bring him round by giving him work."

"What sort of trouble, Mrs. Hutchinson?" I asked.

"Mainly on account of his wife, I believe. Nora discovered her one day selling shoelaces in the Ward and asked to draw her. Nora told me this woman, Rose, had just the look that expressed the soul of the neighbourhood. Peculiar when you consider Rose grew up in Belgium."

I showed Myrtle Hutchinson the sketch in Nora's journal of the woman I believed had been effaced from all the portraits lying about the Elizabeth Street studio.

"Yes, that's Rose. She had what Nora described as a tragic face, sublime somehow. Our Lady of the Ward. Nora put her in the mural design so we would have her image before us every time we worshipped here. But I suppose no husband wants his wife used as the symbol of a slum. Lou didn't want the notoriety for her or for himself. For one thing, he didn't want to be labelled a bad provider. He was always out of work for one reason or another and until Nora hired him was thought unemployable."

"Who by?"

"Everyone — including himself, I think. There might have been more to his dislike of publicity; I don't know the details."

"Where can I find him?"

"I wouldn't know. The rector might, or at least have an address for Mr. Pan. Lou worked under his direction. Albert Pan he called himself. I believe he came from Hong Kong."

I sent Ned up to the chancel to see what he made of Mr. Pan's scaffold while I took the opportunity to ask the rector's wife a few more questions.

"Mrs. Hutchinson, did you ever give Nora Britton anything to eat or drink when she came to the church? Or did you ever pass on to her food or drink on behalf of any of the parishioners?"

"Certainly. Last Monday I baked four dozen hermit cookies. Do you know them? They're mostly brown sugar and dates — and spices. People are always dropping in. Naturally I gave Nora a few to keep her going through the night."

"Did you give her a sandwich too?"

"No, she said she'd made one for herself."

"What about coffee? She had a half-full Thermos with her in the church."

"No, she must have brought that with her from home as well."

"How did Miss Britton strike you when you saw her last Monday?" I asked. "Did she seem in good or poor health? Exhausted? Energetic?"

"Hale and hearty. She told me she'd taken Sunday and Monday off and had quite caught up on her sleep."

"On Monday evening, did you give her anything beside the hermit cookies to eat or drink?"

"No, I didn't. Are you asking if I poisoned her?"

"Did you?"

Myrtle Hutchinson compressed her lips, brushed a wisp of hair behind her right ear and looked at the floor. Her cheeks were colouring. She was plainly fighting to keep her temper.

"Forgive me, Mr. Shenstone. I've never met a detective before, and I don't know what to expect or what to say. I imagine you'll tell me to just answer your questions and not waste your time by taking offence."

"If you think of a sweeter way of saying that, I'll have it printed on a card to hand out to everyone I interview."

Myrtle laughed despite herself. "If I told you I was fond of Nora, whatever her personal morals — that I was protective of her and would never wish her harm — would you believe me?"

"What about her personal morals?"

"Oh, I thought that was supposed to be my motive for disliking her, the clergyman's wife condemning the adulteress."

"Adultery? Who with?"

"I see I've put my foot in it. I wouldn't tell you if I knew with whom, but the truth is I don't."

I took a deep breath and tried to keep my disbelief from showing in my face. I didn't see Myrtle Hutchinson as one of those careless talkers that let secrets just slip out. I doubted she put her foot in much she wanted to step around.

"What exactly made you suspect her?" I asked.

"I merely saw her passionately kissing a man sitting behind the wheel of an open car. Her back was to me; I couldn't see his face at all. I was going to ask her to eat supper with us, but when I saw that kiss I turned and went back in the house. So I never got a look at the man."

"When was this?" I asked.

"The Wednesday before last, ten days ago, at about five o'clock. I remember because Wednesday evenings our daughter and her son come over. Viola's husband died at Passchendaele. Our grandson is having to grow up without a father. I thought of inviting Nora because she liked Johnnie, took an interest in his drawing. A day later, I asked her innocently what kind of car her husband drives. She said Herman didn't have a car. And she saw right through me. She said she and her husband had a non-exclusive marriage; each of them reserved the right to have affairs with other people. That was something new for me. Not adultery, of course — but the frankness about it. New for Toronto too, I'd think, however they do it in Hollywood or Paris or New York. I confess, I was speechless."

Myrtle was quiet again a moment, remembering her shock.

What was new for me, listening to the rector's wife, was the possibility that Nora as well as her hubby had been taking advantage of the non-exclusivity of their marriage. Something new perhaps since Greenwich Village days when only Herman appeared to be playing the field. Nora — the Nora I'd built up in my mind from images and hearsay — became a fuller woman for me, less of a plaster saint. And, yes, I was a little jealous. More to the point, I now had another potential suspect to investigate. Who could have been at the receiving end of that passionate kiss?

"Did she say anything else?" I asked.

"That she didn't expect me to approve, but that she'd try to be more discreet. I haven't told the rector about this, and I hope you won't either. I'm afraid it would change the way he thinks of her."

"You asked Nora what kind of car her husband drives. What kind of car did you see?"

"Open, as I said — a roadster. I didn't catch the make."

"What colour was it, Mrs. Hutchinson?"

"I didn't notice."

"Was it light or dark?"

"Light."

"Ivory? Tan? Pearl grey? The colour of your sweater?"

"I told you I didn't notice the colour. I didn't. Now I'd best be getting back to the knitting circle. Please close the door when you leave: it locks itself."

"Do you know if anyone else gave Miss Britton anything to eat or drink on Monday?"

"No, I don't."

"No one left anything of the kind with you to give her?"

"No."

"To your knowledge, did any member of the Stillwater family come anywhere near Nora or the church or the rectory that day?"

"Not at all. I believe my husband was right to tell you what various generations of Stillwaters said about Nora, but to my knowledge none of them came anywhere near her or her kit last Monday."

"Do you believe Nora Britton was murdered?"

"I don't know. When her body was found, I accepted that her death was an accident. Despite her claim that she was well-rested, after a few hours of work she could have got light-headed. I wouldn't have climbed up on a scaffold like that myself. Now? Well, now the possibility of murder has been raised, I think it's just as well that someone like you is investigating."

"Someone like me," I said, tasting the oddity of the expression. It was as if she were reluctant to say *the police* or *a detective*. "Someone like me usually finds in an investigation that small details have large consequences. I'd like you to think about the colour of that car and tell me if it comes back to you."

"All right."

I thanked Myrtle Hutchinson and told her she could go. Watching her walk neither slowly nor quickly towards the north door, I wondered how much of what she had told me had been the truth. Her voice had been calm, light, unemphatic, even when she'd been angry with me. By her own admission, she kept secrets from her husband. I wondered what she was keeping from me. And why she had been so keen to plant the idea, all the while pretending it had just slipped out, that Nora Britton had a lover.

When I approached the scaffold, Ned Cruickshank was already climbing down the ladders with cans of paint and thinner dangling by their wire handles from his wrists.

"I may have found the poison, Paul," he said. "Green paint — something arsenite. I've heard of kids in a green-painted bedroom wasting away."

I told Ned that because of stories like that, Paris green was now only used as a pesticide, not a paint.

"Maybe she had old paints. Don't you think something like that could be what made her dizzy?"

"Let's see the cans. What you've got there looks new. And there's no poison warning label."

"This can is closed, but not sealed," Ned persisted. "Paris green could have been added to the harmless green paint powder Miss Britton bought. It might look the same."

"Let me sniff." I took the can from Ned and pried off the lid with my pocket knife.

Ned opened his mouth to warn me off, but changed his mind and just ran his tongue nervously over his lips as I stuck my nose in the can.

"No garlic smell," I said. "I don't believe there's any arsenic compound in there. And, even if there were, the poison wouldn't pose the same inhalation risk in a large space like this church as it would in a cozy children's bedroom."

Ned was ready to move on. "These cans were all I could carry in one trip. I better go up and get the rest of the painting supplies."

"I'll come along." I followed Ned up the first of the two ladders leading to the platform where she had been working. "Odd, isn't it," I said, "that green was the only colour she'd used before she died? She had a long way to go."

"There are touches of brown too," said Ned.

"Where?"

He pointed to one dark, drop-shaped patch two feet above the level of the first platform. It didn't appear to bear any relation to the charcoal sketch that covered the prepared white wall. In fact, it looked to me more like a spatter than like an intentional application of paint.

"Another up here," Ned called from the platform above me. I climbed up and looked at a bigger spatter.

"Did you find any cans of brown paint, Ned?"

"No. On closer inspection, it doesn't even look like paint."

I had to agree. I put my nose close to the mark. I wasn't sure if it had an odour, but something about it — maybe just the colour — reminded me of Nora's knapsack. I figured whatever had soiled the knapsack had soiled the wall as well. Finding no more spatters on the wall, I climbed down to the floor of the chancel and crawled under the scaffold at a point directly under the marks on the wall. The dark brown wooden floor in this underlit recess of Christ Church didn't make the stain easy to see, but I could feel a crust, like a dried puddle. There was no chance that a spill from Nora's Thermos of coffee had created the spatters above or the pool below. Coffee is too thin. Nor could this substance be her blood: the rector had seen no wounds or signs of bleeding anywhere on her body. Although I didn't take my pulse, I'm sure it picked up a few beats. I used my knife to scrape some of the deposit from the floorboards into a clean handkerchief and backed out from under the bamboo scaffold.

"What do you think it is, Paul?"

"Professor Linacre will say for sure, but I'm betting it's Nora Britton's vomit. Her death may still have been an accident, but she must have been exposed to something very nasty. Taking what's on her knapsack together with what's on the wall and the floor, we're dealing with a lot of puke."

"Are we going to Linacre's lab now?"

My watch told me it was not yet four. Three hours too early to get Linacre's report on Nora's meal.

"How about you go there and take this." I handed Ned the folded handkerchief containing the scrapings from the chancel floor. "Tell the professor we suspect it's the same stuff that's on the knapsack. After you've talked to him, if you're still keen, there is something else you could do."

"Say the word."

"You've had a look at the scaffold. Anything strike you about it?"

"It's a new one on me. It looks flimsy, but feels solid. Pretty ingenious, I'd say."

"Anything odd from a safety point of view?"

"The railing along the outside of the top platform seems low. That's what struck me. I'd have to go over the thing in detail to make sure there was nothing else."

"I was struck by the same thing," I said. "Now you heard Myrtle Hutchinson say two men worked on that scaffold, Albert Pan and Lou Sweet. You also heard her say that Sweet had a history of ill will against Nora. It looks as if he ransacked her studio on Elizabeth Street last night, cutting all likenesses of himself and his wife Rose from the pictures he found there. What I'd like you to do is track down Pan and Sweet."

"To find out why that rail is low?"

"Bingo. We don't know what Pan thought of Nora, so try to find that out too. As for Sweet, the rector's wife thinks Nora managed to smooth things over with him, but his vandalism last night suggests otherwise. See if he had a strong enough motive to kill her. And, if so, how he might have done so."

"The low railing apart?" said Ned.

"By itself that would have been too hit and miss. What opportunity might he have had to give her whatever made her throw up?"

"Where and when do I report back?"

"Do as much as you can or feel like," I said. "It is just about Saturday night after all. Write down what you find out and leave notes on my desk at City Hall before you go home."

"What will you be doing, Paul?"

"Suspicions about foul play arose from some loose talk by members of a family called Stillwater. It's about time I paid them a visit."

Chapter 8

When I was growing up, Yorkville still had the character of the village it had been before its annexation by Toronto. Now this residential suburb was being drawn into the ever-widening whirlpool of the city. According to the papers, the new public library branch was setting records for loans, including to borrowers living far outside its immediate neighbourhood. The new Mount Sinai Hospital had settled in on Yorkville Avenue, and corner lots on Bay Street were selling to commercial interests for upwards of twenty thousand dollars.

Despite the large number of new businesses, Stillwater Jewellers was not hard to find. I stopped across the street to admire a storefront entirely of glass, including a glass door. With no protective grillwork in evidence anywhere, the façade seemed a cheeky challenge to those coveting the valuable merchandise inside. Although it was still an hour till sunset, the electric sign outside was already lit, and all four of the electroliers suspended from the tin ceiling had been turned on to create dazzling reflections off the polished stones. Through the glass I saw that a stout, well-dressed gentleman with a black moustache had the store to himself. He stood behind the counter arranging gems in the display case. Even at a distance of fifteen to twenty yards, I could see that he was a generation too young to be Jordan Stillwater, the retired pharmacist. I had a remarkably clear view of him, from his pomaded hair to his glittering cufflinks. There was little pedestrian or vehicle traffic at this hour. What shops there were — and these were interspersed with private dwellings — had for the most part closed early for Saturday.

I was about to cross the street when a black Ford approached from my right. It was a four-door touring model with the canvas top up. I waited for it to pass, but it stopped in front of a closed lingerie shop next door to Stillwater's. The driver, a man whose turned-up collar and pulled-down hat hid most of his face, stayed in the car with the motor running. A woman got out of the back seat on my side of the car, her face mostly concealed by her cloche hat and fur collar. Someone also got out from the front right passenger seat. I couldn't see much of him at first, but as soon as the two car doors closed, the driver pulled ahead and stopped again in front of Stillwater's without killing the motor. Then I got a look at the man on the sidewalk. He was wearing a hat and suit, no overcoat. He took a nervous look around and patted his right side jacket pocket, which sagged and bulged. A few words were exchanged with the woman, who took his arm. He shook her hand off, but she put it right back with some sharp rebuke. I could hear her voice but not the words. This time he let it stay. The two headed for the door to the jewellery shop.

As soon as they were inside, I approached the Ford and spoke to the driver.

"Get out of here now. Just drive away."

Two-days' stubble decorated the man's lean jaw. He took a quick look at me and my badge, then fixed his eyes on the road ahead.

"What law am I breaking?" A toothpick bobbed in the corner of his mouth when he spoke.

"None — I'm trying to keep it that way. Scram or I'll handcuff you to the outside of this tin Lizzie and neither one of you will be able to move."

The driver released the handbrake.

"Don't come back," I said.

The car pulled away. The couple had entered the jewellery shop and were making like fiancés, getting the man behind the counter to show them rings. I quickly checked that the Ford was still driving straight down Yorkville Avenue. When I looked back, the husband-to-be was holding an automatic pistol on the jeweller while his future bride scooped the diamond rings off the counter into her handbag.

Events were moving faster than I'd anticipated. I moved to the edge of the window to be less conspicuous. I didn't like leaving a citizen at the wrong end of a gun, particularly a gun in the hand of a robber so inexperienced-looking. But the jeweller was holding his hands calmly in the air and appeared to be avoiding any movement that would startle or provoke the gunman. My entry might be just such a movement and increase the risk of bloodshed. With any luck, the robbers would soon be leaving. I could make my move then without endangering anyone but myself.

The woman closed her bag and turned. Seeing no getaway car, she got scared. Then she scared me by grabbing the gunman's right arm. He managed not to clench his finger on the trigger, but when he turned the sight of the empty curb spooked him. Leaving the woman, he ran to the door and out onto the sidewalk where I felled him with my best rugby tackle. Supine on the concrete, he was still holding his firearm.

"Throw the iron away," I said.

He tried instead to get it pointed at some piece of me. A shot was fired — but not by him. From inside the shop. I couldn't yet afford to look in that direction. Sitting astride my man, I punched him in the face. That loosened his grip, and I was able to take possession of the Colt Hammerless .38.

The woman stumbled into the street clutching her right hand, from which blood was dripping.

"God, Lou," she wailed, "why did you leave me behind?"

"Can it, Iva. Where's that husband of yours?"

Lou? I took a closer look at the man I'd just socked and saw a long upper lip, a mole on his left cheek. When I pulled off his hat, I was less than astonished to see he was bald in the centre of his head with dark hair slicked back over his ears to either side. I hadn't had leisure previously to make an identification, but even under more relaxed circumstances I might not have twigged right away that this pathetic creature was the heroic soccer player Nora Britton had portrayed. Lou's blue eyes were watery and self-pitying rather than coldly focused.

I pocketed his gun and put my handcuffs on him. Having already parted with my own handkerchief, I searched Lou for his. I found it none too clean, so suggested Iva let me have hers to tie around her hand. The bullet had gone right through. I told her I had to take possession of her handbag anyway. The thin square of white lawn I found inside didn't do much to slow the bleeding. Having just been abandoned by two men, however, she gave me a look of gratitude for the attention.

"They're bound to have a better bandage inside," I said, hustling them both into the shop.

The jeweller held a pistol in his hand and was pointing it our way.

"You can put that down, sir," I said. "I'm a police officer."

"Anyone can say that." The jeweller's voice was tight. The lavish lighting now had another surface to reflect from, the slick of nervous perspiration on his well-fed face.

"Anyone can — but I have the man that robbed you in cuffs. May I approach and show you my badge?"

I felt Iva slipping backwards from my side towards the door. I reached back and pulled her forward. Luckily she was to my right, so I was dragging her by the unhurt hand.

"Never mind the badge," the jeweller said in a more reasonable tone. He plainly didn't want the three of us crowding in on him. He set down his revolver — a Smith &

Wesson Safety Hammerless, from what I could see — on the counter before him.

Freed from the threat of being shot a second time, Iva sobbed in relief.

I told Lou to go sit with his back against the counter where I could see him, and he complied. He raised his linked hands to his mouth to feel his teeth — presumably to see if I'd loosened any. Since I'd put the cuffs on him, he hadn't uttered a peep. There was one straight-backed chair on the customers' side of the counter. I put it facing me two yards from Lou and installed Iva there.

"Mr. Stillwater?" I said to the shopkeeper.

"Yes."

"I'd like to use your phone. But first this woman has a wound that needs dressing."

"Serves her right. Don't waste your sympathy."

"I'm sorry you were held up," I replied. "But the person in greatest need here is the woman you shot. Now do you have a first-aid kit or do you want her to go on bleeding on your fancy tile floor?"

Stillwater put his gun in one drawer and from another took a roll of gauze, which he shoved across the counter in my direction. I traded it for Iva's purse.

"See if all your gems are in there," I said.

"Your name and rank?"

"Detective Sergeant Paul Shenstone. Check with City Hall." I gave Stillwater the number of the detective office. "And pass me the phone when you're done."

I wound most of the gauze over the handkerchief and tied it. I told Iva to hold her hand up above her head.

"Cripes, that hurts," she sobbed. She had big eyes in a narrow face, and big teeth now biting into her lower lip. She was trying to be brave and not doing too bad a job.

"Stay tough," I said. "It's hot in here, and I don't want you to faint. I'm going to unbutton your coat."

"I can do it." She did it with her left hand.

"What about your hat?"

"I'll keep it on."

I guessed the pigeon grey felt wrapping around her face gave her some sense of privacy.

"Mr. Shenstone," Stillwater called to me. "Deputy Inspector Crate vouches for you. He wants a word."

I quickly covered my smile with the telephone mouthpiece. There was no such rank as deputy inspector, but Rudy had improvised brilliantly, and nothing would have sounded more reassuring to Stillwater than Rudy's Mayfair accent. I could look forward to some pretty strong reminders that I owed the English-born detective sergeant a favour. Meanwhile, I kept up the farce.

"Yes, sir," I said. "I pretty well stumbled on a jewel robbery in progress. Could you send around a couple of constables to take custody of the perpetrators. Yes, sir. A man and a woman. She's been shot and needs to visit a hospital before being locked up. He's got a colourful bruise developing around the mouth, but nothing to trouble a doctor about. Right, sir. Straight to the cooler."

While waiting for the uniformed officers, I had Stillwater bring out another couple of chairs. The shopkeeper took one while I placed the other for myself opposite Iva and Lou, who was fine on the floor.

"I take it you're not Jordan Stillwater," I said to our host, who appeared from his bearing and complexion to be in his mid-fifties at most. His hair showed no grey, but that could have been black dye.

"Certainly not. What gave you the idea I was?"

"It's just that on the telephone this afternoon, Mr. Fred Stillwater told me Jordan would be here till five."

"I'm Fred. That must have been my father you were talking to. He likes his little jokes."

"My arm sure is getting tired sticking up there," said Iva. "It's like trying to get the teacher's attention in class."

"Yeah?" said Lou through swollen lips. "And you always wanted to show her you knew the answers, didn't you, Iva? The girl with all the smart ideas. 'Make like lovebirds so he'll bring out the ice,' you said. Worked out just dandy."

"It would have too if the copper hadn't chased Lloyd away."

"Wish I'd never met either of you," said Lou.

"Same to you with knobs on." She turned to me. "So, mister, can I put my arm down?"

"Sure," I said. "Only if blood comes through the bandage, stick it up again."

When the constables took Lou and Iva off in different directions, there were no fond farewells. I'd be seeing them both again, but for now I stayed with Fred Stillwater. I started by getting him to hang a closed sign on his glass door and taking his statement regarding the robbery.

I got him to write out a detailed description and evaluation of each of the three rings that had been taken and recovered. He put their combined worth at about eighteen hundred dollars. Permit requirements for possession of firearms had been repealed six years earlier. Permits to carry were still required, but he assured me he never took his revolver out of the store. As to his reason for firing, he said he'd had no time to think it through. His only thought was to prevent the robbers from getting away with his merchandise.

"Did it occur to you that you were firing towards a public street and might have hit a passerby?" I asked.

"That's safety glass," said Stillwater. If my questions made him uncomfortable, he didn't show it. He sounded as if he were used to being on good terms with the police.

"Safety glass won't shatter, Mr. Stillwater, but it still lets bullets through. Have you ever done any target shooting to familiarize yourself with your weapon?"

"No, detective, I haven't had time."

He said he'd been in the jewellery business for more than thirty years, but that this shop was new. Among the security measures he hadn't had time to install was an electric burglar alarm.

I said I wanted to ask him about the robbers. Had he ever seen either of them before?

"Not that I recall."

"I have reason to believe the man's name is Lou Sweet. Haven't you seen him in or around Christ Church Grange Park?"

"That's my church, but no — I don't think so. The name means nothing to me either."

"I understand he was helping erect the scaffolding used to paint the war memorial mural."

"Ah, I wouldn't know. I was never in the sanctuary while that work was being done. Is he a church member?"

"I'm told not."

"Good. I'd be sorry to think a member of our own congregation would rob me."

"Mr. Stillwater, did you oppose giving the mural commission to Nora Britton?"

"Forgive me, detective, but what has my opinion on that have to do with the robbery?"

"I didn't find myself in front of your store this afternoon by chance," I said. "I'm investigating the death of Miss Britton."

"I thought that death was ruled an accident."

"It may have been, but there remain questions I'd like answered."

"I didn't approve of her design, if it *was* her design and not her German husband's. It doesn't express grief as British people feel it. The servicemen depicted are armed and whole. They don't represent the fallen whose names are to be inscribed beneath the painting. I also didn't feel a woman would be capable, even with help, of executing a project on that scale. And unhappily I've been proven right. The whole idea of blind judging was a mistake in my view."

"Did you share your view with other members of the congregation? With your family?"

"Certainly. Within the family we were all agreed, and a respectable segment of the congregation agreed with us as well. Nevertheless, we had no power to keep the project from going forward. Last year we stopped the commission going to the Hun, Nora Koch's husband. But if her design had not been accepted, we would have lost both our rector, Mr. Hutchinson, and the church's principal benefactor, Sir Joseph Deane. There are other generous members of the congregation, and our family does its bit, but ours is not an affluent parish, Mr. Shenstone. We encompass the Ward and most of Kensington, the poorest areas in the city."

"Would you have considered Mr. Hutchinson's resignation a great loss?"

"Without a doubt. He doesn't like our family much, but that doesn't blind me to his merits. He has an orderly mind where most clergymen in my experience are well-meaning dunderheads. His intelligence serves him in the pulpit and no less so when it comes to grasping the church finances. And then he understands the value of showmanship. I don't know if you've heard any of his radio broadcasts, but they brought new members and new money into the church. Don't think he hasn't been offered a bishopric. He's turned down more offers than one. Why? Because he believes the work of the church is done at the parish level. And he does it well."

"So from your point of view Miss Britton's death is the best of all possible outcomes. You lose the mural you disapprove of without losing your rector or Sir Joseph."

"That's an unpleasant way to put it, Mr. Shenstone. I regret Mrs. Koch's death, but at the same time I feel she brought it on herself."

"By provoking the German-haters?"

"No." Fred Stillwater's voice was cold and controlled. "By undertaking work that was beyond her, or anyone of her sex."

"I understand that you have a son named Archie, who predicted that Nora Britton would 'fall off her scaffold and break her neck.'"

"I didn't hear Archie say that, but I might have said the same. Did she break her neck?"

"As good as. The cause of death is still under investigation. Where was Archie last Monday?"

Stillwater ran a plump finger between his neck and his tight collar. His voice started to rise in volume. "Are you trying to pin a murder on my boy? Push that line and I'll be having words with the police commissioners."

I managed not to tremble in fear.

"Fortunately," the jeweller continued, "Archie's alibi is iron-clad. He's a cook on a freighter that was sailing on Lake Erie."

"Nothing to worry about then," I said pleasantly. "Was food from your house ever sent to the rectory or to the church?"

This question seemed to cause more surprise than anger. "What on earth for?"

"For church functions, or just to support the rector's household, or to feed Nora Britton while she worked on the mural."

"Our family supports the church and its works with cash, not cucumber sandwiches. We had no interest in supporting Koch's wife in any way, and nothing was sent to her from our house."

"Where were you last Monday?"

"Will you be asking as much of every Christ Church parishioner that disapproved of that woman's daubs on our wall?"

"I'm asking you."

"I lunched at home Monday and spent the afternoon here conferring with the electrician on the lighting and with other workmen putting the finishing touches on the shop. In the evening, I had dinner at the Board of Trade Club. I was home by ten thirty and didn't go out again. Do you require a list of witnesses?"

"Not at present. Do you know where your father was during the same period?"

"He was also out of town."

"Where?"

Stillwater hesitated. "Montreal. He was visiting friends. You'd have to ask him for particulars."

I let my eyes travel around the shop while wondering if there was anything else I should be asking. "What reason might Mr. Hutchinson have for not liking your family, Mr. Stillwater?"

The jeweller's face relaxed unexpectedly into a smile. "He's a teetotal priest — not a common crotchet among Anglican clergy, but just our luck. Ours is not a teetotal family."

I thanked Stillwater for his time. He did not thank me for saving his rings, but asked if he would have to appear in court. I said not if Lou and Iva pleaded guilty, which I intended to persuade them to do. In return, I urged him to install grillwork in his shop windows and a burglar alarm. While I was folding up the jeweller's statement and putting it in my pocket, he tried to sell me a waterproof watch.

"I caught you glancing at my ad for the Rolex Oyster, worn without the least damage by Miss Mercedes Gleitze on her swim across the English Channel last week."

I told him I rarely had much to do with water and took my leave.

Chapter 9

Back at City Hall, there was a note on my desk from Ned informing me that Professor Linacre would be at his lab till eleven tonight if I cared to drop around. The acting detective said he'd report later on what success he'd had tracking down the scaffold-builders. I hoped he was starting with Albert Pan and not wasting his Saturday evening tracking down Lou Sweet. I left him a note to the effect that we already had that criminal mastermind under lock and key.

I deposited Lou's pistol in the evidence locker and made my way to Lou's cell for a chat. It started with my asking questions and his mumbling back as he made the most of his bruised mouth. Tedious as it was to get him to repeat answers, I was grateful that he wasn't the strong, silent type. I didn't even have to promise that in exchange for his co-operation I'd keep him out of prison; I did no more than issue the standard promise that if he played ball I'd put in a word.

"You've had a busy day, Lou," I said. "You didn't just try to rob a jewellery store. You also broke into Nora Britton's studio and defaced several works of art."

"What makes you say that?" Lou mumbled something further. When repeated, it came out as, "I don't even know where her studio is."

"Sure you do, Lou. It's just down the block from your house, the house Miss Britton made look so bad in her paintings of the Ward. What was it about those paintings that got your goat?"

"She showed the rough cast cracked and falling off. I did that stucco work myself." Mumble mumble.

"Say it again, Lou."

"That's my trade, and I'm telling you it was well done."

"You didn't like Miss Britton's pictures of Rose either. That's why you defaced all the ones of her in the studio. It had to be you. Who else would have felt so strongly about them? Who else would have cut you out of the mural design?"

Mumble mumble.

"Again, Lou."

"She made Rose look poor, as if I didn't look after her."

"Is stealing diamonds your idea of looking after her?"

"I just can't find work right now, nothing in my line. I overheard someone in Christ Church say a gent called Stillwater was opening a jewellery store in Yorkville. I told Lloyd Hanson, and he checked it out. Said there was no alarm and we could hold it up easy. I shouldn't have listened to him."

"Nora Britton gave you honest work and you wrecked her studio."

"She was dead by then." Lou was no longer mumbling.

"How did you manage that?"

"What? I had nothing to do — "

"You worked on the scaffolding she fell from."

"Talk to the Chinaman. I did nothing but what he told me to do."

"The top railing was low — easy to fall over. Why was that?"

"The dame asked for that herself. Some scatterbrained idea about wanting a backrest for when she ate her lunch up there."

"Did you ever give her anything to eat or drink?"

"Hell no. She could afford to feed herself."

"Did you see her last Monday?"

"No. Our work was done by then and paid in full. There was no reason to see her again."

A clerk from the detective office chose this moment to appear outside Sweet's cell and tell me there was a phone call for me. I wasn't sorry to go. I'd run out of questions for the moment, and if I thought up some later, well, Lou wasn't going anywhere.

"That pistol of Lloyd's I was carrying," Sweet said as I started upstairs, "it wasn't loaded."

"I noticed," I said, "but the law doesn't care. It was still armed robbery."

On the stairs, I asked the clerk if the caller had given a name.

"He called himself Joe Deane."

That put a spring in my step.

Upstairs, I grabbed the candlestick off my desk and jammed the earpiece tight against my head. "Shenstone here," I said.

The voice at the other end of the line was a satiny baritone. "Glad to have caught you, Mr. Shenstone. I understand you're looking into Nora Britton's death."

I didn't deny it. I figured Deane had been talking to Eric Hutchinson.

"I'd be happy to help. Happier than I've been about anything since I heard the awful news. Why don't you come over to the house this evening?" He gave an address on Jarvis Street.

"What time, Mr. — Sir Joseph?"

"Now. Sooner the better."

I thought about suggesting I come after supper, but that would have been fishing for an invitation. I took the Yonge streetcar north and walked two blocks east on Gloucester Street to Jarvis.

Along the way, I made a mental list of the people I'd talked to since tying my shoelaces this morning — Carl Moretti, Jordan Stillwater (briefly, by phone, when he pretended to be Fred), Ned Cruickshank, Myrtle Hutchinson, Lloyd (the driver), his wife Iva, Fred Stillwater, Lou Sweet. I followed that by listing the items left on my personal agenda. The main attraction had to be getting briefed by Dalton Linacre on Nora's vomit and the remains of her lunch. But I also wanted to grill Jordan Stillwater, check Archie Stillwater's alibi, find out what Ned had learned about Albert Pan, speak with Nora's family, and identify Nora's mystery boyfriend.

I understood the bohemian theory of non-exclusive marriage, but wondered whether the flimsy human intellect might not on occasion find itself insufficient to tame such a stubborn beast as jealousy. Any cop will tell you that, even in this enlightened age, love triangles often end in violent death. And Nora might have figured in two love triangles — one with Herman and her roadster-driving sheik, another with Herman and a sheba of his. I thought I might want another word with Koch's neighbour through the secret door, Ernestine Lopez.

The strange thing was that Joe Deane had figured on none of my lists, even though he'd played a central role in the mural project.

I expected Deane's house to be impressive, and wasn't disappointed. Twilight had faded into night, but the street lamps clearly illuminated a pink brick and stone cube of between fifteen and twenty yards in each direction — a cube relieved by turrets, galleries, bay windows, and more architectural gewgaws than I had words for. With its wide, semi-circular arches and window tops, it appeared to be the same style and vintage as City Hall. Which meant Deane, who could not have been more than a teenager at the time of construction, had acquired it rather than having it built to order. This impression was confirmed by the entwined initials C.C. carved over the front door.

The doorbell was answered by Sir Joseph himself, wearing checked trousers and a canary yellow cardigan. I recognized his cleft chin and full head of centre-parted, springy white hair from newspaper photos. In person, he was slighter than I expected, short and thin. Out of scale, somehow, with his massive dwelling. My first question was what C.C. stood for.

"'Choo-Choo' is my standard answer, and believe me you're not the first to ask." Joe Deane's amused smile and merry blue eyes suggested he didn't mind the repetition. "The house was built for some poor chump that put too much money into the Grand Trunk Railway and lost it all. He would have done better to invest in timber leases. No need to embarrass him by giving his name — though a sleuth like you would have no trouble finding it out. Come through to the study, Shenstone."

The study was at the back of the ground floor, which gave me a chance to appreciate the quantity of art hung along the way. As to the quality, I was prepared to give my host the benefit of the doubt. Deane led me into an oak-panelled room with a library table as well as a large desk. At the former, two places had been set with cutlery, napkins, and plates of cold meat and salad.

"I should explain." Deane was pouring us large glasses of lemonade, about my tenth- or twelfth-favourite drink. "My wife, sister, and youngest daughter wanted to drag me to the Royal Alexandra tonight to see *The Vagabond King*. They think I'd love operetta if only I'd give it a chance. And this was to be the last performance. I told them not to miss it then, but that regrettably I had to work. It's true that I'm expecting a phone call I can't afford to miss, but while waiting I have time to talk to you. Cook put this snack together on short notice. You'll hurt her feelings if you don't eat up."

We both ate and Deane drank. The potato salad, grated carrots, and pink roast beef were terrific. I went easy on the hot mustard.

"What did you want to tell me, Sir Joseph?" I said.

"Eric Hutchinson said you wanted to see Koch's mural design." Deane pointed over my shoulder.

I turned and stood up to face the wall behind my chair. If I'd noticed the painting hanging there at all, I certainly hadn't connected it with Koch. The only other work of his I'd seen was the one of a gale on Georgian Bay, and that scene contained no people. This painting was executed in the same imprecise, patchy style as that landscape of his, but looked older — perhaps because of its religious topic. How old I couldn't say, but like something I might have seen in a church in Flanders during the war or in Cologne when my regiment occupied that city after the Armistice. In a meadow dotted with wildflowers (including the inevitable poppies), Koch had placed two female figures to either side of a sarcophagus. The stone lid had been dislodged and turned partway. Above this opening, and appearing to have emerged from it, hovered a radiant male figure with arms extended horizontally and bent skywards at the elbows. Of the two women, the one on the left was weeping. Her face, partially hidden by the hood of a slate-grey robe, was turned down towards the base of the sarcophagus, on which was engraved a maple leaf. The figure on the opposite side of the grave was not looking at it, but up at the resurrected man. She wore the same grey cloak as her sister, but the hood had fallen off her tilted-back head, and her face in profile was full of wonder and peaceful joy.

For me, death is final, and there's nothing left for the survivors but mourning or forgetting. But Koch's representation of Grief and Hope struck me dumb. It was the best possible memorial for a church. Not only that, but — in spite of my most considered conviction — I wouldn't have thought kindly of anyone that tried to destroy the vision of the woman on the right and plunge her back into the agony of the woman on the left. I thought of fallen comrades, seasoned brother officers and recruits fresh from Ontario farms and towns, the best of soldiers and the best of friends. I tried to imagine how sweet it would be to be able to believe them all whole and happy in a better place.

Deane allowed time for all this to sink in. Eventually he said, "There was a Frenchman on that first panel of judges. He swore that for conception and execution you wouldn't find a better painting of this kind in any country." He shrugged. "The relatives of the Christ Church war dead didn't like to see the risen man wearing nothing but a loincloth, thought it disrespectful somehow. I'm told the Germans have a different attitude to the unclothed body."

"It's a swell picture," I said, "but it was Nora Britton's design I asked the rector about."

"Ah — now *it* exists in several versions. I have one I haven't framed yet."

Deane went to a wooden filing cabinet behind his desk and returned with a watercolour sketch, which he set beside my plate.

The layout was familiar to me from the vandalized painting in Nora's studio. So too the style. In the watercolour, the outlines were even cleaner than in the oil version, the colours clearer. Seeing it so soon after a work of Koch's further heightened the sense of contrast.

"Beautiful, isn't it?" said Deane.

I thought the answer too obvious to need saying. I was looking more closely at the individual figures.

"So which would you choose, Shenstone? Koch's or Britton's?"

I waved away the question. "I'm no judge of art."

Privately, I was thinking I'd choose his for the wall of the church and hers for my apartment wall. Nora, impossibly lovely in her pauper's dress, stared at me out of the picture, while at her side in the uniform of my regiment and with an infusion of backbone stood the studio-wrecker and failed robber Lou Sweet. On the other side of the central cross, I saw Lou's Rose for the first time in the dress of her native Belgium and beside her — not Koch as in the studio oil, but a beefed-up, rejuvenated Sir Joseph Deane. Deane and no mistake, with cleft chin and ballooning hair from which all trace of silver had been removed.

"Koch's is great," said Deane, "but I appreciate the way Nora Britton honours our heroes with good, crisp lines. I wish I'd known her when we were designing war bond posters."

"When did you first meet Nora Britton?"

"Not till after she'd won the contest. Last February. God, Shenstone, I can't believe she's gone."

I gave him a moment, then asked, "How much did you see of her in the eight months from last February till her death?"

"Quite a bit," Deane said, while the look on his face said, *Not nearly enough.* He cleared his throat and continued. "There were arrangements to be made about her schedule and her expenses and so forth. I represented Christ Church Grange Park in most of those dealings with her. There were also some fine points of the design to be ironed out."

"Would you meet once a week?"

"Not so often. Perhaps every two weeks. I did have her around to the house to meet the family. And then, when I found out she was living on her own, to eat with us from time to time."

"Did she have any closer friend than you? Perhaps someone she saw every day."

"You mean a man?"

"Or a woman — a confidante, someone I could ask about the fine detail of her life."

"No, I don't think so. I never heard there was anyone like that, of either sex."

"How often did you sit for her?"

"Just once. She was busy finishing up other commissions and clearing the decks for our project. During that one three-hour sitting, she made a lot of sketches, but nothing came of it."

"Except this." I passed Nora's watercolour to Deane and pointed to the image of him holding the Lewis gun.

"That's not me." My host blushed. "Is it? Well ... maybe."

"You know it is."

His foolish grin broadcast the middle-aged man's delight at being petted by a younger woman.

Deane hurried to explain. "She was playing a prank. This would never have made it up onto the church wall. I told you there were design points to be ironed out. One of them had to do with her choice of her husband as a model for this machine gunner. It was her way of taunting the Christ Church congregation for their prejudice. Of course, I told her she couldn't do that. The mural would have been defaced for sure. This sketch was her way of paying me back."

"You had a playful relationship with Nora Britton."

"When I do business with people, I make friends."

"You bought two canvases from her for five hundred dollars each. How businesslike a deal was that?"

"I likely paid a little more than she'd have got elsewhere. I still think I made a shrewd investment."

Deane pointed towards an oil hanging over his desk. It was perhaps one of the ones Lou Sweet objected to. It depicted a house with a broken window and crumbling stucco siding. Construction debris littered the sagging porch, and the front door hung from one hinge. And yet the scene was bathed in gentle sunshine. The soft colours made the slum inviting.

Deane summed up the contradictions. "Too pretty some would say, but I believe it shows a warm heart."

"The other painting you bought was a nude."

"What makes you think that?"

"Can you show it to me?"

From the sharp look Deane gave me, I suspected this was the moment when he started to wonder if he'd been smart to ask me over. Why *had* he asked me? I was still in the dark. He hadn't yet told me anything about Nora's death.

"The other painting I bought is a portrait of Eric Hutchinson — not a nude, I assure you. I loaned it to the Christ Church Ladies Auxiliary for their meeting room. The rector can arrange for you to see it next time you're over that way."

"You won't object if I phone the rectory from here to confirm the purchase date?"

"What hangs on that?"

"I'm talking about two paintings you bought this month, October 3. One was a streetscape, which you've shown me, the other a nude."

"You sound as if you believe you've seen some sales records of Nora's."

"I have her journal, found in her studio. Can you advance any reason why she would have recorded there that she had sold you a nude if she hadn't?"

A moment of silence followed, broken by the explosive ring of a very loud telephone bell. Deane answered, then asked me to step outside a moment. This was the call he had been waiting for. He invited me to prowl around the rest of the rooms on the ground floor if I was interested in contemporary art.

As I left Deane's study, I was frankly more interested in whether the room had a second exit through which he might give me the slip. There were no other doors I could see, but the possibility of movable wall panels and secret staircases wasn't altogether to be ruled out in the homes of the rich: I'd heard about Sir Henry Pellatt's former home, Casa Loma.

Perhaps I was exaggerating Deane's determination to avoid questioning, but it did seem to go beyond run-of-the-mill prudery. I chose a room to wait in that had a window on the same side of the house as the study. Opening the window, I sat on the ledge, prepared to follow if Sir Joseph left the house. It was no more than five and a half feet from the sill to the ground, an easy drop even for a shortish man not in his first youth.

After five minutes or so, I relaxed my guard to the extent of turning on the light and inspecting my surroundings. I was confident that I'd still notice if Sir Joseph tried to bolt. I found I was in the dining room. I counted fifteen paintings hanging on the walls. Some of them depicted northern forests — possibly not the ones Deane had enriched himself by cutting down. These were daubed with the loose, energetic brushstrokes I associated with Koch. More of the paintings, however, were portraits in a sharper-edged style, pictures of women prominently among them.

In time Deane came to find me. He mentioned the artists' names — Jackson for the forests, Newton for the portraits — before inviting me back into his study. A fresh burst of cordiality suggested whatever deal he'd negotiated on the phone had gone his way.

"Look, Shenstone, I asked you over because of my regard for Nora. Some thought she was risking her life on that scaffold. Not me — for me her death was a bolt from the clear blue. Grief can make you cruel: I find myself wishing death had struck any one of her critics instead." Deane's jaw tightened. A look of steel came into his blue eyes, which a moment later — just as suddenly — were glittering with moisture. "Anyway, tonight I wanted to commend you for looking into what happened and to help you every way I can. The thing is, modern artists and collectors understand the importance of life drawing. I was just afraid a policeman like yourself might see truthful depictions of the human body as smut."

"Try me," I said.

"I didn't see how showing you this picture could help your investigation, but I guess I should let you be the judge of that."

Deane went to a massive, dark wood wardrobe in a corner of the study. He opened one creaking door and, pushing aside some winter coats hanging inside, he drew from the back a framed painting roughly three feet tall and half as wide. When he brought it under the light and propped it against his desk, I saw it was a portrait of a woman in a northern landscape of rocks and pines with a lake in the background, all conveyed in the sharp detail I had come to associate with the artist. Nora had once again taken herself as her model. She stood on a rock, looking over the viewer's right shoulder at something that absorbed her attention — perhaps some hill or bird or person she contemplated painting. One hand rested on her hip; the other hung loosely by her side. She made no attempt to hide her firm, round breasts or thick, dark pubic hair. She wore nothing but a pair of white canvas tennis sandals. The day was warm and, to judge from the even blue surface of the lake, windless. She had perhaps just risen from sunbathing. Her skin was lightly and uniformly tanned.

I thought this picture had more vitality to it than Nora's other portraits, the ones I'd seen. When she painted other people, she seemed to be trying to build them up into something more than they were in life. But she knew herself and didn't need to exaggerate her energy or potential. For even though this scene was quiet, I felt the woman at the centre of it was crackling with purpose.

"Were you in love with her, Sir Joseph?" I was nearly so myself, and believed it must have been impossible for anyone that had known her in life not to be.

"I'll tell you how I happened to acquire this," said Deane, as if he hadn't heard. "It was submitted for the art show at the Canadian National Exhibition this August. And the CNE selection committee turned it down. They said they already had one or two nudes, for which they were expecting to get a good dressing down from the more straitlaced gallery goers. Nora's painting was liable to cause even more of a rumpus — first and foremost because it was a self-portrait and might incite indecent advances against the artist herself. And there were other touches that prevented it from being regarded as a nude in the classical sense. Those tennis shoes changed it from a nude into a depiction of a naked woman. Likewise, the lacquer on her nails."

"Huh?" I looked more closely and realized red varnish had been applied to Nora's fingernails. "What's that got to do with the price of fish?"

"It's modernity raising its ugly head," said Deane. "It spoils the classical illusion and prevents us from imagining we're seeing an Aphrodite of the Canadian Shield."

"So when the CNE wouldn't show it, you bought the picture and hid it with the mothballs."

"Let me tell you, Shenstone, people are always asking if I'll loan some of my collection of paintings to one show or another. Next time, or one time soon, I'll say, 'Only if you hang *Sunny Lake* along with them.' It won't stay in the shadows for long. In time, I expect it'll hang in the National Gallery in Ottawa."

"When did you last see Nora Britton, Sir Joseph?"

"She died the night of October 10 or early in the morning of the eleventh, didn't she? I remember I saw her in the afternoon of the fifth. I dropped off a cheque to cover the cost of some paints she'd had to buy. Then she was here for lunch on Saturday, the eighth. I didn't see her after that. She wouldn't let my chauffeur drive her back to her studio afterwards. Said it would make her too conspicuous in the Ward. Strange now to think of how when I walked her to the streetcar stop I was talking with her for the last time."

"So you didn't see her on Monday, October 10?"

"No."

"Did you or anyone in your house ever give or send her food?"

"She won't have been poisoned by anything she got from us." Suddenly Deane was a porcupine with his quills up. Quickly, though, he recovered and proceeded more amiably: "Still, that's *the* avenue to explore. If she was murdered in that locked church, it must have been by poison. I'll tell you something else too. Everyone that knew Nora knew she didn't like shopping or cooking or organizing meals. So people were always giving her things to eat. She had half the female parishioners of Christ Church Grange Park baking treats for her. When she ate here, we always sent her home with leftovers."

"What leftovers did she take with her on October 8?"

"Nothing noxious, you can bet."

"All the same," I said. "Put it down to police thoroughness."

"Cook may know." Deane went to his desk phone. "I'll have her send up some coffee as well."

"Could you ask her also if to her knowledge any additional food or drink was sent to Christ Church for Nora Britton on Monday, October 10?"

After talking to his cook, Deane reported back that his sister had organized the food packages for Nora and that answers to my questions would have to wait until Mary-Maud returned from *The Vagabond King*.

While waiting for the coffee I asked Deane if he knew of anyone that might want to kill Nora Britton.

"I heard some of the silly things the Stillwaters were saying, but the only one I'd suspect would be young Archie. He has a violent past. You mightn't think poison would be his style, but he is cook on a freighter."

"Which was on the upper lakes from October 8 till after Miss Britton's death. Anyone else on your list of suspects?"

"There was a man named Lou Sweet that had it in for her, but I thought she'd won him over by giving him a job. Besides, I can't see him as a poisoner."

"I know about Sweet, Sir Joseph. I'm just wondering if during one of your meetings with Nora Britton, she might have mentioned any threats or enemies, information she mightn't have given anyone else."

"I don't think I was intimate enough with her for that. She was very discreet. Perhaps you should talk to her family. Do you have the use of a car?"

Deane had touched on a sore point. I was freelancing this weekend, but even on assigned investigations detective access to Toronto police vehicles was far from automatic. And farther still if the vehicle was to take an investigator out of town.

"Which family member would you suggest I speak to?" I asked.

"All of them. She told me her father owns a dry goods and women's wear store on Yonge Street. Her mother is apparently a force to be reckoned with in the Women's Auxiliary of Trinity Church. And they have another daughter, a high school teacher — still living at home, but city-educated and quite modern in her outlook. In awe of no one, whether baronets, parents or — I daresay — policemen." Deane grinned, plainly admiring of such cheekiness. "I met her last month when she came down on a visit."

"I might get authorization for a long-distance phone call."

"You can call from here. In full privacy, of course, and at no cost to you or your department. But better than that, why don't you borrow one of my cars? I suggest you go tomorrow morning. You'll be sure to catch them just after church."

It did cross my mind that Deane might be trying to get me out of town for a few hours. While I was considering his offer, a middle-aged woman in black entered the study with a tray. She unloaded coffee pot, cups, cream, and sugar onto the library table and loaded our supper dishes in their place before exiting as quietly as she came.

"How do you take yours, Sir Joseph?" I asked.

"Black."

I poured two cups of black coffee and handed Deane one.

"Guaranteed poison-free," he said with a grin before taking his first sip. "I'll have a car with a full tank of gas parked in the driveway tomorrow morning from seven o'clock on. You've only to ring the front doorbell and someone will hand you the key. What do you say? On second thought, don't say anything. Sleep on it. If you don't come by, no harm done."

Chapter 10

I didn't wait at Deane's hovel for his sister to get back from the play. He wanted to make some more phone calls before "those idlers in New York" went to bed, and I had to catch Dalton Linacre in his lab before eleven. I figured I had just time to nip by City Hall and collect Ned's report first.

I expected I'd have time to read it on the Bay streetcar, but Ned — ever the dutiful schoolboy — couldn't seem to stop himself from writing complete sentences. As a detective he'd never have enough pockets for all his notebooks unless he mastered point form.

Albert Pan or Pun was born in Canton, China in 1875. He emigrated to Canada in 1904 upon payment of a head tax of $500. Pan owns a fish store on Baldwin Street in Kensington Market. He builds bamboo scaffolds as a sideline, mainly for construction projects in Chinatown. His chief difficulty in both businesses is finding suitable help as immigration from China is no longer permitted at any price. He began work for Nora Britton last spring. At her insistence, he took Lou Sweet as his assistant. He trained Sweet as best he could. Sweet was neither a quick study nor a hard worker. Nonetheless, Pan *assured me that the scaffold as completed meets the highest standards of convenience and safety. His one reservation was the low rail along the outer edge of the top deck, but that height had been requested and insisted upon by Nora Britton herself. There was nothing he could do. He otherwise got on well with the artist, who on occasion treated him to a bowl of ice cream at the shop across from the church. He was paid for the scaffold in full and on time. He understood that Sweet had a less friendly attitude to Nora Britton, but Pan asked no questions and discouraged conversation on the subject. Sweet did tell Pan that he was not married, but needed the work because he had "family responsibilities."*

I located Lou Sweet's dwelling on Elizabeth Street in the Ward. There I found a woman named Rose Mertens and her two children: Theo, aged six, and Louise, aged three. When I identified myself as a policeman, Rose claimed to be Lou's wife. I explained that I was investigating Nora Britton's death and had no interest in the morality of her living arrangements. I had to say this more than once. Gradually I coaxed her to admit that what Lou Sweet had told Pan is correct. She and Lou are not married. She says she is the widow of Hugo Mertens, Theo's father. To support his family, Hugo took mill work up north with Chapleau Forest Industries. He got caught in a debarking machine and died there five years ago. Rose is receiving a pension under the Workman's Compensation Act, but that payment will be cut off if she remarries.

A year after Hugo's death, Rose began cohabiting with Lou. Their daughter Louise was born the next year. To protect her pension, Rose risked being fined or jailed as a common prostitute for living with a man not her

*spouse. Naturally, Rose and Lou wished to avoid any
kind of publicity that might call attention to their
living arrangements. Then, two years ago, the risk
became even greater when the Workman's
Compensation Act was amended to discontinue
benefits to widows living common law. Fearing the
impoverishment of the couple and the children, Lou
was furious at Nora Britton for using Rose and Lou
and their house as models. His vanity was also hurt by
the use of Rose and their house to represent the slums.
His chief concern, however, was economic. Rose
appears not to have shared his worries regarding
Nora Britton. She believes police and government
officials never pay attention to paintings.*

A screech of brakes broke in on my reading. I looked out
the streetcar window in time to see a long, black Studebaker
Big Six touring car shiver to a stop behind the exit doors, just
then opening to let someone off at Gerrard Street. The fabric
top was down, and I had a clear view of the back and side of
the driver's head. It was familiar. Black hair brushed straight
back on top, shaved at the sides. A certain tilt to the head. I
jumped up and rushed forward through the streetcar till I could
see his straight nose. It was the boxer who'd never had it
broken — Jack Wellington — the rising star I'd watched sell
out to professional gamblers just two nights ago. I wasn't in
time to get out and jump on his running board; I didn't in any
case want to miss my chance to get Linacre's report. But you
can bet I stuck my head out the window far enough to read by
lamplight the six-digit number on the licence plate. I hadn't lost
my appetite for a personal word with the bum.

When I transferred to the westbound Carlton car at College
Street, I finished reading Ned's report. The final portion was an
account of a visit to the police lockup. Lou had under questioning
confirmed Rose's explanation of his beef against Nora.

After hearing Lou's account of the Stillwater holdup, Ned had also visited the cell Iva had been brought to following treatment for her gunshot wound. She expressed fears about the jail or prison farm sentence she was facing, but even more about the difficulty of supporting herself when she got out. She'd been able to type sixty words per minute, which had got her a pretty steady succession of office jobs. But the doctors hadn't promised her right hand would ever recover enough for secretarial work, even if she could find an employer willing to hire an ex-convict. Acting Detective Cruickshank's inclusion of these details in his report on the Nora Britton case did credit to his warm heart if not to his sense of relevancy.

Professor Linacre had hung up his worn lab coat by the time I pushed open the door to his lair in the basement of the Mining Building. I'd never seen him looking so tired. Perhaps he'd have been just as glad if I hadn't turned up before he got away, but he gave me a decent percentage of his normal grin and sank with good grace back into his desk chair.

"Okay," he said.

It was the first unnecessary word I could remember hearing from him. He lit a vicious-smelling cigarette and sucked in a lungful of smoke. When he'd got all the stimulus he could from it, he blew it towards the ceiling. Up till now, we'd had much speculation about the role of poison in the death of Nora Britton, but no evidence. The man I trusted to supply that evidence was about to speak.

"As for the lunch you brought me, I found no trace of toxic material in the coffee, the hermit cookies, or the chicken salad sandwich."

"Chicken?" I said. "I thought it was fish."

"You smelled something fishy and assumed it was the sandwich. It was the knapsack, which was covered in the same stuff your colleague brought me scrapings of. Vomit, as you suspected. But what fish it was or why it made her sick, I can't tell."

"Let me be sure I've got this straight, professor. The vomit contained no trace of any poison known to forensic science?"

"None."

"Can we say then that the deceased must have eaten the fish, whatever kind it was, at an earlier meal and that she suffered a delayed reaction to it?"

"That's possible. It's also possible the fish matter was introduced into the other cookie."

"That's too deep for me, professor." I hesitated to say one of us couldn't count. "What other cookie?"

"Reflect that you couldn't bring me all the items the deceased ate, only the three items she left a part of. I found crumbs of a second variety of cookie, and crumbs were all I found so it must have been delicious. I could just make out that it contained chocolate, but there wasn't enough residue for any sort of toxicological analysis. If the fish matter was introduced into this cookie, it may be that the chocolate flavour would have been strong enough to mask it."

"So where do we go from here? I'd like to be in a position by Monday morning to tell the inspector that this is definitely a murder."

"Find out if the woman ate fish earlier in the day. If not, she must have eaten it in the chocolate cookies. Fish matter isn't a normal ingredient in baked goods, so its inclusion can hardly have been innocent. Meanwhile, I'll get an ichthyologist to tell us which species are poisonous to humans, and then you coppers find out where in this town those fish can be bought, begged, or stolen." Linacre gave his scalp a rub, completely tousling his already slightly disorganized hair. "I'd also like to get a fish expert to analyze this muck on the knapsack, but that won't be done by Monday — or, if we have to send it away to someplace like Princeton or Harvard, by the Monday after that."

I couldn't think of a way to improve on Linacre's plan of action, so I thanked him and was about to about to say good night when it occurred to me to ask whether he was taking the

Carlton car westbound. He said he was. We rode together as far as Roncesvalles, where I got off and headed south. He was too exhausted to have much in the way of conversation, but he did confide that since separating from his wife he had been living in a room in the High Park area. His marriage broke up because he was never home.

I mulled that over on my way down to Queen Street West, where my own bed-sit waited emptily for me. It would seem empty only until I'd had a nightcap and dropped into dreamless sleep on my unmade bed. In my mid-thirties and never married, I still believed I'd done well in choosing to put everything into the job.

Except that this night my sleep wasn't dreamless. And in my dreams female companionship didn't stand as something distinct from the job. Nora Britton was both.

And large as life — which was not large at all. Rather petite and clean-edged, demure and sensuous, coolly focused and warmly tender.

Contrary to popular songs, what happens in dreams — my dreams at least — is rarely what you want. The embraces I shared with Nora, all the physical lovemaking, was an elaboration I indulged in as I was waking up. I'm not saying these fairy tales were healthy. I'd have done better to think about how I was going to get together with Ruth, a woman of flesh and blood with all of life before her. Hell, if I wanted a woman of mystery, why not Ruth? Intrigued as I was, I knew almost nothing about her, less than I now knew about Nora.

Soon, I promised myself: I'd see Ruth soon. I just had to answer to few more questions about Nora first.

I did, after all, remember something from sleep, from that place where wishful thinking doesn't write the script. What I remember Nora conveying, with words or looks, was that she wanted the truth of her death to come out — wanted that more than she wanted her killer tried and hanged. As a cop, I didn't see how she could have one without the other.

I pondered over eggs and toast whether I'd better stay in Toronto today and try to find out whether Nora had eaten fish six days ago. The trouble was I couldn't think who in town would know or could give me a decent lead. On the other hand, she might have mentioned the name of a favourite restaurant to her parents or her sister. I was ready for a break with routine. Might as well take Sir Joe up on his offer of a car and head north.

The streetcars ran less frequently on Sundays, so I had many minutes to settle on what description of automobile I hoped to see in Deane's driveway. I didn't want a limousine, in which one man would look ridiculous unless in chauffeur's livery. An inconspicuous sedan with lots of pep would suit me fine, although I'd never turn down a Bugatti racer.

While no Grand Prix champion, the flivver I spotted when I stepped out of Gloucester Street onto Jarvis was a heart-quickening Chrysler Imperial roadster. I bounded up Deane's front steps two at a time. The manservant that opened the big oak door to my knock delivered the key to me with looks of envy and regret. He made it clear I should consider myself a lucky man.

"It's only a year old, sir," he said, "and guaranteed to run all day at eighty miles per hour with no murmur of complaint."

"Does Sir Joseph drive this car himself?" I asked.

"Always. Only in his absence does his driver ever lay hands on it."

It was not lost on me that Joe Deane's personal car was cream-coloured. It also fell into place that the second last day on which Deane claimed to have seen Nora, October 5, was the same Wednesday on which Myrtle Hutchinson, the rector's wife, reported having seen Nora kiss a man in a light-coloured roadster.

Chapter 11

There was no trick to finding Aurora: it was straight north up Yonge Street. Little traffic was circulating. From the hill down into Hogg's Hollow on, I dodged around the lumbering trolley cars of the radial railway and stopped paying attention to speed limits.

I'd left the Chrysler's top down, as I'd found it. The air temperature, although higher than normal for mid-October, hovered in the low fifties, so the breeze whistling around the windshield into my face had a bracing sting to it. New pavement smoothed my ride all the way up to Richmond Hill and then again beyond that dusty village past stubble fields. Some proceeds of the recent harvest seemed to have been invested in repainting the trim on the Victorian brick farmhouses; a shaft of sun broke through the clouds and gleamed off the white front doors. I nudged the speedometer needle up another ten miles per hour and let the wind howl.

The half of my mind not focused on the drive was batting around the question of whether Joe Deane and Nora Britton had been lovers. Apart from the light-coloured roadster and the coincidence of dates, the evidence was a matter of impressions. Deane had shown me that he would rather spend an evening talking about Nora with a stranger, even if the talk shed little light on how she died, than pass an evening with his wife at the theatre. Deane and Nora had a common interest in painting. Lady Deane's interest in operetta was not shared by her husband. Then there was Nora's nude self-portrait. Had Lady Deane seen it? Even if Deane and Nora had never been to bed together, their friendship, it seemed to me, might inspire jealousy in a neglected wife. The last thing I needed was more murder suspects, but if the inspector let me pursue this case, I was resigned to interviewing Deane's wife and anyone that took her interests to heart. That might include her sister-in-law, who had been responsible for the food packages Nora took away from Deane's house.

My plan was to catch the Britton family as they left Trinity Church, but the car ran away with me. In short order, Aurora cemetery loomed up on my right. I wondered if Nora's ashes would ever find their way there. Then, also to my right, rose the war memorial — a facsimile lighthouse without any artistic rendering of warriors to stir up controversy. A mile further on, I reached the centre of the community with three-quarters of an hour in hand.

I didn't have the Brittons' home address, but by asking around soon found their place on Temperance Street. It was a well-kept, two-storey brick house on a wide grassy lot, with a side yard as well as front and back. A property slightly grander than its neighbours. The house faced west, away from the sun at this hour. There appeared to be a lamp on in the front room, so I thought I'd knock and see if one or more of the family had stayed home from the eleven o'clock service.

Before I made it halfway up the front walk, the door was opened by a youngish fair-haired woman in a white middy blouse and a dark skirt so long it swept the floor. Her right hand rested on the door frame. When I got closer, two more things about her struck me: first, the placement of her hand was not casual but for support and, second, she had been crying. Her brown eyes were wet and red, and the handkerchief she clutched in her left hand looked well used.

"Mr. Shenstone?" she said. "I'm Effie, Nora's sister."

"A pleasure, Miss Britton. Did Sir Joseph tell you to expect me?"

"I'd just put down the phone when I saw your car — his car, he tells me. Please come in."

She hopped back into a square hall, at the same time grabbing a worn wooden crutch she had leaned against the wall. If she had a right leg beneath her long, black skirt, plainly it was of no use to her. She turned and led the way to the right into a large living room in the front of the house.

She invited me to sit on a chesterfield with its back to the front window, while she took a wing chair opposite. Beside her stood a table holding the telephone, a lamp, and an open book lying face down. She blew her nose into her handkerchief before putting it away, then looked at me and nodded. Ready.

"What did Sir Joseph tell you about me?" I asked.

"That you're a police detective looking into Nora's death and that it may not have been accidental after all." Her voice was brisk and reasonably steady.

"I take it that possibility is not new to you, Miss Britton."

She shook her head. "Nora wasn't clumsy. I never thought she tripped."

I wouldn't have said that Effie Britton bore any family resemblance to Nora, but I had to remind myself that I'd only seen one photo of the artist. All the other images I took as portraying her were ones she'd painted herself, possibly with a quart or two of self-flattery. Effie's mouth was wider, her face longer, her hair shorter — boyishly short in fact. Her build was more masculine too: she had broad shoulders and large hands. The one thing I saw in the younger sister that I'd seen in the elder was energy.

I came to the point; I judged she would want it and could take it. "Can you think of anyone that might have wanted to kill her?"

"That I can't." Effie swallowed and went on. "No, Nora was the finest person that ever walked this earth. I hero-worshipped her. She was kind to everyone, kind to a fault. And so very talented. And beautiful, with a beautifully free spirit as well. And, although there's an eight-year difference in our ages, once we were both grown-up she never made me feel like a younger sister. She treated me as a friend and an equal. She had first-rate artistic training in New York, but she admired me for having a university degree."

"What do you mean by 'kind to a fault'?"

"Turning the other cheek. There was a man that said terrible things about her, and she gave him work. Work building the structure she fell from."

"Rest easy on that score," I said. "The scaffold wasn't sabotaged. The scaffold didn't kill her."

"I hate that word. *Scaffold.* It makes it sound as if Nora were hanged."

I gave Effie a moment. She was handling the interview well, and it didn't take long for her irritation to subside.

"Did she mention anyone else that might have wished her harm?" I asked.

"She never said a word against Herman, but for our parents he's the source of all harm."

"Do they think he had anything to do with her fall?"

"Not directly. But in their mind he corrupted her, persuaded her to accept a marriage without fidelity, alienated her from her family, sponged on her, and expected her to continue to support him even when he set up a separate establishment. And, to top it all, they believe he had her remains cremated just to spite them — and cremated in haste to deny them the chance to see their daughter one last time."

"Was it Nora's wish to be cremated?"

"She told me she thought it was cleaner and tidier than burial. Father and Mother are against it. Something to do with believing in the physical resurrection of the body. Nora, on the other hand, called burial a waste of God's good earth. She told me in her sweet, quiet voice — full of love and compassion —

that she feared our parents were letting themselves in for disappointment. No golden harvest would result from planting corpses. For myself, I can't see that it matters; when I'm dead, the decision will be out of my hands. Nora acknowledged that too. The fact that there are no crematoria in this province made her all the more doubtful that her wishes would be respected — but she did have wishes."

"So would you say that, in having Nora cremated, her husband was simply carrying out her instructions?"

"And that his haste in doing so was to prevent Dad and Mum from interfering — yes, I would say so."

Koch's mural design came to mind. What he had depicted was a body rising from a sarcophagus, the physical resurrection Nora had denied. Might he, strange as it might seem, share Nora's parents' objections to cremation? I briefly entertained the possibility that he had burned Nora's remains against his own convictions and only to fulfill her request. But I reckoned it more likely that the rising from the tomb in the mural was no more than an artistic stratagem, a pattern drawn from Koch's memory of other religious paintings with no reference to his own beliefs. In any event, Koch's haste in arranging the cremation was convenient if he had any reason to keep a post-mortem from being done.

"Miss Britton, did your sister have a will?"

"She did. But she didn't want our parents to know during her lifetime. I haven't told them yet."

"Let's talk about it before they get home. First, why the secrecy?"

"Because she was leaving Herman two-thirds of her money. They wanted him disinherited entirely."

"And the remaining third?"

"Comes to me. They wouldn't have minded that."

"Do you know much money she had?"

"I haven't been told yet what she had in the bank. She lived as frugally as someone that doesn't cook for herself can. At the same time, she had lots of commissions and — in Sir Joseph Deane — a wealthy patron. She told me she hoped that by the time she died my share would be enough for me to buy a house."

"Miss Britton, when did your sister and her husband start living apart?"

"Before the first mural competition. She told me when she came home for Christmas — the Christmas before last."

"After the separation, how much did Nora and Herman see of each other?"

Effie Britton moved her hands very little when she talked, but now she raised her right hand thoughtfully in front of her mouth. So far, she had appeared quite frank and direct. Now I wondered if she was trying to decide whether to censor herself.

"Nora confided in me a certain amount, Mr. Shenstone, but she didn't tell me everything. She never mentioned seeing him."

"She disliked cooking. Would Herman ever have brought her food?"

Effie let her hand fall back in her lap and smiled for the first time — a large, hearty smile that showed two even rows of teeth. "What a cockeyed sounding idea! I can't imagine it, and I certainly never heard about anything of the kind."

I flashed her a grin back. "Nora was allowed to execute her winning mural design, whereas Herman was denied the chance to carry out his. Is it your impression that he was jealous of her success?"

"If he was, I got no hint of it from her. Nora didn't make any secret of her view that Herman's being snubbed like that was horribly unfair. She believed in her own work, but she went so far as to say that Herman's design for the church was superior to her own. I argued with her about that. It was a wonderful surprise when she won the second mural competition, but I was never in the least doubt that she deserved to win."

"You've told me your parents view of Herman Koch. What do you think of him?"

"Herman didn't corrupt Nora." A pause here filled in by a shake of the head. "I've more respect for my sister's strength of character than that. She subscribed to the mores of Greenwich Village just as freely and deliberately as Herman. He's no Svengali. What's more, as Nora saw and as Mum and Dad can never see, he's one of the finest painters in the country."

"Are you saying that your parents have no appreciation of art?"

"They haven't much, and in Herman's case their judgement is biased. They never disowned Nora or prevented her coming home for a visit, but they regarded her as damaged, morally crippled as I'm physically crippled. By the way, you've done well in twenty minutes' conversation not to refer once to the way I hobble around."

"I'm afraid, Miss Britton, that in my neighbourhood crutches are not such a rarity — although young women without the use of a leg are thankfully in the minority."

"I'm like the lame boy of Hamelin that was unable to follow the Pied Piper." Effie shrugged and continued mildly. "I think our parents would have liked to have Nora live with them here as I do. Not the best situation for adult children to my mind — oh, common enough, but still not ideal. I manage pretty well. I could live on my own and one day may do so, but I suppose I've been letting them look after me to console them for the waywardness of their first-born. They blame Herman for the damage to Nora, and so can't see his artistic talent. In my case, they believe the only blameworthy party is the poliomyelitis virus. Between you and me, I suspect my withered leg was made more useless by the medical treatment I received, which involved extended periods of immobilizing the limb to rest it. The suspicion is that muscles that were not paralyzed before atrophied for want of use, but talk of that would distress Mother and Father to no purpose."

"Your parents are at church?"

"Yes."

"Do you not go?"

"Often I do. But this is the first Sunday since Nora's death. I would have cried buckets and not, I'm afraid, found any consolation in the service. I meant to keep to myself and my very particular grief, but you're helping me through a difficult hour."

"Did Sir Joseph Deane know you'd be home when he called?"

"He stayed away from morning service himself and took a chance I'd do the same. Of course, it would have been worse for him facing that … scaffold at the front of Christ Church and sitting in a congregation that still includes Nora's detractors. People that persist in regarding her as a Kraut-lover unfit to memorialize their war dead."

A clock on the mantel warned me that Mr. and Mrs. Britton would soon be returning. There was a line of questioning I wanted to cover before they did. "You say, Miss Britton, that Nora subscribed freely to the mores of Greenwich Village. Did she have a lover?"

Effie also checked the clock before answering. "Possibly. She didn't tell me yes or no. Or who."

"Might it have been Sir Joseph Deane?"

Effie Britton's jaw dropped. Pink spread over her pale face. She tried to speak, but no words came out. I waited, suppressing my impatience. Eventually she broke the silence.

"Now I know what runs through a policeman's mind in the big city," she said. "Sir Joseph? The idea seems so — so out of kilter. But practically speaking, it's impossible. Nora told me she would never go to bed with a married man unless his wife knew and approved, or at least gave her permission. I believe her: that was her code. Enough — my parents are back."

I turned in my seat to see a woman and man, apparently in their fifties, coming slowly up the front walk. Mr. Britton was balding with a fringe of fair hair the colour of Effie's. He carried a black top hat in his left hand and wore a black

morning coat, black waistcoat, and black trousers. Dark-haired
like Nora, Mrs. Britton held his free arm as she walked. She
wore a black fall overcoat open over her long, dropped-waist
black dress. Effie and I rose to greet them, and Effie made the
introductions in somewhat formal terms. George Britton and I
exchanged first names as well, and I heard him call his wife
Alice. Understandably preoccupied, the couple did not know
what to make of me.

Alice offered to make tea. I could see she was exhausted,
though.

"I won't stay long," I promised. "Perhaps we could all sit
down for a moment."

The women and I did so. George Britton took his wife's
coat and his hat to a closet somewhere. When he came back, he
stood by the mantelpiece and wiped the lenses of his wire-
framed spectacles on his handkerchief. His eyes were red, and
his mouth drooped, but the deep lines in his face suggested
grief of one kind or another was nothing new. At the same
time, he had a solid build and an erect posture. I could easily
imagine him wielding authority in his dry goods shop.

"What brings you here?" Alice Britton asked me.

"Mr. Shenstone is a detective, Mum, from Toronto," Effie
explained, not for the first time.

"I'm making inquiries concerning your daughter Nora's
death," I said. "I understand that this is a difficult time, Mrs.
Britton. I'm sorry for the intrusion."

"Yes. Well…" Alice Britton unpinned her black hat and set
it and the attached veil on the chesterfield between us. I saw
that there was a lot of grey in her black hair and heavy bags
under her eyes.

"Sir Joseph Deane phoned me this morning and asked me to
make Mr. Shenstone welcome," Effie added.

"You *are* welcome," George Britton remarked absently.

"Thank you, sir. Miss Britton has given me most of what I
need, so I won't take much of your time."

I inquired first about Nora's medical history, specifically about the conditions Professor Linacre had identified as likely to cause dizziness. Alice and George exchanged a helpless look. Effie said that nothing of the kind had been identified while Nora had been living at home. Moreover, when she started work at Christ Church on a platform high above the chancel floor, she had assured her family that her balance was excellent.

Next, I asked Nora's parents whether they knew of anyone that might want to hurt their elder daughter.

"That rat Koch!" George Britton spat out. He rolled back his shoulders, as if to ease the tension that thoughts of his son-in-law had put them under. "Are you a churchman, officer — er — Paul?"

My head shake didn't appear to add to his misery.

"There are those in the Church of England that have accepted cremation, but more — including Alice and me — that have not. Setting such differences aside, though, for us not to be granted so much as a glimpse of Nora before…"

George Britton, heartbreak in his face, stared out his front window. What he saw was for dead certain not the street, but the crematorium flames.

"Dad, Mr. Shenstone and I have been over all that," Effie soothed. "He means anyone else."

"I don't understand." Alice Britton sat up straighter, her fatigue set aside. "You're not saying our daughter was murdered?"

"Alice, that's a dreadful thought," George Britton cautioned. "The situation is distressing enough without that."

"It is a dreadful thought," I said, "but it has to be explored — the sooner the better." I was grateful to have for the first time Nora's parents' full attention.

"She didn't tell us anything," Alice burst out. "Well, not much." Nora's mother smoothed her black skirt over her knees while composing her thoughts. "Daughters today are so independent. And then Nora lived in the city, and we had no way of knowing what went on there, except what we read in the newspaper about automobile accidents and crime. Nora was one of the family when she came home for a visit. She helped out at our church bazaar, raising money for us by selling people sketches of themselves. We loved having her here, but she made it clear her life in Toronto was not a subject for discussion."

I asked the three Brittons — as I had Sir Joe — whether Nora had had any close friend in the city, someone familiar with her daily life. None of them admitted knowing of such a person.

"We were told Nora's death was accidental," George Britton said. "We gather she was alone in the church when she fell. How could murder come into it?"

"I'm trying to find out what Nora might have had to eat in the hours before her death," I said.

"You're suggesting she was poisoned." George made his words an accusation. "That beggars belief."

"I gather she didn't like to cook," I bludgeoned on. "Would any of you have any idea where she took her meals last Monday?"

George Britton turned his back and looked as if he might stalk out of the room. His wife was quicker to come to terms with the unthinkable.

"George, if she was murdered, we have to think of poison. But where could she have eaten it?"

Nora's father rejoined the conversation reluctantly. "How the deuce would I know?"

"The question is impossible," said Effie. "I doubt you'd find anyone in the whole of Toronto with eating habits less regular. Sometimes she made sandwiches in her studio. Sometimes she ate at Eaton's cafeteria. Sometimes she ate at Chinese restaurants."

"One in particular?"

"No, lots of different ones."

"Chinese?" said George Britton. "I had no idea."

"And then," Effie raced on, "she often ate at the homes of friends or of members of Christ Church — and church members packed her picnic lunches to eat while she was working on the mural."

I said I understood and asked if any of the three of them had any idea where, of all the possibilities, Nora might have eaten last Monday. None of them did. Nora followed no set rotation and hadn't been in touch with any of her family in Aurora for over a week.

"Might she have eaten fish?" I asked at last.

"That, no," said Alice Britton.

"Out of the question," George Britton added.

"My sister shunned fish and seafood of all kinds," said Effie. "She'd never have eaten it voluntarily."

"Eating fish made her sick?" I suggested.

"No, she didn't have an allergy or anything like that," said Effie.

"She just tried a lot of different kinds and didn't like any of them," Alice put in. "Ten years ago, she gave up trying and swore she'd never eat anything with a shell or fins again."

"Whatever my daughter ate last Monday," George concluded, "you can bet your bottom dollar it wasn't fish."

Unless, I thought, she ate it as the unsuspected ingredient of a chocolate cookie. I didn't see how the inclusion of that ingredient in baked goods could be innocent. I didn't know which fish were fatal to eat, but I was sure that there must be at least one and that Nora had eaten it.

"Why do you ask, Mr. Shenstone?" Effie wanted to know.

"I'll tell you as soon as I can," I said. "Meanwhile, I'm asking you not to mention that I was here today or what we talked of."

I was leaving the Brittons in suspense, but I couldn't risk the killer's getting wind of what the police now knew. What we — what I — now knew was that there was without doubt a killer. All weekend, I'd been acting without instructions on my own initiative. Tomorrow morning I'd be in a position to have Inspector Sanderson open an official murder investigation.

I felt bad knowing that someone had deliberately taken Nora's life, but at the same time eased in spirit *knowing* — rather than guessing and wondering and never being sure. I didn't go into this with the Brittons.

I let them think my evident relief was all gratitude for Effie's assurance on behalf of the family that I could count on them to keep mum.

Chapter 12

As I swung Sir Joe's machine around the block and back onto Yonge Street, my mind went back to what Effie had said about Nora's code. She wouldn't take up with a married man without his wife's permission. This was a new one on me: another artsy variant on the marriage game. Effie had had time to get used to the idea, but the arrival of her parents had left me with a lot of thoughts half-formed. What I was really missing at this point was a fellow detective to bat hypotheses around with.

Effie implied that Lady Deane would not have given Joe and Nora the green light. Of course, Effie might be mistaken or lying, but what about Myrtle Hutchinson? Suppose she were the permissive wife.

"It's maybe a long shot," I imagined myself saying to Harry O'Brian, "but suppose Myrtle made up the story of seeing Nora kiss a man in a light-coloured roadster in order to cast suspicion on Joe Deane and away from her husband. Just because she allowed Eric to make love to Nora didn't mean she wanted the affair known. Hutchinson's a priest, after all, not an artist. Exposure as an adulterer would cost him his position, and Myrtle hers."

"How old is the rector?" I heard Harry ask with amusement.

"Not young, but full of pep. Besides, news that he'd gone to bed with Nora would have been damaging enough, even if he was unable to do much when he got there."

I was making good time back to Toronto when I was flagged down at the corner of Yonge Street and the Stouffville Road. The flaggers were two girls in bright slickers standing beside an open car larger than the one I was driving. Despite the overcast sky, the girls' yellow raincoats, their sky-blue motor, their ruby lips, and round, unpowdered faces shone so brightly it was impossible to speed by.

When I pulled up, one of them dashed across the road in front of a northbound limousine to jump onto the running board beside me.

"We're all turned round," she said. "Can you tell us how to get to Gormley? We're afraid it's going to rain, and we'll get soaked."

The second girl crossed the road more cautiously, but sounded just as excited. "Which way is it to Gormley?"

I said I'd no idea, but that I'd help them put the roof up on their car if they liked. They weren't having any of that. They were enjoying the air — only they had to get to Gormley. They said the name in unison, setting each other off in fits of giggles. Then they looked brightly at me as if my ignorance just wouldn't do.

"I'll see if there's a map in the glove compartment," I said.

There was. I tried to show it to them.

"Oh, just point us the way," coaxed the first girl.

I asked why they wanted to go to Gormley. As suspected, they just loved the sound of the name, no other reason. I doubted if either of the shiny flapperettes was old enough to have a driver's permit. I sent them off eastward down the Stouffville Road, to look — I suspected — for someone else they could ask.

I'd pulled the map from under sundry other items, which I now removed to get it back at the bottom of the glove compartment. There were two golf tees, a bag of humbug candies, a brochure from an art exhibit, a clipped newspaper advertisement for the quality papers manufactured by Chapleau

Forest Industries, a 2B pencil with a broken point, a sharpened 2B pencil, a golf score card not filled out past the third hole, and a key ring with a single Yale key on it.

Elizabeth Street was not on the shortest route back to Choo-Choo Mansion, but I allowed myself the detour in case Carl Moretti had stopped by his shop after church. He had. He was picking up some Great War medals he'd managed to sell to one of his fellow congregants.

Moretti today was wearing the olive jacket that went with the trousers I'd seen him in yesterday, plus a whitish shirt and a Coldstream Guards regimental tie, which I assumed was part of his antiquarian inventory rather than a badge of his own affiliation. I observed that since yesterday morning he had boarded up the door to the staircase leading up to Nora's studio.

"Darn right," he snarled back. "No more people just walking in helping themselves to whatever they fancy."

"Which people?" I asked.

"You yesterday morning, Koch yesterday afternoon."

"Koch?"

"Shoved me aside when I tried to stop him. No consideration for a wounded veteran, but what can you expect from his kind?"

"Do you want to press charges?"

"I can look after myself." An open clasp knife suddenly appeared in Moretti's hand.

"Don't take it too far," I cautioned. "What did Koch take?"

"Some of the artist's work. Claimed it was his right as a husband."

I saw that the part of the door around the handle, which Lou Sweet had split with a crowbar, had been sawn away altogether and a sturdy plank screwed, not nailed, into the door frame.

"What did you do with the lock?" I asked.

Moretti pointed to a bin where a jumble of locks of various makes and sizes awaited the discerning shopper. It didn't take long to find one I thought I recognized.

"Is this it, Mr. Moretti?"

"If it says Yale on it."

The Yale key from Sir Joe's glove compartment fit smoothly in and worked the mechanism.

"I'll take it," I said.

Moretti accepted the receipt I handed him without hiding the fact he'd have preferred a couple of dollar bills.

"How often has Sir Joseph Deane been in here?" I asked.

"How would I know?"

"Beats me, Mr. Moretti — apart from the fact that you're members of the same church and that you attended a meeting where he stood in front of the congregation and defended Herman Koch's design. That was the occasion on which you threatened to spit on the memorial mural if Koch were allowed to paint it. Ring any bells?"

"I haven't seen Deane in here." Moretti was tidying his shop's cluttered counter when he said this, paying particular attention to a box of stereoscope slides. "I have photos of the ruins of Pompeii at twenty-five cents apiece. Ten free if you buy the viewer."

"Is the shop ever open when you're not here?"

"Pay an assistant to steal from me? Do I look like I'm made of money?"

"So no one could have gone through that door and upstairs without your knowledge?"

"Except for the artist woman and anyone she let in. I had to give her a key to my street door."

"You work hard to make a living, Mr. Moretti, and I know you appreciate a deal. Did anyone ever pay you not to notice when he came through the shop?"

"Never." Again Moretti wasn't looking at me when he answered. He'd hobbled over to his shop's front door, which he held open for me while staring out into the dusty street. "I'm locking up now," he said. "It's Sunday."

I picked up a smoked salmon sandwich at United Bakers on Spadina Avenue and ate it while driving back to Jarvis Street.

By the time I reached Deane's place, the family had had their lunch and dispersed to different parts of the large house. The manservant that had handed me the car key in the morning welcomed its return when he again answered my knock. He looked less happy when I asked him to announce me to Sir Joseph. I had to produce my badge for inspection.

Deane came out to greet me in a gold dressing gown worn over shirt, tie, and dark trousers. He led me through to his study where he installed me in a comfortable leather chair and took a seat behind his paper-cluttered desk.

"I'm not a strict Sabbatarian, Shenstone. I'd rather you didn't tell my sister, however. Mary-Maud may suspect I'm attending to business correspondence, but pretends I'm engaged behind my study door in Bible reading all Sunday afternoon. Did you manage to speak to the Brittons?"

"Uh-huh. Thanks for the use of your car."

"Give you any trouble?"

"Only when I tried to hold it back. Speaking of your sister — "

"Having a nap."

Just then raised female voices were heard in the foyer outside Sir Joe's study door. The two of us went out to investigate. Mary-Maud Deane was not napping, as it turned out, but rather remonstrating with a woman some thirty years younger.

"It's not as if I'm going dancing, Auntie," the latter said. "Patients need attention seven days out of seven."

"Nonetheless," the older woman replied, "I don't see that you have to race around in an open car on the Lord's Day."

"But since the car is back from wherever it was, why shouldn't I take it? Women's College Hospital is the other side of the city. Have you even heard of Rusholme Road? I had to look it up on a map. The streetcar on its 'Lord's Day' schedule would take forever."

Sir Joe jumped in before his sister could reply. "Mary-Maud, this is Detective Shenstone. He'd like a word with you."

"Glad to know you, Miss Deane." The angular woman before me reminded me somewhat of Alice Britton, in appearance as well as age, and I wondered if the same resemblance had struck Nora. "But if the younger Miss Deane is leaving," I went on, "perhaps I could start with her."

"Phyllis, Mr. Shenstone." The girl stuck out her hand, and I shook it. She had a Varsity look, wearing a plain but well-cut maroon wool dress and a turban that appeared both fashionable and practical for keeping her hair up in a hospital setting. "Could we make our talk brief? I'm already late."

"Use the dining room for your interviews, Shenstone," Sir Joseph advised. "There won't be anyone to disturb you till dinner time."

"This way," said Phyllis.

I ascertained that no one besides Deane's daughter was planning on going out that afternoon. Only then did I follow her into the long room and take the chair she'd picked out for me.

"Phyllis, would you say you have an inquiring mind?"

"Sure."

"Then you'll want to ask me questions. It'll save you time if you don't ask and I don't have to think up polite ways not to answer."

Short and slight like her father, Phyllis had a rather severe, narrow face, clean of cosmetics. My suggestion, however, did get me a fleeting grin.

"Deal," she said.

"Do you drive the cream roadster often?"

"No, I walk to university."

"Do you recognize this key?" I held it out for her to look at.

"No."

"How well did you know Nora Britton?"

"Not well. She ate here a few times. I might have seen her at church. We talked once about how strange it is that women are now permitted to study medicine, as I'm doing, and yet not all art academies allow them to do life drawing. Perhaps aspiring painters should take anatomy courses."

"Did you ever prepare any food for Nora Britton or give her any food?"

"No. Cook and Aunt Mary-Maud are the only ones that have anything to do with food in this house."

"Did you ever see Nora Britton eat fish?"

"Ye-es, but not much. That was a surprise. Cook served Winnipeg goldeye one night Nora was here, a great treat for all of us. Nora only had two small bites. I asked her afterwards if eating fish made her ill. She said no, she just didn't like the taste or texture or anything about it."

"Miss Britton was separated from her husband. Do you think she was romantically involved with anyone else?"

"No. I think she loved her husband. She spoke quite feelingly of the injustice of his not getting the mural commission. If she'd lived, I wouldn't have been at all surprised if she'd gone back to live with him."

"Did you ever meet Herman Koch?"

"No."

"Do you think he was jealous of her success?"

"I don't know."

"Do you think there was any other man in her life?"

"Lots of men: she had to make her way in a man's world, don't forget. But they would have been like Poppa. Business friends — growing into good friends perhaps — nothing more."

Phyllis was a bright girl, but I thought she might be reading Nora better than she read Sir Joe.

"Is there anyone you believe might have killed her?" I asked.

"No. Is this a murder investigation, Mr. Shenstone?"

"Have you forgotten you're late?"

"No."

"Run along then, Phyllis. And thanks for keeping us on track."

The sound of the front door slamming behind Phyllis brought her aunt from a sitting room into the foyer. Mary-Maud Deane stifled a yawn, apologized, then yawned again.

"Please excuse me, Mr. Shenstone. I'm afraid I've become a creature of habit, and I usually nap at this time. I was going to invite you into a room where the seating is more comfortable, but perhaps the dining room chairs will do a better job of keeping me alert. I suppose a policeman's calling is like Phyllis's: Sunday is no day of rest for you."

I saw I was not going to get through this interview as fast as the last one. The more I saw of Mary-Maud, the fainter the resemblance I'd noted to Alice Britton became. Like Sir Joe, his sister had springy white hair, blue eyes, and cleft chin. I took her to be in her fifties, like her brother, but both had youthful, unlined faces. Mary-Maud was perhaps the elder sibling, but her manner also made her seem older. Her high-collared Sunday dress in deep purple was of a cut that even I could recognize as some years behind the fashion.

I asked many of the same questions I'd put to Phyllis and got confirmation that Nora Britton didn't eat fish and didn't appear to be involved in any extramarital affairs. Mary-Maud didn't drive and denied recognizing the key to Nora's studio. She'd never met Herman Koch. She said she had no idea whether he or anyone else might have wanted to kill Nora Britton. The idea that Nora had been murdered alarmed her. I had to call a halt to my questioning while she composed herself, and I phoned down to ask Cook to bring her a cup of tea.

"We were all so fond of Nora," she said after the first two sips. "I never heard her say a mean word about anyone. I'm not sure I understand her mural, but any of her portraits I've seen are lovely, very kind to the person she's painting. Who could have wanted her dead?"

"Miss Deane, I ask the same question wherever I go. I haven't had an answer yet."

"Such a sweet young woman. Not so young, I suppose, really."

"No," I said. "Thirty-five."

"You know, if my brother weren't so much in love with Lady Deane, I think he could have fallen for Nora."

"Some men love — or believe they love — more than one woman at a time."

"A mistaken belief, depend on it. In any case, Sir Joseph isn't that kind of man. He knows he has only one heart to give and he gives it whole."

A soft, vague smile came over Mary-Maud's face. I didn't know whether romantic disappointments lay in her past, but I assumed that having a man wholeheartedly in love with her was the stuff of her daydreams. I changed the subject.

"Miss Deane, I understand you prepared a package of leftovers for Nora to take away after she ate lunch here on Saturday, October 8. Do you recall what was in that package?"

"That would be a week ago yesterday. I plan the menus and keep a record in my journal. I could check for you, but if memory serves I sent Nora home with a bowl of corn chowder and some fruit salad."

"No baked goods?"

"Not on that occasion. Of that I'm sure: neither Cook nor I bake on Saturday morning."

"Was that Saturday lunch the last time you saw Nora Britton?"

"Yes, it was. She was next due to eat with us this past Thursday, but ... Her death still doesn't seem real."

"I understand," I said, and waited a moment. "Did you send Nora anything to eat between lunch on the eighth and the evening of the tenth?"

"Oh, no. We were going to see her again so soon, and I knew other people gave her food — Myrtle Hutchinson at the church and quite a number of the parishioners."

"Do you know who gave her food on Monday, October 10?"

"No, I didn't hear anyone mention it. It sounds as if you think someone poisoned her. If I'm under suspicion, I don't think I'd better answer any more questions."

"Miss Deane, everyone says Nora Britton didn't eat fish. Did she eat chocolate?"

"Don't most people? I don't remember her saying anything about it. Now that I think about it, though, we did serve her chocolate blancmange once. She ate that all right."

"Did you or anyone in this house ever give her chocolate cookies?"

"No."

Mary-Maud's answer was unequivocal, but uncharacteristically brief. I thanked her for her time.

Rather than come down to the dining room, Lady Deane invited me to her own parlour upstairs where she could play her gramophone while we talked. She favoured the title song from *Rose Marie* and — incongruously in view of Sir Joseph's enthusiasm for lemonade — a drinking song. She said it was from Sigmund Romberg's operetta *The Student Prince*, and that made it all right.

Sir Joseph's wife was more forthcoming than his sister on the subject of chocolate. She recalled Nora Britton's eating chocolate brownies at the Deanes' table and being given some to take away. On Saturday, October 8? She didn't remember.

So saying, she helped herself from a bowl of candied cherries on a table at her elbow. Lady Deane was larger than her husband in every direction, a handsome woman now carrying more and looser flesh than looked healthy.

"Lady Deane, was your sister-in-law ever engaged?"

"Very nearly — to a promising young music student."

"Killed in the war?" I remembered Eric Hutchinson's mentioning that Mary-Maud had opposed acceptance of the mural design by the German-born Koch.

"Oh, no. By 1914, Mary-Maud's Paganini was in New York with one of her sorority sisters."

"He's still there?"

"As far as I know — sawing his fiddle at the Shubert Theatre. He remains perfect in Mary-Maud's eyes. She holds the minx that took him away from her entirely to blame."

Lady Deane's answers to my other questions were for the most part unremarkable. She told me she had only ridden once in Sir Joe's roadster, which she found uncomfortable. She didn't recognize the Yale key. She said she liked Nora Britton and her painting, although art was really more her husband's province than hers. She thought Sir Joseph's interest in painting quite sweet. She couldn't imagine how he found the time and energy for it, considering he had a thriving company to run and a house full of women to keep happy.

There was one member of this joyous female band I hadn't yet interviewed. Cook, a widow by the name of Grace Chadwick, had only every second Sunday off; I found her in the kitchen rolling out pastry for pies. She said chocolate brownies were one of Miss Mary-Maud Deane's specialties. Mrs. Chadwick didn't have the recipe and was not always present when they were being made.

It was time to speak to Sir Joe again. I knocked on, then opened, his study door. He was on the phone. He held up two fingers, tapped his chest, and pointed towards the dining room. I went there and didn't have long to wait. He strode in tugging on the crimson cuffs of his gold dressing gown.

"How do you happen to have a key to Nora Britton's studio?" I asked him before he'd sat down.

"You searched my car, eh? When I bought those latest paintings of hers, she suggested I pick them up whether she was there or not, but in the end she brought them over herself on the eighth, and I didn't need the key. I didn't have a chance to return it before her death."

"Those paintings are too large for her to have brought on the streetcar. Did someone drive her?"

"I presume so, but I didn't see and didn't ask."

"Did she have a lover, someone outside her marriage?"

"I saw no sign of one. But, as I say, she was discreet."

"Last night I asked if you loved Nora. You didn't answer."

Deane got up and walked around his dining room table to straighten one of the landscapes hanging over the buffet. "In a fatherly way, yes, I did love her."

"Did you ever kiss her, Sir Joseph?"

"On the cheek. What of it?"

"Anything more passionate?"

"Never." Deane reddened. "You have a dirty mind, Shenstone. I have one wife, and you ... pollute her house with your insinuations. I see no good that's come of my asking you here. You can show yourself out."

Sir Joseph started to leave the dining room. I was seated nearer the doorway, however. I got up and stood in his path.

"Let me tell you, sir, the good you can't see. As an important person in Nora Britton's last months, you'd have had a call from me whether you asked me here or not. What you did by calling me was save valuable time. You suspected foul play in Nora's death. Today, thanks to you, I was able to interview Nora's family. Thanks to you, I got the evidence that proves you were right. Tomorrow morning at eight o'clock I can put in play all the resources of the city's detective office to find Nora's killer. Take credit for that. Still, by the standards of a normal murder investigation we're several days behind. Eight a.m. is still sixteen hours away. I'm not about to waste that time. If you ever felt affection of any kind for Nora, you won't want me showing myself out until I've learned everything I can in this house. Please tell your sister I need to speak to her again."

Deane glared at me across the half yard that separated our faces. In less than a second, though, a cool smile took over his features. He was again the executive with a talent for and a joy in clean, quick decisions.

"Tell her yourself," he said. "Up the front staircase, second door on the right."

In answer to my knock, Mary-Maud Deane came out into the upstairs hall and closed her door. I took it she didn't want me to see her unmade bed. She wasn't happy to see me again, especially as she had just managed at last to drift off to sleep. Her dressing gown, less flashy than her brother's, featured white peonies on a purplish background.

"When was the last time you gave or sent Nora Britton any of your chocolate brownies, Miss Deane?"

"I'm going to ask Sir Joseph whether I should be answering any more questions."

"Your brother knows I need to speak to you again."

"Does he? What is the need?"

"When you and I talked about cookies, you didn't mention Nora's eating your brownies."

"Detective!" Mary-Maud gasped, her hand on her heart. "Cookies and brownies are as different as chalk and cheese. Cookies bake individually, brownies in one piece like a cake. And consider the ingredients. Any chocolate cookies of my acquaintance use baking soda. My brownies contain only butter, sugar, milk, eggs, flour, chocolate, and chopped nuts. And a little vanilla extract."

I got her to repeat the list of ingredients while I wrote it down.

"And when did you last give Nora Britton any of your brownies?"

"I'd have to consult my journal."

When she went to do so, I followed her through her door into a bright and tidy sitting room, with net curtains on the windows and hand-embroidered flowers on the chair cushions. In a house this size, it made sense that a considerate brother would provide her with a suite rather than just a room. Her bedroom would be beyond a second closed door.

She unlocked the centre drawer of an antique writing desk and took out a leather-bound journal, roughly five by seven inches in size. More than half the lined pages were filled in with a handwritten date at the top, followed by detailed entries for breakfast, lunch, dinner. Mary-Maud showed me the daily menus, starting with the most recent. We had to go back to September before we found a mention of brownies.

Detective work doesn't require a dirty mind, just a skeptical one. I took pains to assure myself, by looking for cuts or tears along the gutter, that no pages had been excised from Mary-Maud's book.

Chapter 13

Despite what I'd said about making the most of the next sixteen hours, I wasn't at all sure when I walked out Joe Deane's front door where I was heading next. I concluded the best place to puzzle this out was my own desk at City Hall. I just had to stop first at a blind pig to top up my whisky flask. The new liquor stores were hunky-dory six days a week, but today wasn't one of the six. I managed to purchase a couple of mickeys. Just as well, because when I arrived at the detective office Rudy Crate was on duty and not slow to remind me of how he'd smoothed things over for me with Fred Stillwater on Saturday night.

"Deputy Inspector Crate." I passed him my flask. "Deputy Banana Oil. Still, you carried it off."

"I'd rather pour from a vessel that hasn't had your mouth all over its aperture. From, for example, one of the bottles that are responsible for the bulges in your jacket pockets."

I tipped a couple of precious ounces from one of my mickeys into the big Englishman's coffee cup.

"Tell me," I said, "why is it that you're always the one the inspector leaves here in the evening and on weekends? Is it just that your posh way of speaking sounds so good on the phone? If so, I'm glad I'm an uncultivated colonial."

Rudy was spared answering by the appearance at the door of a man in a pink suit. With a flourish, he removed a pale felt hat with a high crown and a rolled brim, then slowly peeled off a pair of kid gloves. His hands were stiff and heavily veined, his forehead high, and his yellowish hair thin — albeit freshly barbered in the latest style.

"Are these the offices of the *Toronto Star*?" he asked. "I sure hope so. I understand I'm to confess to the murder of Nora Koch, and I want to get top dollar for exclusive rights."

Rudy was quick to push an extra chair up to my desk. "Have a seat here, sir. Mr. Shenstone will be glad to take your statement."

"Would that be Scoop Shenstone, the crime reporter?" The elderly fashion plate seated himself and crossed his legs comfortably. "My first-born says you've been looking for me."

"If you're Jordan Stillwater," I said, not doubting that he was. "But I'm a detective sergeant and this is police headquarters, not a newspaper office. Do you still want to confess to murder?"

"Oh yes. It was done by poison. I should tell you that as an ex-pharmacist I know my poisons. A little ergot introduced into her red wine, leading to vasoconstriction, gangrene, hallucinations, convulsions, and ultimately death."

"That's not how Nora Britton died, Mr. Stillwater, and you know it. Your son says you like your little joke. Now that you've had it, are you prepared to talk sense?"

"Ah, where's the fun of that?" Rudy chuckled. "I liked it better when we were running a newspaper. I could be sports editor and get paid to go to the races. Or the golf course." He took a practice swing with an imaginary club, then — catching my eye — seated himself quietly on a neighbouring desk.

"Nasty stuff, red wine," said Jordan Stillwater. "Brandy is what I liked to stock during Prohibition, a drink with class, and with enough of a medical reputation that doctors would prescribe it."

"Sometimes," I said, "you sold it without a doctor's prescription."

"What of it? I paid the fines and still made a profit."

Straight talk at last.

"Alcohol apart, what poisons did your pharmacy stock?"

"Arsenic, hyoscine, strychnine, potassium cyanide. And ergot. It's used to treat migraines and stop bleeding."

"Any poisons derived from fish?"

"Fish?" Stillwater smiled broadly, showing a suspiciously perfect set of teeth. "That's a new one on me. I've never heard of fish poison."

"Did you want to rid Christ Church of Nora Britton?"

"Not after I met her. I got to thinking if I married again she might be my third wife. She was a darling little thing."

"At church you were heard to call her something different."

"My opinion changed. Things change all the time. I was born in Canada West — find that on a map now if you can."

"How could you have married her? She had a husband."

"A Hun. That might have been got over."

"How?"

"By running away with her. I may do it yet. Truthfully, I doubt she's dead. Has anyone in your department seen her body?" Jordan turned to Rudy. "You, sir — have you seen it?"

I could see a quip quivering on Rudy's lips, but he contented himself with a subdued smile and a shake of his head.

"Early next week," I said, "I expect to obtain a photostat of the certificate of cremation. In the meantime, why don't you tell me where you were last Monday?"

"Kansas."

This answer didn't surprise me any more than if he'd said he'd been camping on the dark side of the moon. "Really? The state of Kansas?"

"Yep."

"What were you doing there, Mr. Stillwater?"

"Whatever you may think, not looking for the way to Oz. I was receiving medical treatment at the clinic of Dr. Brinkley."

I looked at Rudy to see if the name meant anything to him. Apparently it did.

"John R. Brinkley, the goat gland doctor?"

"The same. When I heard he had a procedure to restore vigour to older men, I made an appointment. I have the clinic's receipt if you'd like to see it."

I inspected the receipt, which was for five nights room and board — October 6 to 10, 1927 — and for medical treatment described as the surgical implantation of goat testicles into the scrotum of Mr. Jordan Frederick Stillwater of Toronto. I had heard people talk amusedly of this treatment as our era's version of the fountain of youth. I certainly never expected to encounter anyone who'd had the operation. I passed the document to Rudy, expecting him to expose it as a prank. He didn't, though.

"Okay, Mr. Stillwater," I said. "I'll keep this until I've made further inquiries. Kindly don't leave town in the meantime."

Stillwater said he had no other trips planned. He pulled on his gloves.

"Tell me," said Rudy, "does it work?"

"There must be something to it," Stillwater answered with another large display of his store-bought teeth. "It's the latest thing! Anyway, I'll be trying my luck at a tea dance tomorrow afternoon. I'll let you know."

"No rush," Rudy chuckled. "I'm not in need just yet."

When Stillwater had gone, Rudy picked up a crossword puzzle he'd been working on.

"By the way, Paul, what's Canada West when it's at home?"

"A pre-1867 name for Ontario. He was just telling us he's over sixty, but we knew that already — over by nearly twenty years, I'd guess."

I sat quietly at my desk for the next ten minutes and did some thinking. Eric Hutchinson, rector of Christ Church Grange Park, had been right and wrong. His suspicion that Nora Britton's death was not accidental appeared well-founded. The painter had eaten some poison derived from fish. On the other hand, his two chief suspects — Archie and Jordan Stillwater — both had alibis. Alibis that could be checked.

For my money, the likeliest murderer was Herman Koch. He was the person that had made an autopsy on Nora impossible — and was the chief beneficiary of her will. He had reason to be jealous of his wife's professional success. She had taken the commission that should have been his, and at a time when he was short of funds. She had, on Mrs. Hutchinson's testimony, taken a lover as well. For all his bohemian philosophy of sexual freedom, and his own adulterous affairs notwithstanding, he was not used to being cuckolded. He might have found that sauce for the gander was not necessarily sauce for the goose.

Koch was a gifted painter. Even a boor like me could see that. To hang him would deprive our world of many fine pictures, perhaps masterpieces. Artistic sensitivity, however, was no guarantee of innocence. Awareness of one's exceptional talent might even confer a sense of entitlement to break rules made for the ungifted masses.

Turning from the topic of motive to that of opportunity, I realized I'd made no progress in determining who would have been in a position to obtain the poison and introduce it into Nora Britton's last meal. Myrtle Hutchinson was the only person I'd talked to so far that admitted to having given Nora anything to eat or drink Monday, but what Myrtle said she'd contributed to Nora's meal — the hermit cookies — had not contained the poison. Somehow Nora had come by another dessert. Who besides Myrtle could have provided that dessert?

I went down the hall for some water to mix with my next shot of rye. Rudy was talking on the phone when I got back.

"Hey, skipper," he greeted me. "Professor Linacre's called to talk to you about — guess what — fish poison."

I lunged at my phone. "Shenstone here."

"I talked to a fish man named Keller. He named two toxins, practically indistinguishable. They are…" In the brief pause, I could hear paper rustling; then Linacre's flat, calm voice came back on the line. "Yes, saxitoxin, which under certain conditions accumulates in shellfish, and tetrodotoxin, which accumulates in certain organs of the pufferfish."

I got the professor to spell the two toxins.

"None of my criminological sources mention these poisons," he said, "which leads me to believe they have never been identified in a murder case. Are we dealing with murder, Shenstone?"

"Yes, sir. The deceased never ate fish voluntarily, and so wouldn't have had it for lunch."

"Keller believes these are the strongest poisons known to science. If she'd ingested even a few milligrams of either of these substances at noon, she wouldn't have survived till mid-afternoon, let alone evening. If she ingested any during the evening, she'd have been dead before she toppled to the floor. I'm giving Keller the vomit samples to analyze, but that'll take a few days and he's not promising definitive results. In the meantime, I'd guess you're dealing with the puffer. Tetrodotoxin is reliably found to be present in the liver and ovaries, whereas with saxitoxin it's hit and miss, depending mainly on whether the shellfish in question has been exposed to something called red tide."

"What's that?"

"Certain reddish algae that appear in the ocean in high concentrations from time to time. Ask a marine biologist if you need more. But my bet is the pufferfish — also called fugu — always poisonous irrespective of time and tide, and yet safely edible if properly prepared; therefore, commercially available."

"Where, Professor Linacre?"

"Keller says they're chiefly eaten in the Orient — China, Korea, Japan. Whether they can be bought in Toronto, I leave to you coppers to discover. I'd search first the fish shops in Asian neighbourhoods."

"Before I let you go, sir, you told me you'd found crumbs of chocolate cookies in the deceased's knapsack. Could they have been brownie crumbs instead?"

"All I could identify in the crumbs was chocolate. It could have been brownies she was eating. When I said cookies, I suppose I was speaking loosely."

"That would be a first."

"One more thing, Shenstone. It should be possible to extract the tetrodotoxin from the puffer without bringing the fishy odour with it. Your murderer wasn't a scientist, it seems. He must just have hacked out of the beast one or two organs and chopped them up. Good thing too or we'd never have known the lady was the victim of foul play."

I said I appreciated Linacre's call — which was putting it mildly. The university should have named a building after him.

Talking to the professor had left me restless and frustrated. I couldn't start checking fish stores till tomorrow. In the meantime, I gritted my teeth and got down to the drudgery of typing up my notes on the case so far. I was expecting that in the morning Sanderson would open a formal investigation and assign additional detectives to carry it out, so I made a couple of carbon copies to help brief my colleagues. That done, the copies all sorted and stapled, I couldn't think what to do with myself. I called the *Daily Dispatch* on the off chance that Ruth Stone might be sitting at her Remington as well, writing up a story for Monday's edition. She was.

"Hey, Paul." Her voice sounded playful, but she got straight to business. "You have a crime scoop?"

I didn't really. I couldn't announce a murder investigation until I'd spoken to the inspector, and it wouldn't have been prudent to tell the public, including the murderer, about my interest in tetrodotoxin.

"I have some free time," I said. "I thought if I could tear you away from your labours, we could go to an art gallery."

"You know any that open Sunday night?"

"How about dinner?"

"I brought something from home. I have to file this advice-to-the-lovelorn column tonight."

I imagined her pushing her wild red hair back from her face as she talked.

"Work, Paul. You know what that is?" Once again, she didn't leave me time to respond. "Call me any time you've got something for me."

"I'll come by the newsroom right away and we can flirt a little."

"I'll punch you in the eye."

"One fight taught you to box?"

"Night, handsome." With that endearment — pleasing, I grant you — she hung up on me.

I sat thinking how I'd parry her freckled little fists, then get inside them and grab her by the waist. *Lovelorn* would have been too big a word, but I did have a question for Ruth's newspaper column: what if the only girl that could save you from obsessing over a stiff is too busy to see you?

I was just starting to think of taking the Queen car back to my bedsit, opening a can of stew for my supper, and looking on my bookshelf for something soporific to read when Ruth called back.

"Did you ever catch up with Jack Wellington?" she wanted to know.

"I saw him last night in an open car, but not to talk to. I can use his plate number to find his address when the Ontario government offices open tomorrow."

"Don't bother. He lives on Lonsdale Road." She gave me the number.

"How'd you find that out?"

"I'd like to pretend it was brilliant sleuthing. The fact is he's just around the corner from where my parents and I live on Dunvegan. Daddy's talked to neighbours that complain about his noisy parties. Don't thank me; just tell me something sometime."

"You're the — "

"Something I don't know."

"You might have a better chance as a crime reporter if you wrote under a man's name, something like — I dunno — Frank."

"Funny! There's a Frank here that writes as Flossie for the women's pages. I've already done all I can to fit in: you'll never see an article by me under any name but Ruth Stone."

As soon as she rang off, I gathered my coat and headed for the northbound Bay streetcar, which turned west at Bloor and then north on Avenue Road and west again on St. Clair. The intersection of Lonsdale and Dunvegan was just two blocks north of where I got off. If Jack was at home, I was counting on my badge to get me in the door.

The house was red brick with the front door in the middle of its ground floor and two windows to each side. Five windows on the second floor lined up with door and windows downstairs. There didn't appear to be a third floor: no windows poked through the sloping roof. And no pillars bracketed the door. So, a palace by my standards, but modest for the neighbourhood. Jack likely hoped to do better as a result of more fights won — or profitably lost.

The man that opened the door had the shape of a gorilla and a less friendly expression. He looked more like one of the toughs that had escorted Jack from the Coliseum last Thursday night than like a butler. I didn't believe him when he said Mr. Wellington wasn't at home. What was the point of a bodyguard where the body wasn't? I was even more skeptical when I spotted over his wide shoulder two people descending the curving staircase that took up the back half of the front hall. A grey-haired man wearing an overcoat and carrying a black medical bag was coming down two steps ahead of a woman kitted out in white: dress, cap, and shoes.

The doctor may have been hard of hearing and not have realized how loud his voice was. He pretty certainly didn't notice the proximity of an eavesdropping outsider.

"The ribs will mend," he told the nurse without turning around. "The nose too, although he'll never look the same. His pride's hurt most of all, so try not to refer to the fight."

I was exerting myself to prevent the bodyguard from closing the door on me and missed half the nurse's soft rejoinder. I did think it included the name Dr. Telford.

"Tell the girl that replaces you tomorrow morning, won't you? I'll look in, but likely not till midday."

The doctor pulled up before the door, noticing for the first time the struggle taking place there.

"You, stand back so this gentleman can get out," said the bodyguard.

I ignored his request.

"I'm a police officer, Dr. Telford. I need a word with you. It'll be more convenient indoors where it's warm."

"Let him in please, Begg," said the doctor.

Begg stopped pushing on the door. "I'll have to tell the boss."

"Yes," the doctor assented. "You do that."

Begg went to a phone table in a corner of the front hall and kept an eye on us while he dialed. It was no surprise that by *boss* he meant Pork Chops, not Jack.

"Detective Sergeant Paul Shenstone, Dr. Telford. Will Mr. Wellington or the other party be wanting to lay charges?"

"I shouldn't think so. If you're with the Toronto department, the matter's outside your jurisdiction anyway."

"Could it be the fight occurred at Mr. Lariviere's club across the river?"

"I have to be going, detective. I suggest you address any further questions to Begg."

"Just one more thing, Dr. Telford — is there any medical reason why I can't talk to Mr. Wellington himself?"

The doctor ran his hand over the pale stubble that had grown in on his long face since his morning shave. He was tired of me — and, I suspected, of this case. "He was in bed but awake when I left him. Miss Julien will show you up."

"Just a moment," Begg called, covering the mouthpiece of the phone with a broad hand. "Mr. Lariviere would like a word with the policeman."

"Gladly," I said, as Dr. Telford slipped out the door. "Would you mind waiting a moment, Miss Julien?"

I'd never seen or spoken to Pork Chops, although I knew the stories everyone knew — how he'd taken over his father's butcher shop, selling cuts of meat in the front while running games of chance in a back room. As his fortunes grew, his stock in trade changed from dead pigs to live horses. Many of the nags he bought won races in smaller tracks across the country and in the States. Competing stables sometimes suffered ruinous fires, not that anything was ever pinned on Pork Chops. To date he'd won nothing as prestigious as the Kentucky Derby or the Queen's Plate, but no one thought he'd stop until he had. Boxing was a relatively new interest, and — again — there were suspicions he used shady means to make his bets pay off. Buying a ref, for instance. As I'd told Ruth, however, paying a good fighter to lose to a palooka wasn't something my little corner of the boxing world had seen before. If that's what the man I was about to speak to had done, I'd happily have seen *him* under a doctor's care.

I picked up the phone and identified myself. "Am I speaking to Mr. Lariviere?"

"Indeed, my friend. But what business has a hard-working city policeman like yourself up at Jack Wellington's?" A smooth voice with a hint of a chuckle behind it.

While Lariviere was speaking, I thought of the last photo of him I'd seen in the papers. Despite his porcine name, he had looked trim and fit in his Savile Row suit. He'd phrased his question to imply I might be out of my social depth.

"I've followed Jack enough to know he'd be hard to beat in a clean fight," I said. "I was just wondering who put him in bed with multiple fractures."

"Wondering as a boxing fan then, not as an officer of the law. What if I told you that the truth was quite uninteresting, that Mr. Wellington tripped on uneven pavement?"

"That's not what he told Dr. Telford."

"Well, whatever happened, my friend, will not require any action on your part." Lariviere's amused tone of voice was by now only a memory. "Begg has instructions to show you out when we're finished talking."

"Then I suggest you give Begg new instructions. I'm not in your East York club, Mr. Lariviere. This part of Forest Hill is within my jurisdiction."

"You can't just barge into a private dwelling."

"I was invited into Jack's house, and I'm not leaving until I've seen him. If Begg tries to prevent me, he'll be in the kind of trouble with the law you won't want. Where was he, by the way, when Jack got busted up? Some job you did of protecting your investment." I heard nothing from Lariviere's end of the line. "Begg," I said. "He wants another word with you."

"Stay right here," Begg growled at me as he took the receiver.

He could have saved his breath.

"Shall we go, Miss Julien?" I said, starting up the stairs. "Left or right at the top?"

I turned and let the nurse pass me. She had a round face bordered under her cap by severely pinned dark hair. A rough complexion and an unsmiling, thin-lipped mouth made her look a bit hard-boiled, but she answered me readily enough, with a charming French accent.

"Around this way, sir. Follow me."

Wellington was lying on his back in bed in the room over the front door. One low-wattage lamp was burning in a far corner, and the illuminated dial of a radio shone from a bedside table.

"You have a visitor, Mr. Wellington," said the nurse. "Would you like to sit up?"

"Uh-uh."

The voice softly drifting from the radio speaker was that of Charles Hart singing "Are You Lonesome Tonight?" Not the song to snap Jack out of his self-pity. When I approached the bed, I could hear his breath coming and going in short gasps.

"Who is it?" he asked, turning his face with its cracked centrepiece my way.

"Paul Shenstone," I said. "A police detective and an admirer — at least until recently."

"Marie, get Begg to throw this bum out."

"He won't, though," I said. "Instructions from Lariviere."

"Nurse!"

Marie Julien looked at me. I shook my head.

"The quickest way to get rid of me, Jack, is to tell me who broke your nose."

"He'll get his, don't worry."

"One man did all this?"

"It wasn't a clean fight."

"You should have been right at home then."

Jack Wellington sat up at that, dropping his long legs over the side of the bed. Then, wincing, he got to his feet so he could look down into my face.

"If Begg won't send you packing, I will." His fist came flying at my jaw with all the speed Wellington was famous for. I hadn't a hope of parrying. Still, it was just a warning punch, not hard.

"That's the spirit, Jack," I said, stepping back. "You're not badly enough hurt to be lying around in bed with round-the-clock care."

I fancied I was ready for his next punch, but he redirected it at the last instant from my face to my gut, and it hurt plenty. I come off well enough in barroom brawls, but I'm not fast enough to contend with pros like Jack. As I doubled over, I thought of head-butting him in his damaged rib cage, but didn't have the heart. Couldn't even bring myself to threaten charges of assault. I no longer wanted to punish him for throwing the Lucan fight: someone had beaten me to it and done a more than adequate job. What a contrast tonight's sorry casualty made with the sheik I'd seen cruising Bay Street behind the wheel of his Big Six just twenty-four hours before!

"I'm leaving, Jack," I said, retreating further. "Just one thing..."

Apparently winded, Jack didn't follow me. "Yeah," he gasped.

"Your fists are the fastest I've seen. What did this dirty fighter throw at you, a crowbar?"

Still gasping, Jack might not have answered at all, but then he decided to confide. He still couldn't get out a sentence of any length.

"Boots! Boots with metal plates in the heel. He kicked me in the face. In the chest."

"Try to take deeper breaths, Mr. Wellington," said Marie. "Remember what Dr. Telford said about your needing to clear mucous from your lungs."

"Ah, dry up! Stupid hag. You'd think Lariviere — "

"What about him?" I said.

"Could have sent — a pretty nurse."

"She's a better nurse than you deserve, Jack. Treat her right."

Marie Julien flashed me a tight-lipped grin she made sure Jack didn't see.

Chapter 14

With the cars on Sunday schedule, I was late getting home. My stomach was telling me it was as empty as my bank account, but hurt too much for me to think of putting anything solid inside. If it felt no better in a day or two, I figured I'd have to get a doctor to tell me whether Jack had ruptured anything important. Meanwhile I medicated my hunger with a belt or three and went to bed.

I wanted to arrive at City Hall no later than Inspector Sanderson on Monday morning and lost by no more than a nose. I wasn't used to sitting in his poorly ventilated office before eight and found that one big bonus was that he considered it too early for his first pipe of the day. The inspector remarked on my keenness.

"You must have had a relaxing weekend, Paul. Do any serious courting? A man your age should be married."

"More productive than relaxing, sir. I believe I have enough to open an investigation into the murder of Nora Britton."

I laid out the evidence that some fish-based poison, probably tetrodotoxin, had been slipped into the artist's last meal. The motive, I suggested, was not anti-German feeling. More likely it was jealousy, professional or sexual or some combination of the two. To shore up this hypothesis, I reported that Mrs. Hutchinson claimed to have seen Nora with a lover. I showed the inspector the ribbon copy of my case notes.

"So your top suspect is the deceased's husband, supplanted both professionally and sexually?"

"Yes, but there's digging to do before we can make an arrest. I'm asking you to assign some men to look into this full-time."

"How many? I can let you have Rudy Crate."

"Rudy's fine in the office, but I'd rather have Harry O'Brian in the field along with Acting Detective Cruickshank."

"You'll have to see yourself if Ned can be spared." Sanderson uncapped a thick fountain pen and pulled a sheet of office stationery off a pile on a corner of his desk. "I'm writing a note authorizing Rudy and Harry to work with you till Wednesday night. We'll see then if the game's worth the candle."

"Three days? I'd call that chintzy for a murder case."

"Bear in mind the only member of the public asking for an investigation is Eric Hutchinson, and I understood you to say he's barking up the wrong tree."

"I think he is, but there are alibis to check and new leads the public isn't aware of. We need to know what happened to Nora Britton. So do her family."

"Hell, Paul!" Sanderson seldom cussed and even more rarely shouted. Today he kept his voice low and disdainful. "You haven't been speaking to the grieving parents, have you? Guaranteeing them justice?" He redirected his gaze from my irksome face out his office window into the cramped room where we detective sergeants had our desks. Maybe he was looking for someone less disappointing. I flattered myself that he didn't see one, for he continued more matter-of-factly, "If they paid taxes in this city and felt they could take your promises to City Council, I'd string you up by your thumbs."

"I promised nothing," I said, "but I think they're owed."

"Not by me — you're on your own." Sanderson glanced at the clock and stuck a pipe in his mouth.

I'd taken the hastily scrawled note from the inspector's hand and was on my way out the door when he called after me, "Did Nora Britton leave a sister?"

"How did you guess?"

"It's the women with you, Paul, always the women. Report Wednesday night."

Ned Cruickshank worked out of Station Number One. My first order of business was to phone over and request his services for a few days. Once that loan had been approved, they were able to put Ned himself on the line. I wanted him to see if he could get a photograph of Herman Koch from one of the city newspapers and have four copies made. The artist was famous enough that there had to be a portrait in some rag's files. Ned was to keep one of the photos and leave the other three on my desk.

Then I wanted Ned to find out where in Toronto you could come by a pufferfish complete with liver and ovaries. He was to show Koch's picture to every supplier and see if any of them recognized a customer.

I started a note for Rudy Crate, but was glad to see him drift into the detective room before I had it done. We were equal in rank, so I couldn't appear to boss him around. I suggested he field any further calls from the university about fish poison. I said we were waiting for an analysis of some regurgitated specimens from Nora Britton's stomach. He was to pay special attention as to whether tetrodotoxin was detected. The Englishman acted insulted when I offered to write the word down for him.

I praised his scholarship and asked if, while waiting for the toxicological results, he could test the alibis of the two threat-uttering Stillwaters, Archie and Jordan. Both men had criminal records, so there would be police photographs. He should get copies to the two local constabularies, but this would have to be done by mail and would take time. Neither the city of Toronto nor any of its newspapers yet had machines for sending photos by wire. Meanwhile, Rudy was to make whatever phone calls would tend to confirm Archie's presence in Sandusky, Ohio and Jordan's in Milford, Kansas at the time Nora must have been given the chocolate dessert.

Rudy was less happy with assignments requiring exertion and asked to see Sanderson's note, which he examined carefully, but in the end he said okay. The whole goat gland business seemed to intrigue him.

I left him one of the carbon copies of my case notes.

I still had to decide how to deploy Harry O'Brian. Sanderson had tasked him with compiling data for the Chief Constable's Annual Report, a labour from which my request for his services in a murder investigation temporarily saved him. When I dropped Sanderson's note onto his desk, his round face broke into a wide, dimple-cheeked grin. Unlike Rudy, Harry was a man of action who compared desk work to being confined in the stocks.

I considered taking him to again help me interview Herman Koch. I found it hard to think beyond (a) Koch's plausible motivation for murder and (b) his suspiciously rapid disposal of Nora's remains. At the same time, we still had to establish that he'd delivered the toxin to Nora. We had to connect him to the poisonous fish and to the chocolate dessert in which the fish poison had been disguised. The more I thought about it, the less likely it seemed that Koch would reveal those connections under any pressure Harry and I could ethically apply.

Ned would, I hoped, connect Koch to the fish. But what about those cookies or brownies? There are people that tell someone about every incident in their lives, right down to the brushing of their teeth. It would have been convenient if Nora had known someone she'd have mentioned those chocolate treats to — a confidential friend. I hadn't found one yet.

If Harry was expecting a thrilling assignment, I had to disappoint him. In the end, I sent him to speak with everyone he could on Elizabeth Street, starting in Nora's block. I wanted to know if there was anyone that had heard or seen what the artist had in her knapsack when she left her studio one week ago tonight. He should also be asking if anyone on the street had seen Nora with a man, particularly a man in a light-coloured roadster.

Once everyone knew what he was doing, I pulled on my trench coat and headed for the westbound King streetcar stop. After a mild Sunday, Monday was cooler than usual for this date in October, and the look of the sky made me think I'd be rained on before I was done. As I neared the site of the old Central Prison chapel, now providing studio space for two artists, I decided to start by having a word with Ernestine Lopez.

When she answered my knock at nine fifteen, it appeared she had already started work. Her blue-checked house dress bore fresh, damp stains, and she was wiping clay from her hands with a rag as she looked me over. Recognition wasn't immediate, but when it dawned the expression in her lined face changed from inquiring to unfriendly.

"What are you doing back here?" she growled. "Haven't you caused enough grief?"

"What grief is that, Miss Lopez?"

"Throwing accusations around, making the best painter in the country incapable of work."

"I want to hear more. May I come in?"

"And if I say no?"

"Think before you do. When I was here before, we didn't know whether Nora Britton died accidentally or not. Now it's clear she was murdered. There's an official investigation. I'd rather talk to you here, but I do have the authority to take you to police headquarters for questioning."

Ernestine Lopez fell back from her doorway to let me by. In a gesture of acknowledgement that she wouldn't be back sculpting right away, she pulled off the man's cloth cap she had been using to keep her curling black hair out of her eyes.

Upstairs, the same clay infantryman stood on her work stand. His boots, rough blobs three days ago, now showed shape and detail. In clay she had rendered the creases across the toes, the worn laces, and the places where the leather disappeared under the cloth puttees that wrapped the soldier's legs.

The artist stood defiantly with her back to her work, her hands in her dress pockets, and her dark eyes fixed upon my face.

"Just keep your voice down," she whispered, gesturing at the partition wall. "He's been up all night and may just have fallen asleep."

"What's keeping him from working?" I asked in an undertone.

"You! Your suspicions, your not believing that he loved Nora too much to kill her. Fear, too — fear that even though he's innocent he'll be tried and hanged for Nora's murder. Mother of God — I had more reason to kill Nora than Herman did."

"Why?"

"I did, that's all."

She was spitting mad. I moved a garbage pail so I could grab and set beside her the kitchen chair she'd offered me on Friday.

"Ernestine, why don't you sit down?"

She blinked, hesitated, finally shrugged and sat. I stepped back so as not to crowd her.

"Are you Herman's lover?" I asked.

She glared at me.

"It happens." I left her time to speak. She didn't. "Am I way off base?"

"I *was*."

"When?"

"Until the end of September — until he got Nora's letter."

"What letter?"

"The letter — " Ernestine covered her face with her hands for a few seconds, then wiped her eyes and nose and continued: "The letter she wrote — she was asking to…"

"To do what? To come back?"

"I could have killed her. I daydreamed about it."

"So he told Nora he'd take her back. He broke with you."

"Herman and I were to go back to being pals, like before. I tell you, the only way I could get through those days was to

plan how I'd feed her poison, how I'd disguise the taste. Pals?
How could I think about that?"

"Did Herman keep this letter?"

"Like a holy relic."

Ernestine Lopez was hipped on Koch; I couldn't doubt it.
But I wasn't sure yet whether he and Nora had been about to
set up house together again or whether that was just Ernestine's
way of convincing me Koch hadn't killed his wife. I did have
an idea as to why Herman wasn't working. In the open garbage
pail I'd moved, I noticed — among the apple cores and
cigarette packages — a bottle for toothache medicine.

"The humiliating thing is I couldn't bring myself to give up
this studio. Look at the light." Ernestine gestured towards the
many tall windows piercing each side wall of the former prison
chapel. "Think of the storage space downstairs. The Inglis
company will throw us out eventually, but meanwhile the rent's
a bargain. I'd have swallowed being their neighbour, pals or no,
listening in on their lives. I don't know which would have been
worse, hearing them argue — Herman loves that — or hearing
them make up. I'm glad she croaked before she could move in."

Pulling off a pair of scuffed and clay-stained saddle shoes,
Ernestine Lopez set about massaging her toes. She was no
longer boiling over with anger. I had the impression that
everything she'd just told me she had rehearsed often enough
in her mind that, while the animosity was real, the fire had
gone out of it. Nora was not worth any part of the energy that
belonged in Ernestine's sculpture. I didn't see her as a
murderess, but I still had questions.

"When did you last see Nora Britton?"

"A year ago, maybe more. Not since Herman took the other
half of this building. Nora was older than I am, but looked
younger. Pretty in a neat and tidy, schoolgirl way. It was clear
to see she had not a drop of passion in her veins."

"You daydreamed of poisoning her. Did you send her any
food?"

"No, I'd have waited till she came here."

"You mentioned disguising the taste of poison. How would you have done that?"

"Combine chocolate and chili: the strong tastes plus the fire in her mouth would mask any other flavours."

"I bet. Only wouldn't so unusual a mix be suspicious?"

"Not at all unusual. Do you eat chop suey? Do you eat spaghetti?"

"Sure — anything as long as it's cheap and filling."

"Suppose I invite you to try the cuisine of Mexico."

"Where they eat chocolate with chili?"

"Since the days of the Aztec Indians."

"Did you ever tell Herman that recipe?" I was thinking about Professor Linacre's report on the crumbs found in Nora's last meal. He hadn't said anything about chili, but likely hadn't tested for it either.

"Of course not," Ernestine snapped. She seemed to forget we were speaking quietly. "Herman loved her; he wanted her back."

I thought I heard a nose being blown on the other side of the partition wall. I needed to catch Herman Koch before he had a chance to go out.

"One last question, Ernestine. What poison would you have used?"

"Arsenic, I suppose. I never got around to working that out."

I figured the secret door in the partition wall was behind Ernestine's bookcase. I told her she'd made a good case for crossing Koch off my list of suspects, but that it'd pay him to grant me another interview. Did she think she could get him to move the piano and let me through? I had to coax her a bit more. I spoke of how we both admired Koch's art and both wanted him back at work. In the end, she swung the bookcase, which must have been mounted on concealed hinges, away from the wall.

"Hermie, the cop is here, the plainclothesman. He knows you didn't kill Nora. Will you see him?"

"Does he have a hair of the dog with him?"

"I do, Mr. Koch. I've refilled my flask. But wouldn't you rather have cocaine?"

Silence on the other side of the wall.

Ernestine glared at me. Before she could start scolding, I put my finger to my lips, and to her credit she held her fire.

"What makes you say that?" Koch asked at last.

"We can talk better if you open the door."

No answer.

"Mr. Koch, your wife was murdered. That's the crime I'm investigating. Would you rather talk to the drug police?"

I could hear the piano being rolled aside. The low connecting door forced Koch to stoop as he came through. When he stood up, I had the impression he hadn't bathed or shaved or brushed his teeth since Friday. His right cheek above the beard line was marked by a large, irregularly shaped scab he appeared to be trying, without much success, to keep from touching and picking at. He still wore the trousers of the brown corduroy suit I'd last seen him in, although he'd shed his jacket. His green knitted tie was loose, his white shirt creased and stained. Whether with blood or food I couldn't tell.

"God, it's cold in here." Koch's voice was hoarse and he appeared to be shivering. "Give me a drink."

"Sure," I said, "if you show me the letter you got from Nora Britton at the end of September."

He tried to grab my flask out of my side pocket. I got hold of both his wrists. It didn't take lightning-quick reflexes on my part. He was far from peak form and, I suspected, had never been much of a brawler.

"Enough of that. I don't want to put you in handcuffs."

"Let go."

"My pleasure." And it was: his breath smelled of rot. "The letter?"

"It's private."

"I'm discreet."

"I burned it."

"Like you did Nora? Miss Lopez says not."

Koch turned on the sculptress. "Some friend you are."

"Baloney, Herman. She cares enough for you to want you cleared of suspicion in your wife's murder. Just give me the letter and satisfy me that you didn't kill Nora Britton; then I can get on with putting a noose around the neck of the bastard that did."

"And if I say no?" Herman scratched at his cheek, then forced his hand away.

"You can delay but not stop me. You know I can fill in forms and use the powers of the police to get the letter in the end. But if you make me go that route, your troubles won't end there. You've been abusing cocaine all weekend. The empty tooth drop bottle in Miss Lopez's trash pail bears a prescription date of October 15. No toothache could use up that much medicine in two days. You're the one that drained the bottle, not Ernestine. You maybe thought the drug would stimulate you enough to get you painting again, but you overdid it and now you're hooked. You have to get more. If I have the RCMP put you under surveillance, they'll catch you soon enough with either drops or powder, and you'll go away for seven years."

"You cops — ah, where's that drink?"

I was prepared to follow him back through the wall, but he took a creased wad of notepaper from the left hip pocket of his corduroys. Handing it to me, he collapsed with a fit of shivers on the chair Ernestine had vacated when she let him in.

His surrender appeared to relieve the sculptress. She had been following our back and forth like a chair umpire at a tennis match; now she turned away and with a wooden tool began to worry away at her clay soldier.

I unfolded the pages Koch had given me. While no handwriting expert, I concluded after noting the slant, the margin widths, the letter size and spacing, and the sparing use

of loops that the same person had most probably written both
the letter and the journal I'd found in Nora's studio. I passed
the painter my flask and started reading.

September 27, 1927

Dear Herman,

*When I asked for your advice on fixing the colours of
the Christ Church mural with waterglass, I'd no idea
you'd treat me to a recipe for making the goop —
correction, three recipes for (1) potash waterglass,
(2) soda waterglass, and (3) double waterglass.*

I blinked at the letter. Waterglass was familiar to me, from
the newspaper ads, only as a liquid in which eggs were
preserved. Evidently it was part of the artist's bag of tricks as
well. I read on in hope of coming to something less technical.

*Forty-five pounds of quartz? Twenty-three pounds of
anhydrous carbonate of soda? Three pounds of
powdered charcoal? I can quite understand that you,
who take infinite pains over every detail of a work,
would never trust to others to make what you could
make for yourself. And perhaps, if I had won the first
mural competition instead of you, I'd have worked
myself up to do as you suggest. Now, however, time is
short and I have no appetite for going the extra mile,
not for this congregation.*

*I do want to create a lasting memorial if only to vex the
more prejudiced members of Christ Church. And so I
appreciate the advice you gave me as to the preparation
of the surface to be painted. I found the plaster quite
sound and free of efflorescence. After the scaffold was
up, I was able to get straight to the first application of*

(store-bought) waterglass to the wall. Once that was dry, I proceeded to a second application and now as a new month is about to begin I am ready to start drawing and, soon I hope, painting.

I considered your offer to help with the work. I even installed a bolt on the inside of the vestry door to the Christ Church sanctuary so that no one should barge in on us and find you there. But someone might still see you coming or going. Why risk inflaming short tempers and jeopardizing the entire project? As I benefit from your counsel, you are here in spirit. Incidentally, I chuckled when I read your advice not to mention to anyone the originators of the waterglass technique as all have German names. It was brave of you to joke about it.

I know how you distrust any praise that does not come from yourself. Still, I must tell you I do admire how you have risen above your disappointment without the least resentment of my success. I was disappointed too. Your painting in the chancel would have adorned not just one small Anglican church but the city as a whole. More than an attraction to be gawked at by tourists, a treasure to be studied by artists and scholars. You showed such character in never mentioning your pain. You simply got down to giving me the benefit of your years of study.

With the foundation problems, thanks to you, settled, I have been able to spare some thoughts for the significance of this memorial. As I begin outlining my warriors in charcoal, I ask myself what they would have to say about the cost of winning the war. Some Canadians lost limbs. Some lost the ability to open their arms in welcome.

You have applauded my success with the judges. You tell me to pay no nevermind to what came before. I can't do that. I shall fulfill my commission, but always aware that my opportunity arises from a wrong done to you.

That's not all, though. The way you set aside that wrong to encourage me moves me right down to my boot laces. Two years ago, when I took the studio on Elizabeth Street, we decided that neither of us could have the freedom we both value and at the same time live together. The world was wide and wonderful and full of opportunities for the unencumbered. There are still opportunities, ones I do not mean to let slip. At the same time, it has been borne in on me that some people are less wonderful than others. I believe the best use of my freedom is to draw closer to the person my heart recognizes as the most wonderful of all. I'm asking you, Herman, if we might again live together. Being reminded of the sweetness that runs through your temperament, as through your art, makes me miss all the more the sweetness of your touch. I miss everything about you. Please read between the lines. That small-town upbringing still makes it hard for me to say some things. Harder still to write them.

You have dinned it into me that life should be lived with enthusiasm. The most enthusiastic life I can dream up for myself would be one lived at your side and in your arms.

Love,

Your Nora

I took a deep breath and looked around, surprised to see that the studio with its high windows and plank partition was the same space in which I'd started the letter. If either

Ernestine or Herman had spoken while I was reading, I hadn't heard them.

I'd expected Nora to sound more up-to-date, more like Gussie perhaps. Both women accepted the age's sexual freedom. But Nora's way of expressing herself had taken me out of that age, not simply to a smaller town but to an older time. It made my murder victim not stuffy but even more exotic, and did nothing to lessen her hold on me.

The way I saw it, the man she addressed in this letter was exceptionally lucky in his wife and exceptionally unlucky in losing her less than two weeks after receiving it. I was glad to get a glimpse of the more competent Herman Koch, the knowledgeable artist, the creator of the two brilliant paintings I'd seen — the Great Lakes landscape on his easel and the winning yet rejected entry in the first mural competition, the vision of the man in the loincloth rising from the sarcophagus between figures of grief and hope.

"I'll return this, Mr. Koch, as soon as I've made a copy. How did you respond to Nora Britton's request?"

Koch still appeared to be suffering from the cocaine user's itch. He scraped at his forehead with his untrimmed nails and continued to finger the scab on his cheek. On the other hand, the rye he'd consumed had stopped, or at least tamed, his shivers. I intercepted the flask as he was again putting it to his lips.

"I'll have that back now," I said. "You're no use to me sozzled."

"You're a bully. You know that?"

"Pray you never meet a worse one. Did you tell Nora you'd live with her?"

"Of course he did," Ernestine spat out, looking up from her work.

"Miss Lopez," I said, "let him speak for himself or I'll have to take him away to the station."

Ernestine said nothing, but gave up the pretense of sculpting. She wrapped a damp cloth around the clay figure and directed all her attention to my interrogation. Whether on account of the whisky's mellowing influence or of my threat, Herman became more cooperative.

"Mr. Koch?"

"She's right. Nora's the woman I love."

"As I understand it," I said, "you've had many lovers."

Koch waved away the relevance of his liaisons. "Not the same thing."

This must have been hard for Ernestine to hear, but she had the consolation of being the survivor, the only woman left to Herman and the only one he was likely to have in his present unenticing state.

"Did you tell Nora in person?" I asked.

"Yes, I went to her studio."

"When?"

Herman struggled to concentrate; his hand went to his cheek. "I don't remember."

"It was a Saturday," Ernestine prompted. She handed Herman a cleanish handkerchief. "You're bleeding again, Hermie."

Herman dabbed at the wound he'd just opened. "Yeah, that's right — the first Saturday in October, late."

"October 1 — after Moretti's shop closed?"

Herman nodded. "Nora said she had things to tidy up that would take her a few days. She hoped to be able to move here by the middle of the month."

"Did you see her alive after that?"

"After? No, I remember. She was going to write me when she was ready."

"So you didn't see her on Wednesday, October 5?"

"No, I've told you."

"Then the man she was seen kissing on the afternoon of Tuesday, October 5 was not you?"

"What?"

"Four days after you and Nora agreed to live together."

"Who says?"

"So you didn't know Nora was intimate with someone else after she wrote you this love letter?"

Herman jumped out of his chair. "Of course I didn't know. Because it didn't happen. Who says it did?"

"A source I've no reason to doubt. Suppose that source is right and suppose that you did discover Nora's connection with this man. In that case, Nora's letter here wouldn't tend to remove your name from the list of murder suspects. You might have fallen for the letter and then found out she was playing you for a sap. In that case, you might have been sore enough to slip her some poison, not so?"

"Drive the bayonet in and twist it. Good sport, eh?" Herman squared his shoulders and fixed me with mournful eyes. "When you look at me, what do you see? A Kraut like the ones you cut down during the war?"

"Not a bit, Mr. Koch. You're not tough enough. What I see in you is an artist drowning his talent in self-pity and making a lame play for sympathy."

Ernestine's weathered face broke into a smile. Some part of her must have agreed with me. Perhaps too the idea that Nora had been playing a double game with Herman gave her hope that he'd stop mooning after his dead wife.

That wasn't the way it played out. Koch shoved his hands resolutely into his trouser pockets.

"This is all I'm going to say, detective, whether you take me to the station or not. If Nora kissed another man after I saw her, it was to say goodbye. It was one of the things she wanted to tidy up before she came here."

That's all he did say. And, after poking at and prodding him a bit more, I started to think he just might be right.

Chapter 15

Riding back east on the King car, I started reviewing the remaining suspects on my mental list. If Nora had had a lover, and if at the time of her death she'd been in the process of leaving him to return to Herman, then that lover might have been jealous enough to bump her off. I thought Sir Joseph Deane the likeliest candidate for the role of lover, but too fond of Nora to have slipped her poison and also too anxious to be of assistance to my investigation. The same arguments applied to Eric Hutchinson if he had been breaking his marriage vows with the painter. Both men, however, had women in their lives that might have resented Nora.

Effie Britton believed Nora would never have had an affair with a married man without his wife's leave. I bet there were loveless marriages in which adultery might be freely okayed, even in our sexually orthodox town. But permission might also be granted insincerely or under duress. Or the wife might, having given the green light, find herself more liable to jealousy than she expected. Both Hutchinson and Deane were public figures. An additional motive for the removal of a mistress might be the protection of the great man's reputation.

I had already entertained the possibility of such a motive in the case of Myrtle Hutchinson. The man in the light-coloured roadster she had claimed to have seen kissing Nora might have been no more than a fiction to divert attention from Eric. Joe Deane lived with three female family members: any one of them might have resented an infidelity on his part or feared the consequences of its exposure. My conversation with Deane's daughter Phyllis had aroused no suspicions, but had been too brief for me to rule her out. As a medical student, she might be familiar with poisons. Lady Deane I had also spent too little time with to either suspect or clear. She struck me as too indolent to be a criminal. Of the three, Joe's sister Mary-Maud was the person I thought likeliest to have made away with Nora. She had the most involvement with the kitchen. Judging by her own case, she also tended to blame the other woman for a man's disloyalty.

It ran against the grain for me to think of women as murderers, but I had to admit that when women did kill, poison was often the method of choice. The administration of noxious substances requires no brawn and sorts well with the art of cookery.

When I got to City Hall I found on my desk three photos of Herman Koch and a message that Ruth Stone had phoned from the *Dispatch* and wanted a call back. I didn't waste a second.

"Hi, Ruth. You miss me?"

"Non-stop. Say, I hear Jack Wellington has had a few of his ribs cracked and his nose broken. Did you do that for him?"

"Whoa, Emma! That would be against the detective's code of conduct."

"So it's pure coincidence that yesterday afternoon I gave you his address and the next thing I hear he's confined to bed with hot and cold running nurses?"

"His injuries were incurred Saturday night. And, while I appreciate the compliment, Ruth, I doubt if I could have inflicted them. I'm not in his class for speed." My stomach didn't ache enough to keep me from looking forward to lunch, but was still sufficiently tender to make me glad I wasn't Jack's regular sparring partner.

"Too bad. I could write such a good story, having been at the fixed fight and everything. Would it wreck your career if I used your name anyway?"

"Would it hurt yours if you took a jump in the lake?"

"So you saw him yesterday?"

"Uh-huh."

"How did you find him?"

"In bed all right, but scarcely confined."

"Who do you think messed him up?"

"On the record?"

"Not for attribution."

"Jack didn't say, and frankly all that mattered to me was that someone had dealt with him. I couldn't arrest that someone even if I wanted to. The encounter happened outside my jurisdiction."

"At Lariviere's club, I'm guessing."

"That's the impression I got."

"Anything more you can give me?"

"Lots. If you'll see me, I'll show you."

"About Jack's injuries, Paul. Try to concentrate."

"Not for attribution then. He said the damage was done with high kicks. Can I take you to an art gallery this weekend?"

"Never thought I'd hear that from you. Kicks, eh? Bare feet?"

"Boots. I've become a real fan of paintings in the past week. What about it?"

"Not one of those Oriental styles then. Sounds like savate."

"French." I was impressed and didn't care if it showed. "You know more about fighting than you let on."

"Girl's gotta keep up. Any murder investigations underway?"

"I'll tell you Saturday."

We agreed to work out details later in the week.

In a celebratory mood, I trotted off for a fish salad sandwich at Uneeda Lunch. Tucking myself into the last seat at the counter, I found myself sitting beside an equally ebullient Harry O'Brian, just back from Elizabeth Street. His sandwich was baked beans with plenty of onions. He smacked his lips, finished it in four bites, and ordered another the same — none of which convinced me that his choice was anything but disgusting.

"Good news, Harry?"

"A couple of things to show for my morning," the tall man beamed down at me. "First, the car. A cream-coloured roadster was seen parked in front of Nora Britton's studio at various dates up to October 5. Always during daylight hours. I have the word of four different people — a housewife, a rag-and-bone man, a laundress, and a ten-year-old boy who sells cigarettes he makes from discarded butts. Do you want their names?"

"Not if you have them written down. Anyone see a driver?"

"Only the boy, and he just got a glimpse of the back of a middle-aged male closing the car door and walking into Moretti's shop. This man had white hair with a centre part, seemed short standing beside the car, and was dressed in a well-cut charcoal grey suit."

"Not after October 5, Harry? How can they be sure of the date?"

"The laundress's hands had become so irritated by the bleach she has to use that she was taking a day off work. It was warmer than usual for the season, so she went out on her porch. She was sure of the date, and the temperature squares with my memory. The two of us agreed that the next day, when she was back at work, was even warmer. Anyway, sitting there on her front stoop, she missed seeing the driver, who had already gone inside, but she got an eyeful of the car all right. She remembers exchanging a remark with the cigarette boy about it and his telling her what he'd do with a boat like that. Oh, I forgot to mention, when I spoke to him he told me it was a Chrysler Imperial. After October 5, the laundress hasn't had another day off till today, so she couldn't have seen the car even if it had been there."

I was sure the roadster she and the boy had seen was the Chrysler Imperial I'd driven to Aurora just yesterday, but there was nothing suspicious about any of it. Deane had told me he'd delivered a cheque to Nora on the fifth.

"Any more neighbours left to interview?" I asked Harry, who was now slurping down a second cup of stale coffee made palatable by four lumps of sugar.

"I'll go back after lunch and see if there's anyone home now that was out this morning."

"Stop by my desk first and take one of the photos of Herman. He says the last time he saw Nora alive was October 1. I'd like to know if anyone on the street saw him with her or near her studio since then."

"Sure thing. But, meanwhile, would you like to hear about October 10?"

I nodded.

"The last day of Nora Britton's life."

"Enough of the 'coming attractions,' Harry. What have you got?"

"A woman on the street named Rose Mertens. She's posed for Nora Britton."

"Ned Cruickshank spoke to her. The man she lives with had a grudge against Nora — so he thought. Is that what this is about?"

"Ixnay — it's about diet." The habitual grin left Harry's face. "You wouldn't call Rose Mertens blooming with the appearance of good health, but she is full-figured, not wasting away. In motherly style, she used to coax Nora to eat more. Now Rose happened to be out on an errand on Queen Street on the afternoon of Monday the tenth when she bumped into Nora. Nora was on her way to Christ Church, where she intended to paint till morning. The two women didn't talk long, but Nora mentioned that someone had dropped in the evening before and given her half a dozen chocolate cookies for her midnight lunch. A new style of cookie — had Rose ever had chocolate mixed with chili? Rose hadn't. Nora said neither had she, but if they were as good as they sounded, she might please Rose by putting on quite a few pounds. Hearing that wasn't fun I'll have to say. I couldn't help thinking how little she must weigh now."

"Buck up, Harry," I said with exaggerated gruffness. "It'll be better for your mental balance if you don't think of a pile of ashes as *she*. Who was this cookie-bearing someone?"

"Rose asked — it seemed such a curious combination — but Nora never answered questions about who came to her studio. All she would say was a friend had brought her this dessert. It was supposed to be a Mexican recipe."

"I'll bet."

I couldn't have answered in a word how this bombshell made me feel about Herman. If he hadn't killed Nora, I felt sorry for him. Just as it was starting to look as if he were in the clear, this new thundercloud rolls in over his head. On the other hand, it had just become far easier to believe he was a wife-killer. How many people on my list of suspects had convenient access to someone with so arcane a formula for disguising the taste of poison?

I filled Harry O'Brian in on my morning interviews at the former prison chapel.

"Have you considered the possibility that Ernestine Lopez killed Nora herself?" he asked.

"But then why would she tell me about the chocolate-chili mix?"

"Bad conscience perhaps. Last year, one of my first assignments as a detective was to catch an embezzler. The guilty party couldn't bring himself to confess directly, but deliberately dropped so many hints that Parsons and I were able to book him."

"The only poison she mentioned was arsenic. Professor Linacre found no trace of that."

"What I'm suggesting, Paul, is she's of two minds. One wants to own up; the other wants to escape suspicion."

"Maybe," I said. "But on the face of it what she said doesn't make things look good for Herman. My first thought is that he got the cookie idea from Ernestine and the fish poison idea from a source she knew nothing of."

"So you still believe Herman's our murderer?"

"I do, Harry," I said. "And the hell of it is I don't want to. We've already lost one talented artist this month. I don't want another one executed. So I'm going to try my damnedest to resolve this case some other way and prove myself wrong."

"I didn't know you were so hipped on art."

"Me neither."

I asked Harry if, before returning to Elizabeth Street, he could go out to Ernestine's studio and ask who else in Toronto might know of the chocolate-chili cookie recipe. Whom had she told about it? Was it to be found in any English-language cookbook, newspaper, or magazine? Was it used by any local restaurants or bakeries?

Meanwhile, I returned to the detective office to see what Rudy Crate had to report. He said no one had phoned with further news of the fish poison. On the other hand, he had obtained Sanderson's authorization for two long distance calls. The first one the operator put through was to Dr. Brinkley's goat gland clinic in Kansas. The office manager there proved by an accurate description that he well remembered the dapper Mr. Jordan Stillwater, who had shown a thoroughly official-looking Canadian birth certificate during the admission formalities. The second international call yielded the news that Archie Stillwater had also had to show his birth certificate in the United States, in his case to the Sandusky police on being arrested in connection with a bar fight. Under the circumstances, Rudy asked me if I was satisfied that both grandfather and grandson had sound alibis for the period in which Nora Britton received the poisoned treats. I didn't think he still needed to bother mailing off the two men's photographs, did I? I said I did — then thought of something else I could ask him to do.

"Say, Rudy, are you Church of England?"

"At one time I suppose I must have been."

"When you've got the photos off, could you drop in on Myrtle Hutchinson, the wife of the rector of Christ Church Grange Park?"

"A bug-eyed Betty more than likely."

"No, quite a doll and much younger than her husband."

I referred Rudy to the place in my notes where I'd recorded Myrtle's claim to have seen Nora Britton with a lover. I'd left her with the task of trying to remember the shade of the boyfriend's roadster; now I wanted Rudy to find out if she'd made any progress. I also wanted him to form an opinion of her truthfulness and to try to find out if she suspected her husband of adultery.

"Sorry, sport," said Rudy. "I don't think that sort of questioning's in my line at all."

"You'll think of a classy way to do it, Rudy. I've every confidence in your resourcefulness."

"Not the right job for me."

"Okay. We also need someone to pay a call on the Deane household and see if any of the family might have been anywhere near Elizabeth Street on the evening of Sunday, October 9." I had been saving this as the more complicated job for myself, but was just as happy to let Rudy go. "Nora is reported as saying a friend came by with a gift of cookies."

"Choo-Choo Mansion on Jarvis Street? I've been wondering what the inside looks like."

"Once you see it, you may want to move in. But if you'll take advice from one that's been there, all the tact in the world may not protect you from some resident's taking offence. Don't let thin skins keep you from pressing your inquiries home."

I left Rudy at his desk and phoned the Christ Church rectory. I was told Mrs. Hutchinson was out visiting the shut-ins of the parish, but was expected back by tea time.

Detective Sergeant Parsons at the desk next to mine was marking the birth of an adorable granddaughter by lighting a monstrous weed. The first whiff curdled the air in my nostrils, and the cigar's dimensions guaranteed no relief any time soon.

I took myself off to the evidence locker to reacquaint myself with Nora's picture of the soccer players. I couldn't imagine Nora making love to either Lou Sweet or Carl Moretti as I had seen them. Sweet — the vandal and failed hold-up artist — I thought of as weak, mean, and homely. Moretti, by contrast, stood on his own two feet. One foot, actually. But he seemed to be supporting himself. Fine features and a good head of ginger hair might make him appealing to a woman that could see beyond his missing leg. On the other hand, his extreme graspingness and parsimony were scarcely calculated to attract female attention, and he'd made a very convincing show of having nothing to do with his upstairs neighbour.

One glance at the pastel I'd taken from Moretti's shop sufficed to show that Nora could see these two men through eyes very different from mine. She had depicted both of them, along with her husband Herman, as princes. I could choose to believe that one or both of the depictions were charitable flattery. Still, I didn't know if I could rule out the possibility that she had actually felt some magnetism coming from one or the other of the two men — and that she had responded to it.

My next destination was the Department of Public Works and Highways. Lou Sweet, I discovered, did not now and had never owned a car. Carl Moretti owned a 1912 Overland Model 59 Roadster, the colour listed as white. Well, you couldn't get lighter than that. I just didn't see how he could have driven it over to the church with one leg. Had he added some ingenious hand control to work the right pedal? Had Nora driven it for him? Neither alternative struck me as very likely. And yet the tightfisted Carl Moretti had spent money year after year keeping his registration up to date.

I dropped in on him on my way to Christ Church Grange Park. As usual, Moretti was sorting through the items in his shop, treasures that never appeared better displayed or organized when he left them to move on to the next bin.

"That car has been sitting on blocks since I enlisted," he said in answer to my inquiry. As when I'd had to deal with him two days earlier, he sounded aggrieved at having to speak to a fellow member of the human race, but there was a shoulders-squared air of pride about him as well. "I pay rent on a garage just to keep it there, and I pay the registration — you bet. In case you were wondering, it's not for sale, at any price."

I made him hang a closed sign on his shop and take me round to see the machine. It was as he'd described it, up on blocks, no tires on the rims, and no hand controls. He clearly kept it polished, though. The roadster's whiteness gleamed angelically in the dingy shed. When I left Moretti, I took away the impression that this chariot was the monument to his dashing and whole-bodied youth.

My arrival at the Christ Church rectory followed Myrtle Hutchinson's by no more than a minute. She was still standing in the vestibule, her fall coat unbuttoned, her cloche hat in her hand, when she opened the door to my knock. The sight of me elicited a little hiccup of surprise. She clapped her free hand to the pleated front of her white blouse.

"Are you telepathic, detective? I was just about to phone your office."

"You remembered the colour of the car you saw."

"Well, yes." She gave me a quick smile, recovering her poise. "Come in and shut the door. Eric is sensitive to drafts."

I came in and shut the door. "What colour was it?"

"Come through to the drawing room, won't you?"

I came through. The drawing room was for its spacious dimensions sparsely furnished. Fresh upholstery fabric in a variety of floral patterns livened up three battered armchairs and a sofa. A harmonium, a couple of Windsor chairs, and stacking tables — scattered from their nest — filled in as much of the remaining floor area as they were capable of. The walls were decorated at wide intervals with photographs of clergymen and their wives and framed reproductions of well-bred, old-country landscapes.

Myrtle hospitably gestured me into the most comfortable-looking of the armchairs. "I'll order tea for you if you like. Forgive me if I don't join you. I've had at least a cup at every house I visited this afternoon."

"None for me either, thanks. And, just for the record, I don't read minds."

"Then I'll need to keep talking about tea. Excuse me a moment."

Myrtle went to speak to someone in the kitchen. When she returned, she pulled the door to, then sat on the sofa and leaned towards me. "I was just in the home of a young Varsity man, victim of a terrible accident. He dove into a pool where the water was too shallow, broke his neck, and is now without the use of both legs and both arms. His widowed mother is a great believer in the health-giving properties of green tea, and — although I think she realizes quadriplegia is beyond even this beverage's power to cure — she has grown fond of the flavour and serves guests nothing else."

"The car was tea green."

"I believe it was, detective. The colour of weak green tea."

"The whole outside, or were the fenders — say — a different colour?"

"No, every part of the body. When I looked into my cup, the white porcelain inside appeared just the palest shade of green, and that was the colour of the roadster Nora's lover was driving. If it had been lettuce green, I'd have been able to tell you right away, but I simply had no word for a shade of green this light. When I tried to remember, I thought the car must have been white or grey, but somehow I knew it wasn't."

I was excited, but not jumping over the moon. If Myrtle was talking straight, it wasn't Joe Deane's Chrysler she'd seen. On the other hand, I didn't know anyone with a tea green roadster. I wasn't betting any company sold cars that colour; possibly it was a custom paint job. Or had Myrtle made this car and its driver up?

"Have you any other clue as to who this lover might be?" I asked.

"Not a one, I'm afraid."

"The make of car? The man's height? A glimpse of anything he might have been wearing — a hat, for instance?"

"No hat. Nora was standing on the running board and leaning into the car. Her hands were on the sides of the man's head, covering his ears, and her head hid the rest of his features. I might have caught a glimpse of the shoulder of his suit jacket — charcoal grey or black."

"A wisp of hair?"

"Possibly, but I couldn't tell you what colour."

"Think it over," I suggested. "There are fewer choices than for car colours. Do you think he might have belonged to Christ Church?"

"I don't know, detective." Myrtle shrugged. "And I refuse to throw around wild guesses that might hurt innocent parties."

"All right. Have you ever been to Nora Britton's studio?"

"No. I was at Carl Moretti's shop once picking out costume jewellery for a pageant. But that was before Nora moved in upstairs."

"Did you or Mr. Hutchinson visit Nora on the evening of Sunday, October 9?"

Myrtle's long blonde eyebrows went up in surprise. "No, neither one of us. Normally I wouldn't presume to answer for Eric, but Sunday evenings you can count on the two of us being fully occupied around the church, with lots of witnesses to tell you where we are."

"Were you aware of anyone's having gone to Nora's studio that evening? Perhaps you overheard the chance remark of a parishioner."

"No. I presume you think the poison was delivered to Nora that evening."

"How old is your husband?"

"Seventy-two."

"How is his health?"

"Good. I think he smokes too much, but he's more vigorous than most men ten years younger. Why do you ask?"

"Mrs. Hutchinson, the police have questioned plenty of folks since you and I first talked, and you are the only one to report that Nora Britton had a lover."

"I can't help that. Do you suspect I was hallucinating?"

"I do not."

"Then you suspect I'm lying. And why would I do that? Not to gratuitously blacken the reputation of a friend. Oh."

Myrtle dropped her eyes. Her hands, which had been folded in her lap, now were clenched. When she looked up at me at last, her cheeks were flushed.

"You suspect I was lying to protect Eric. Would you believe me, detective, if I told you I would know if Eric were unfaithful?"

"Yes," I said. "I believe you would." I had for this belief not only my estimate of Myrtle's perceptiveness, but also Effie's assurance that Nora would never have slept with a married man without his wife's permission. "Was Mr. Hutchinson Nora Britton's lover?"

"No, he was not. Will you have to speak to Eric about this?"

"I've no plans to at present," I said.

I was about to thank Myrtle for her time, but decided instead to just sit quietly across from her for the minutes it took her to collect herself. Eventually, she took a handkerchief from her purse and blew her nose, then gave me a smile that started small and sad, growing slowly into the full, impersonal rectory smile expected from the priest's wife as she saw off departing visitors.

Chapter 16

Outside the rectory, I asked the first passerby where I'd find the nearest service station. It was a four-minute walk. The owner was able to direct me to an automotive paint shop, which gave me a folder displaying samples of available fast-drying pyroxylin colours. The closest shade to what Myrtle had described was called Whisper Green. When I started asking questions about it, the smooth-talking sharp-dresser behind the counter went to the shop area and brought out a man in goggles and paint-stained khaki overalls whom he called Sam.

"Do you know of any cars that come straight from the factory in this colour?" I wanted to know.

Sam, in his forties by the look of him, pulled off one leather glove and scratched his sandy moustache. He spoke with an Irish lilt, his *there* and *the* coming out *dare* and *da*.

"Any there are would be coming from General Motors. They're boasting how much choice they offer, compared to the competition."

I assumed he meant Ford, still wedded to black. "Have you ever repainted a car in Whisper Green or anything like it?"

"See any traces on my boiler suit?" With a soft chuckle, Sam turned slowly around to allow for a thorough inspection. "That colour hasn't been out a year," he added. "It's never been used in this shop to my knowledge."

"Has anyone bought the paint to take away?"

I turned from Sam to the counterman, who consulted his files and told me no.

Before leaving, I asked the two men how many car-paint competitors they could name and carried away the beginnings of a list. Before visiting any of these shops, however, I went back to the rectory to check the colour of the sample against Myrtle's memory. When she'd recovered from her surprise at finding me back on her doorstep so soon after I'd left, she said, "Yes, that's it — or maybe that with five per cent more white mixed in."

The shade was distinctive enough that all the paint shops I was able to visit in the hours before closing time were able to answer my question with certainty. Unfortunately, the answer in every case was no — they hadn't used Whisper Green or anything like it on any vehicles of any sort. They hadn't sold any either. I also managed to reach a General Motors dealership. They told me none of their products were in what I was starting to think of as "my colour."

I returned to the office tired and hungry close to eight o'clock. The official investigation into the murder of Nora Britton was twelve hours old. I hoped the rest of the team had progress to report.

The only one of my three musketeers I found in the detective room was Rudy Crate. He was jolly and full of the fine time he'd had at Choo-Choo Mansion. Mary-Maud had served him brownies. He'd discussed with Sir Joseph the relative virtues of Constable and A.Y. Jackson as landscape painters. He'd chatted with Frieda — that is, Lady Deane — about the depiction of François Villon in *The Vagabond King* and the perpetual appeal of the artist/criminal. He'd discovered nothing we could use, but it didn't matter now that Myrtle had made it clear that the light-coloured roadster she claimed to have seen was green, not cream like Sir Joe's.

I couldn't think of anything further for Rudy to do at that moment and told him he could go home. He said he might as well stay a bit longer. Professor Linacre or some ichthyologist might still phone about the fish poison. While I thought this a curious display of keenness after the way he'd spent his afternoon, I told him to suit himself.

I asked around the detective room to see if anyone had anything I could nibble on while waiting to hear from Harry and Ned. No one did. I sat at my desk and drew up a list of suspects with Herman's name at the head. The Deane household was now in the clear. Under *Herman* I wrote *Ernestine* — but how could she, without arousing suspicion, have delivered the poisoned cookies? Nora might not resent her, but I'd had no indication that she regarded Ernestine as a friend. Finally I added *Myrtle* with a question mark and the possibly fictitious *man in the green car.*

Twenty minutes later I was still scratching my head when Ned called from the pay phone in the lobby of his apartment building. He'd already been home and eaten some of his mother's good meatloaf before speaking to me. I told him he'd done right and asked him not to tell me anything more about the meal unless he wanted my drool in his ear.

Ned reported that the first fish shop he'd tried informed him that, however much of a delicacy poisonous pufferfish or fugu might be in the Orient, it was not sold in Toronto. Skeptical, he sought a second opinion, a third, and so on till he'd canvassed twenty retailers — starting with Albert Pan in Kensington Market and ending with Ye Olde Fish Shoppe in Forest Hill Village. Those listed in the directory he phoned; those without phones he visited. Ned was pressing in his inquiries. He feared that fishmongers might have one story for government agents and another for gourmets. If — as seemed reasonable — customs officials made difficulties about allowing the importation of food that might kill, smuggling or deliberate mislabelling might still make that food available for a premium under-the-counter.

What convinced Ned in the end that no shop sold fugu flesh, legally or otherwise, was the food-preservation argument.

While experiments with rapid freezing promised a brighter tomorrow, today's freezer technology was still not good enough to bring dead fish across the Pacific to Toronto in peak condition. Simply put, any fugu you could have put on your dinner table would have been too mushy to be worth the price you'd have had to pay to get it there.

So it was that Ned came to believe that the creature that interested him was more likely to be found in a menagerie than a food store. He contacted the Riverdale and High Park zoos. Neither had the fish; neither knew where one could be found. He visited the Walker House Aquarium attached to the Walker House Hotel at Front and York Streets. Aquarium director James Palmer had in his collection exotic goldfish, fighting fish from Siam, and a pair of piranha, but no pufferfish. He was just suggesting Ned direct his inquiries to the New York Aquarium in Lower Manhattan when an associate recalled that the owner of a private zoo had shown up last winter with a selling price for various fierce or poisonous fish, including a two-year-old female fugu. The Walker House specialized in smaller and more colourful fish, and since the curious but less decorative fugu could grow to three feet in length, the offer had been declined. The fugu and other exotic fish had subsequently been advertised for sale in the daily papers. The seller called himself Wild Bill Templeton, and kept his creatures on an acreage outside Whitby, a town forty miles east of Toronto. Ned told me he could do no more until he got authorization from Inspector Sanderson for a long-distance call.

I undertook to speak to the inspector on Tuesday morning.

I'd just rung off when Harry got in.

"You should be at home changing diapers or building a playpen," I told him. "It's late."

Harry shrugged off his fall coat and grinned. "Think the old man will give me a day off after I solve this case?"

I perched myself on the edge of Harry's desk while he slouched in his chair. "Are you close?" I asked.

"No further than from here to Timbuktu. First, Ernestine. The chili-chocolate mix was family lore. She later looked for it in cookbooks. Not there."

"So who did she tell?"

"Maybe a few people, in idle chat. She doesn't remember who, except — she's unshakable on this — she never told Herman. Not that it was a big secret, but it never came up. He didn't cook and didn't care what he ate. She just started thinking about chili and chocolate again when Nora suggested a happy family reunion."

"Anything new from Elizabeth Street?

I told Harry we now had a better idea of what shade of car we were looking for, but he had no new roadster sightings to report. In the afternoon, he'd talked to a number of Nora's neighbours, both ones he'd missed in the morning and ones he'd spoken to before he had Herman's picture to show. The bright boy that sold cigarettes thought he'd seen the party in the picture over two weeks earlier, which squared with Herman's claim to have visited Nora's studio on October 1.

"The problem with spotting Nora's visitors," said Harry, "is that she shared a street door. Any friend or lover of hers might get lost among the antique fiends and bric-a-brac addicts that dropped money at Carl Moretti's shop."

"What about after shop hours when Moretti locked up and went home?"

"Well now, there I learned something interesting and pretty well useless."

"Spill, Harry."

"There's a fella on the street that calls himself Grummy and dresses like a bookie, though he won't admit to having any occupation. This afternoon he told me he regularly cuts down the lane behind Moretti's and has on occasion after dark seen a rope ladder hanging from the second-floor window."

"Do you buy it?"

"I didn't until I met two more residents that claimed to have seen the same thing. So someone could have visited Nora without showing his face on the street."

"Or her face," I added, although I had trouble seeing Myrtle as this someone. She'd told me she wouldn't have ventured up the painter's scaffold, a stable structure compared to a swinging rope ladder. "There was no ladder in the studio Saturday morning," I told Harry. "But by then it could have been removed by Nora, her night visitor, or Lou Sweet, the oaf that broke in."

"Think he could have brought her the poisoned cookies?" Harry asked.

"Where could he have got them?"

"If you've no better use for me tomorrow, I could see if I can establish any link between him and Ernestine."

"Let's decide in the morning. At least we know where to find Lou. He couldn't make bail today and is remanded in custody pending his trial."

After Harry left, I apologized to Nora for having got no nearer to finding her killer. There was no kindly ghost to forgive me. Drained and depressed, I took myself to the King Edward Hotel and treated myself to a steak dinner that, food and tip, cleaned my wallet out but for the last three shinplasters. I put these together with two dimes and a nickel from my pocket and bought myself a ride home in a dollar taxi.

Chapter 17

Tuesday morning I ate a bowl of corn flakes, recharged my flask and my wallet from home stores, and found a complimentary reference to myself in my morning paper. It was the *Dispatch*, which I picked up at the car stop to pass the time on my ride down Queen Street to the office.

I checked first for any article by Ruth. There wasn't one. Looking for something else to read, I flipped past the *Dispatch*'s usual rant about which races made the best immigrants and allowed this headline to snag my eye: "Firing squad painting sold to New York gallery for $2,000." I didn't recognize the byline, but I did the name of the artist. Oscar Craig was quoted as saying the work's actual title was *Dawn Muster*. "I was angry last Friday evening when a perceptive friend said he thought it depicted a firing squad, but on reflection I appreciated his direct approach." Craig went on to tell the journalist about the actual execution that had inspired him. The boy they had had to kill — yes, Craig had been the corporal placed in charge of the unhappy squad — had been caught near Boulogne wearing a nurse's uniform. The "compassionate" sister that gave him her spare kit did him no favours.

I sympathized. During the war, while not all deserters were shot, they stood little chance of clemency if caught in disguise.

In short order, however, a sign I saw out the streetcar window drove the young soldier's fate from my mind. That sign was for Panzer's Automotive Repair and Repainting. I got down at the next stop, Bathurst Street. Panzer's shop wasn't open yet, but a fiftyish man with stubbly cheeks and uncombed white hair came and unlocked the door for me when I knocked. He knew Whisper Green. He'd painted a Model T roadster in the colour when it first came out a year ago. He couldn't describe the man — did I think he had the memory of an elephant? — but he might recognize a photo if I had one to show him. I told him not yet.

All in all not a bad start to the day. When I got to City Hall at ten past eight, I bounded up the pink front steps whistling "Blue Skies."

In the detective office, I found Ned Cruickshank seated at my desk.

"I've just been going over your case notes, Paul," he said by way of greeting. "Do we know if Fred Stillwater has a green roadster?"

"Stillwater? You think he might have been Nora's lover?"

"He lied to you about where his father was on the day of Nora Britton's death. He said Jordan Stillwater was in Montreal when we're pretty sure he was in Kansas."

"True. I thought he was just embarrassed by the nature of his father's surgery."

"All the same, I wonder if he might also have been hiding the extent of his involvement with Miss Britton. Even if he disapproved of her being given the mural commission, he might have found her an attractive woman."

"From what I've seen, she was one."

"Married, but nevertheless…"

However dogged Ned was as a detective, and despite his clean-cut good looks, he had still to find or be found by his first girlfriend. Anything to do with sex had the power to make him blush.

"Married but available?" I volunteered. "Well, if you like we could explore that angle."

I could hear the lack of enthusiasm in my voice. My eye had caught on Ned's photograph of Herman Koch. Easily recognizable with his widow's peak and dressed in his perpetual corduroy suit and knit tie, Nora's husband stood face-on to the camera in front of a wall full of paintings. So far Ned's photo was the same as the ones he'd given me for my own use and to distribute to Rudy and Harry. But Ned's photo showed another person as well. Beside Herman and towering over him stood Oscar Craig. Oscar and no mistake with his wide neck, dark eyebrows and moustache, and curling dark hair.

"Ned, what's this?"

"A mistake — nothing serious."

"Go on."

"The picture was taken at the opening of last year's Group of Seven exhibition at the Art Gallery of Toronto. It was the best photo of Herman Koch I could find for our purposes, so I asked the paper that ran it to print four copies from the negative. The first one came out like this. Once it was done, I asked if they could print just the portion showing Koch so as to avoid confusion. That's how you and the others got the pictures you got. I thought if I had to show the photo, I'd just cut this other gentleman out of my copy or hold my hand over his likeness."

"I know him, Ned." I shoved my paper in front of the acting detective. "That's his painting being written up; he's the artist being quoted. I was talking to him just last Friday. He said he hadn't seen Koch for years."

"Did he know Miss Britton?"

"Barely, to hear him tell it." I was remembering Ruth Stone's assertion that Oscar Craig knew every female in Toronto. Ridiculous, but maybe not if restricted to women artists and art lovers. Nora, for example. Ernestine Lopez.

"But you don't believe him," Ned put in.

I don't know what expression on my face led Ned to say this. What it felt like on the inside was a certain amount of mental furniture being moved around into new positions.

"On Friday night," I said, "he talked as if Herman likely killed Nora. He sounded plausible to me at the time. He drives a Model T roadster, black now and dented but perhaps looking different thirteen days ago when Myrtle saw Nora kissing her lover."

Ned was listening to me and at the same time studying the newspaper article, including the part that came after I'd stopped reading. It featured Oscar's life story. Ned gave me the highlights.

"Art lessons in New York before the war — served 1916–18 on the Western Front — unable to make a living as an artist when peace came — enlisted in the French Foreign Legion — saw action in the Rif War, whatever that is — stationed briefly in French Indochina — returned to Canada in 1925 at the end of his five-year term of service."

"The Rif War," I said, "was fought in Morocco between the Berbers and the Spanish, later helped by the French." I thought back to the innocent desert sketches in Oscar's classroom. "From what I've heard," I went on, "a ruthless, take-no-prisoners business. Anything strike you about his deployment to Asia?"

"A good place to meet pufferfish?"

"None better."

I was starting to think I'd been too glib in sorting the tough guys and the poisoners into two mutually exclusive classes — the scrappers and the schemers. Might not Oscar the painter/soldier be just the man to have a foot in each camp?

"Want to interview him?"

"At his home, this evening. Not at the school where he works."

"You think he could be dangerous."

"I have seen something of his rough side. Besides, there are a few things to check into before we talk to him."

I asked Ned to get three more copies of the Oscar photo and bring them here on the double. He was to get a picture of a

Model T roadster as well. He was back soon after the other team members got in. I asked Harry to take his copy of Oscar out to the Central Prison chapel to see if it lit any light of recognition in Ernestine's eyes. Ned went to show Oscar to Mr. Panzer. Rudy surprisingly agreed to show both Oscar and Herman to the menagerie owner in Whitby if I could get a police vehicle to take him. I passed the buck to Inspector Sanderson, who promised to do what he could. In less than half an hour, a traffic patrol officer arrived to take the Englishman off on the back of his Harley-Davidson. That left me to see if Myrtle Hutchinson recognized either Oscar or the shape of his car.

When I came down the front steps of City Hall, my state of mind was very different from when I'd earlier climbed them. Different, not worse. I couldn't have explained it at the time because the good thing now was not conscious cheerfulness but rather absorption in the job I was born for — detective work. Did it bother me to think Oscar might have killed Nora? Yes, it had to. And when I was next at leisure it would bother me a lot. Oscar had exaggerated in calling me a friend, but we'd been increasingly friendly acquaintances. Right now I didn't have time to feel disappointed. The task was all that mattered.

My business with Myrtle was soon done. She didn't recognize Craig's photo, although she saw nothing in it that ruled out his being Nora's lover. The shape of the car I showed her elicited a more positive response. She couldn't be sure, but the Model T roadster "looked right" — in shape if not in colour.

Although I hadn't thought that far when I set out from headquarters, showing the photos as well in Leavitt's Polar Treat Ice Cream Parlour scarcely counted as a stroke of genius. Simon Leavitt in his white jacket and a brisk-looking younger man with curly fair hair were preparing for the opening at ten a.m. The shop owner saw me at the glass door and unlocked it for me. He introduced his son Michael, a medical student, who treated me to a firm handshake and a steady, memorizing sort of look. His fine features likely made him more conquests among the coeds than he had time for.

I explained my errand and laid the photo of Oscar Craig on Leavitt's counter. He didn't look at it.

"You said, Mr. Leavitt, that during August and September Nora Britton sometimes came in for one of your fresh fruit sundaes. Did she ever come with this man?"

"I don't notice who anybody comes in with," he said.

"Some things have changed since Friday, sir. There is now an official investigation under way — an investigation into the murder of someone you called 'a sweet woman.'"

Leavitt met my expectant gaze without comment.

"That's a murder not twenty yards from your front door," I said. "You're a responsible citizen with a strong sense of justice. Think. Do you really want to leave this crime unpunished?"

Michael Leavitt, who had been setting up tables, came over to look at the photo we were talking about.

"I saw him in here almost two weeks ago, holding hands with a woman. Was that Nora Britton, Dad?"

"I didn't see," his father answered uncomfortably.

"Describe the woman you saw," I asked Michael.

"Mid-thirties, I'd say. Dark, straight hair with a centre part. Clear complexion, maybe a bit pale."

"Nose?"

"Straight, with a rather pronounced philtrum — "

"Nose ditch, right, doc?"

" — connecting to the cupid's bow upper lip."

"Full lips?" I asked.

Michael nodded. "Hair pulled back and done up in a knot of some kind — would that be her?"

"You bet."

"The fella had a car he parked across the street, a pretty unusual green colour — three whopping scoops of vanilla plus a half-teaspoon of pistachio." The serious young doctor-to-be cracked a smile. "I remember thinking the days when every Model T was black are finally over."

"This would have been October 5?" I asked.

"Round about then."

"Did either of you see him any other time?"

"I didn't. Come on, Dad. Tell him what you know. You don't want murderers walking in here."

Simon Leavitt looked at his son and then at me. "I served the two of them maybe four or five times," he said. "They sometimes ate from the same bowl."

That sharing seemed to upset Leavitt to a degree I couldn't understand. I hazarded a guess.

"You saw them acting intimate in other ways."

Again Michael helped out by giving his father a nudge.

"One time he stroked her leg under the table," said Simon. "She didn't slap his hand away. She was a fine person, but children come in here. If it had happened again, I'd have had to speak to them. Did he kill her, mister?"

"You're helping me find out, Mr. Leavitt."

In retrospect I realized I should have pressed him harder at our first meeting. I'd been too influenced by Eric Hutchinson's assurance that Nora had no lover. If I'd got descriptions last Friday of the men Nora ate ice cream with, I might have found Oscar without chasing paint colours. On the other hand, I might not. I suspected the city held more big, dark-haired men like Oscar than it did Whisper Green roadsters. Oscar must have thought the same or he wouldn't have bothered repainting his car black.

My next stop was Dalton Linacre's lab in the bowels of the University of Toronto Mining Building. I wanted him to go back to those cookie crumbs and see if in addition to chocolate they might contain traces of chili peppers. I asked also what progress Professor Keller had made analyzing Nora's vomit for traces of tetrodotoxin. Linacre said he'd inquire, but didn't hold out hope of any news on that score before the end of the week.

At the Department of Public Works and Highways I looked up Oscar's car registration to find out his address. It turned out he rented quarters a few blocks east of mine. I took the Queen car out to have a look. Whereas my building had three storeys of apartments running back from a narrow frontage, Oscar's consisted of two residential floors above a row of shops. Bay windows and tricky brickwork in the upper façade suggested construction had been well-funded. Fresh paint on the window trim showed the landlord's interest in keeping up appearances and rents.

I puzzled over whether to show Oscar's picture around the neighbourhood in the hope of learning something of his movements, but concluded such inquiries weren't worth the risk of Oscar's finding out and being put on his guard. For the same reason, I decided we wouldn't stake out his building just yet. I bought a sardine sandwich on whole wheat and took it back to the office.

Riding the streetcar in, I had to remind myself that Nora's lover was not necessarily her killer. Perhaps Oscar had murdered Nora out of jealousy when he found out she was returning to Herman. Or perhaps Herman had poisoned her because he suspected she was not in fact breaking with the other man in her life. The kiss Myrtle had seen on October 5, after Nora's promise to Herman to return to him, might have made anyone suspect that Nora's extramarital affair was by no means over. Could Herman have found out about that kiss or about equally intimate recent dealings between Nora and Oscar? If so, Herman's sense of betrayal might have snuffed out whatever was left of his bohemian renunciation of sexual jealousy.

In the course of Tuesday afternoon members of the team returned to headquarters with their reports. Ned and Harry's were anti-climactic.

Yes, in the summer of 1926 Mr. Panzer had painted Oscar's car Whisper Green. Panzer had predicted the owner would be back within the year to have the car restored to its original black, but this hadn't happened. Ned had asked around other neighbourhood paint shops to no avail and had concluded that Oscar had done this repainting job himself.

And yes, Ernestine had shared a flat with Oscar soon after his return to Toronto. She thought she remembered that in the course of a boozy conversation about the perfect crime she had mentioned to him combining chili and chocolate to disguise the taste of poison. Once again she denied categorically that she had ever told Herman. Harry had his doubts: he believed that Ernestine was sweet on Herman and would say anything to protect him from suspicion. While at the prison chapel, Harry had visited Herman's studio as well. Koch was taking veronal to help overcome his incipient cocaine habit and was consequently drowsy, but less irritable than I had found him the day before. Harry asked the painter if he knew that Nora had been having an affair with Oscar Craig. Herman said not — adding that, if Craig had been Nora's lover, Herman was sure she had broken with him before her death.

Anti-climactic also was the phone call from Professor Linacre confirming that the cookie crumbs contained traces of capsicum as well as chocolate.

The big news I was waiting for would come from Rudy Crate. Assuming he survived his chilly motorcycle ride, he would tell us whether Herman or Oscar or neither had acquired, in whole or in part, Templeton's pufferfish. I passed the hours from lunch to dinnertime writing up case notes, attending to other neglected paperwork, and from time to time walking out to the front door of City Hall to see if I could spot Rudy's approach.

Meanwhile I could think of no more assignments for my teammates. Acting Detective Ned Cruickshank went back to his regular base, Station Number One — stipulating that someone phone him there as soon as Rudy came in. Detective Sergeant Harry O'Brian sat at his desk and reluctantly returned to his work on the Chief Constable's Annual Report. Whenever I glanced over in his direction, Harry seemed to be consulting his watch, which made me check mine as well.

Three fifteen. Herman or Oscar?

Four twenty-five. Oscar or Herman?

However hard I tried to concentrate on other work, my mind kept circling back to this one question. I wondered if Nora would have told Rose Mertens that a "friend" had given her the chocolate-chili cookies if they'd come from Herman. On the other hand, if companionate marriage flourished in Greenwich Village, the artistic set might see friendly marriage as nothing peculiar.

Four fifty-four...

"Ants in your pants, Shenstone?" Parsons at the desk next to mine was holding out a pack of Player's Navy Cut in my direction. "Try a cigarette, good for the nerves."

I looked into my neighbour's untroubled, wrinkled face. He was retiring in January, but after forty-six years of police service was already taking it easy.

"Ever been to Bill Templeton's zoo in Whitby?" I asked.

"Wild Bill? Certainly." Used to my declining his smokes, he put them away without insisting. "We went a lot when the kids were teenagers. There was a shark tank then, a whole aquarium in fact, as well as animals from raccoon-size on up. Then we didn't go for a few years, until last summer when some of the grandchildren were old enough."

"What was it like?" I asked.

"Pared down — more exciting, though, in a way. Wild Bill had got rid of the fish altogether. He'd taken to strutting around in khaki jodhpurs with a bullwhip clipped to his belt. Said he was concentrating on dangerous animals he fancied he could train. He put on a pretty good show for the kids. There weren't enough visitors to bring in much money, he told me, but he thought he could use the bears and big cats to make movies. He involved in a case of yours?"

"Just as a witness."

Parsons chuckled. "Then you better hope that lion of his doesn't close its mouth while his head's inside."

Chapter 18

Harry O'Brian sat slouched in his chair looking about as relaxed as a hungry tiger on a short chain. I was perched on the edge of his desk. The clock hands stood at six ten, half an hour past sunset. Rudy had been back from Templeton's menagerie less than five minutes, and you can bet we didn't give him time to treat us to any local colour. He pulled his chair up to Harry's desk and, still dusty from his motorcycle ride, told us that Wild Bill had recognized the purchaser of his pufferfish when shown the photograph of Oscar Craig. With a flourish, Rudy handed me the bill of sale.

"Do we have enough to get an arrest warrant?" Harry asked.

"Doubt it," I said.

"We know Oscar was Nora's lover."

"Yes."

"She was dumping him, so he killed her. Come on, Paul. Craig's our man. I never thought it was Koch."

"At one time you thought our 'man' was Ernestine. We know she had an affair with Craig. What if they stayed in touch? Suppose she heard about fugu poison from Oscar, and when Oscar acquired his very own pufferfish, she bought or stole it from him for the purpose of eliminating Nora."

"Ah, phooey," said Harry. "You don't believe that."

"I can't disprove it."

"Why did Craig buy that fish in the first place, Paul? It's not a normal pet."

"My short immersion in the world of artists," I said, "makes me think they haven't much use for normal. But if you're saying Oscar bought the puffer in February for the purpose of poisoning Nora, then you'll have to come up with another theory of his motive. It was September before Nora formed the intention of returning to Herman. Read her letter."

I produced the document from my inside jacket pocket, but Harry waved it away.

"Folks get a thrill," I went on, "out of cozying up to dangerous creatures."

"That's Templeton's stock-in-trade," Rudy put in.

"Detective Sergeant Parsons was just reminding me. Wild Bill sold the puffer because he couldn't fit it into an act the way he could his cats. For Oscar, though, it could well have been exciting enough to share his apartment with a poison more deadly than cyanide."

"Even if he never contemplated using that poison?"

"I think so, Harry. Maybe. But the question for us is not whether he contemplated using it someday, but whether he used it on Nora Britton. Suppose we jump to the conclusion he did, then arrive at Oscar's apartment to find his finny friend swimming around in a big tank of water. We don't have proof yet that parts of Oscar's fish got into Nora's picnic — or even that she ingested pufferfish poison at all. They're still analyzing her puke over at the University."

Neither Harry nor Rudy put up an argument.

"Based on what we have," I went on, "I can't ask for a warrant against Oscar. I would like to question him, though."

"I'll come along," said Harry.

"Good. Rudy, you've been jostled around quite a bit today. Go on home if you like."

"No need. I keep a razor in my desk. I'll just have a shave and a wash and be good as new."

While Rudy was freshening up, I gave Ned a call. Unsurprisingly he wanted to come too. The four of us amounted to an excess of manpower for a simple interview, but I had a reason beyond team loyalty for excluding nobody.

Harry seemed to read my mind. "This bird liable to give us trouble?" he asked.

"Could do."

"Take your Colt, Paul. I'll have mine, but I want to know you're armed as well."

I nodded. I hadn't contemplated gunplay inside Oscar's apartment. Judging by the flimsiness of the partition walls in my own building, stray bullets could easily pass through and into an unsuspecting neighbour. Still, Harry was asking no more than that I follow the rules.

I didn't doubt Harry's courage. Harry, though, had what I did not — a family to go home to — and that rightly made him less reckless. I went to my own desk and unlocked the side drawer where my Police Positive rested in its shoulder holster. I had the revolver cleaned and loaded by the time Ned arrived at headquarters.

"We don't know how close we are to wrapping up this investigation," I told my three teammates when we were all assembled. "But, just in case, we all want to be in on this next task. Oscar Craig's building has two outside doors, one in front and one up from the basement into the side alley. I'm suggesting that Rudy and Ned each stand guard at one of these doors and stop Oscar if he gets away from Harry and me. When I say stop, I don't mean arrest."

"The common law right of investigative detention," said Rudy.

"We'll quote you. Now, if Oscar's not in, there's the Night Owl coffee shop across Queen Street where we can wait."

The four of us got off the Queen car at Lansdowne and walked west. It was just a few degrees above freezing; I turned up the collar of my trench coat. When I spied Oscar's building, there was a slim woman with frizzy hair going in the door to the upstairs apartments. She had well-shaped legs and, to show them off, was wearing a jacket too short for the season. I ran and caught up to her while she was looking at the names on the mail boxes.

"Hi, Ruth."

She gave me a more than friendly smile. "Hello, Paul."

"What a coincidence!"

"That Oscar should invite us both for the same time?"

"Don't go."

Harry joined us in the vestibule. Through the glass door I could see Ned and Rudy waiting outside.

"What do you mean don't go?" said Ruth. "I have an interview arranged. Say, are all these he-men with you?"

"Interview about what?"

A steely firmness came into her jaw; her emerald eyes turned hard as diamonds. "I'm going to get him to admit to having busted up Jack Wellington — the story that scoops me right out of the women's pages. Don't get in my way."

Harry gave her an admiring look, but left the play to me.

"Wait with one of the detective sergeants in that coffee place and I promise, Ruth, you'll have a bigger scoop before you go home."

"Do I have a choice?"

"One of us will hail you a cab now if you prefer."

"Damn you, Paul. Break your word and while you advance your career I'll be writing about hat shapes and hem lengths till I'm a hag of sixty. Then, believe you me, I'll tell the world in my haggish croak that it was Chief Shenstone that ruined my life."

Rudy took Ruth to the Night Owl, from where he could keep an eye on the front door of Oscar's building while Ned went down the alley to cover the side door. Harry and I went up to the second floor and found the door marked twenty-one.

Harry knocked, not hard like a cop.

"Come in. It's open."

Oscar must have thought it was Ruth.

He was occupied with a corkscrew and a bottle of red wine, perhaps unaware that she didn't drink. He was wearing a new-looking white pullover tucked into the waist of freshly pressed tweed trousers. All gratifyingly neat and fitted with no place to hide a weapon. His room was swept and tidy, sparely furnished, with nearly all available wall space displaying his own paintings and sketches. Some of the landscapes looked African, some European, both featuring scenes of wartime devastation. Three or four large canvases were of boxing matches. In all of these the gloves and faces of the combatants bore traces of blood.

When Oscar looked up, an expression of annoyance crossed his face and disappeared. "Paul — I was expecting someone else."

"A last-minute complication prevented her from coming. I know she wanted to. Oscar, this is Harry O'Brian."

"You a policeman, Harry?"

"And a friend," I said, jumping in. "I was hoping he'd have a chance to see some of your art. This is an impressive display."

"Very." Harry moved away from me as if he wanted to look more closely at the pictures, all the time keeping an eye on Oscar.

A couple of table lamps lit the room unevenly. A fixture in the middle of the ceiling was turned off.

"Have some wine," said our host, producing a third glass. "French. Pity to waste it."

"Sure," I said. "Thanks. Did they give you good wine in the Foreign Legion?"

Oscar snorted disdainfully. He'd been expecting a flirtatious evening, maybe more, and still couldn't see how it had turned into a police interrogation.

"Odd Ruth didn't tell me herself," he said. "You're mistaken, you know, if you think she's your girl."

"Smart cookie, Ruth." I took one glass of wine to hand to Harry and one for myself. "She figured it out that you're the one that gave Wellington a lesson in fighting clean."

"What are you talking about?"

"Don't be modest, Oscar. You know — but Harry may not. Last Thursday, a quick and promising middleweight threw a fight Oscar and I were at. I wanted to have a word with the lad afterwards, but Oscar got to him first and used his boots to such effect that the gambler that bought Master Jack had to send a nurse to his bedside."

"Am I being accused of a crime?" said Oscar.

"Not at all. I understand Wellington struck first."

"Why don't we sit down then and enjoy our Bordeaux?"

"You sit, Oscar. We'll look at the art."

None of us sat.

Oscar took his first sip of wine. I followed suit. I could feel Harry's disapproving glare, but I'd seen the bottle opened and watched the wine poured. And I was thirsty.

Harry set down his glass. "Say, Oscar," he said, "mind if I use your jakes?"

"Follow me."

There could be no possibility of Harry's losing his way, but by walking ahead Oscar was able to close a bedroom door as he passed. I understood that my job would be to take up enough of Oscar's attention to keep him from supervising Harry's return trip.

"You know, Oscar," I said when our host returned, "your bout with Wellington was outside my jurisdiction anyway — but I wish I'd been there to see it. I'll bet Jack was too busy watching your fists to notice your feet. Perhaps he'd been drinking Lariviere's liquor."

"Jack's used to dancing around the canvas surface of a boxing ring."

"Whereas the floors of the club...?"

"Polished and smooth with little throw rugs here and there."

"Did he step on one and slip?"

"Something like that. Come clean, Paul. What are you playing at here?"

"I wanted to congratulate you on the sale of *Dawn Muster*. That must feel fine. I guess Friday night they were still keeping you in suspense, maybe trying to drive down your price. That's why you seemed tense."

"It's all bushwa, Paul. You wanted to show Harry my art. You wanted to talk about Wellington. You wanted to congratulate me on the sale. Lots of reasons — and none of them makes sense."

"In that newspaper article, you referred to me as a friend. If I'm your friend, why so suspicious?"

Oscar didn't answer, his attention taken by a movement in the back hall. "Don't open that," he called, charging after Harry. "You've no business in there."

"Sorry," said Harry. "I just wanted to see your pufferfish. It's not everyone has one of those. But she's not there. There's just a big, empty glass tank."

"Do you have a search warrant?" Oscar growled. "If you do, I want to see it. And if you don't, I want you both to leave."

"You invited us in, remember?" I said. "Now let's all cool down. Oscar probably took the puffer to show his students at Central Technical School. Shall we all go and look at it there?"

"I was inviting Ruth Stone in, not a pair of bulls."

"You mentioned no names. We believed in good faith we had leave to enter. Now about that fish — it is at Central Tech, isn't it?"

"I don't own a fish."

"You bought one from Wild Bill Templeton in Whitby on Tuesday, February 8. He identified you from a photograph." I took the paper I'd got from Rudy from my jacket pocket and held it up. "Here's the bill of sale."

"That fish died."

"Really? She was only two years old. Pufferfish live a lot longer than that."

"Maybe my tank was too small."

"It must have been an incredible experience, Oscar, sharing a bedroom with the source of such a deadly poison. Part of the thrill must have been knowing how easy it would be to execute anyone you decided needed execution. Of course, you had to choose carefully. Who offended you enough for you to be willing to carve up the fish with the toxic ovary?"

Oscar stood facing us in a loose but wary stance. He must have felt the tightness of the spot he was in, but with his six feet two or three inches of height, broad shoulders, and thick neck he looked strong and tough.

"You call me a poisoner," he said with a wry smile, "and yet you drink my wine."

"I don't think you're suicidal," I said. "You're a punisher, and I don't imagine you think you deserve punishment. The army made you the unwilling killer of that young deserter, and now you want to judge and punish by your own rules. Besides, Harry has drunk none of your wine and will want words with you if I fall dead."

"What a lot of blather!"

"I'll happily shut up and let you talk, Oscar. I'm sure you'd like to tell your own story in your own words."

"Get out, both of you."

"Reticent as always, eh? You know, Harry, when I asked him on Friday Oscar said he didn't know Nora Britton. Now it turns out he was her lover. It's hard to be discreet — isn't it? — when you've got a car the colour of no other."

"You're trespassing, officers. The only talking I'll be doing will be to a lawyer."

"When was the last time you saw Nora?"

"Out now. I need to use the pay phone on the corner, and I'm not leaving you here." Oscar no longer looked so cool and loose. A vein was standing out on his forehead as he struggled to control the exasperation in his voice.

"Did you see her after the evening of Sunday, October 9?" I asked.

"Let me past."

"Certainly. I just want to know if you saw Nora Britton at all after you went to her studio a week ago Sunday."

"No! Now…" Seeing that I was not moving from my place in front of the door to the stairs, Oscar turned and took a step towards the darker side of the room.

"So you admit to climbing up the rope ladder to Nora Britton's studio that evening?"

"I admit nothing."

"I heard you." I glanced at Harry.

"So did I," said the detective.

"I take it back."

"As a matter of fact," Harry added, "I saw a rope ladder just now rolled up in a corner of Mr. Craig's bedroom."

"I wonder," I said, "if you have any cookies to go with the wine. I hear you make ones that combine chocolate and chili. They sound mouth-watering, eye-watering too. Chili and chocolate — what else is in the recipe?"

"Shall I have a look around the kitchen?" asked Harry. "See if there are any left?"

Shadows hid half Oscar's face. No matter. More lights could have done nothing to strengthen the impression of hostility it conveyed.

"Maybe later," I said. "You took some cookies to Nora that night, didn't you, Oscar? The night before she died. She told a neighbour she was looking forward to trying them. By then she'd told you she was finished with you and going back to Herman. I guess when you heard Nora had been cremated before a post-mortem could be done you thought you were home free. But Nora threw up. The nasty stuff from your late pufferfish will be found in her vomit."

Oscar Craig's hand shot out towards one of the paintings on the dimly lit wall, a picture of a revolver. Only it wasn't a picture, but the wall-mounted weapon itself.

Harry and I were standing too far apart for him to cover us both. Harry was shot before he could draw. Oscar's pistol was swinging towards me when I dropped to a crouch and put a bullet into his right arm. I don't believe his gun had hit the floor before Harry shot him twice in the chest. Oscar went down on his back.

Sitting on the floor, Harry kept his gun on Oscar while I got a chair cushion to press over Harry's leg wound. From the meagre flow of blood, it was clear the artery hadn't been hit. Oscar hadn't been as lucky. His arm was bleeding badly — but not for long. Almost immediately his heart stopped pumping altogether. He was dead from Harry's two bullets. Harry had done as he had been trained and aimed for the larger target.

I left him to go downstairs and call for a couple of ambulances.

Chapter 19

I asked Harry if he'd like me to go to the hospital with him. "Someone to explain the circumstances in case you pass out," I said.

"Hell no! You'd be a chump to stand up that red-haired newsgirl. Besides, I need you to tell her it's O'Brian A-N, not E-N."

Once the ambulances had come and gone, I got Ned and Rudy to search Oscar's apartment.

Ruth was on her feet at the window when I entered the Night Owl coffee shop. A half-eaten piece of pineapple upside-down cake and a pot of tea stood on the table behind her.

"You going to spill the beans, Paul?" she asked.

"As soon as I've made one phone call."

The call was to Inspector Sanderson. I didn't want him reading in the press anything about his department that he hadn't been told first. He didn't resent my calling him at home and dragging him away from a "thrilling" game of contract bridge. I could hear the smile in his voice. And the frost that followed when I had to break it to him that one of his men had been shot. I didn't blame him. I was pretty unhappy about that myself. All the same, I gamely pointed out that in a day or so Harry would be back at City Hall and quite up to desk work, which was all the inspector had had him doing anyway. Once the Chief Constable's Annual Report was off to the printers, I expected Detective Sergeant O'Brian to be well along the road to health. In France, a corporal in my platoon had recovered from a leg wound as grave as Harry's and gone on in time to lead trench raids. And other men, Sanderson retorted, men with apparently trivial injuries, limped around with a cane the rest of their lives. I couldn't argue. It might easily have been me Oscar shot at. There would have been more justice in that: the plan for this interview had been mine, and my plan had put my partner in harm's way.

I found Ruth Stone back at her table, scribbling on a large notepad, the sleeves of her navy cardigan pushed back from her wrists and her hair pinned back from her face. I called to the counterman for coffee as I dropped into the chair across from her. She studied my face a moment before speaking.

"You've had a rough evening."

"Not as rough as the two other fellas," I replied. "Harry wounded, Oscar dead."

"Dead — really? I guess there's no question."

"None at all."

"So what happened, Paul? Give me some sort of statement."

"Okay, but not for attribution. And you'd better not mention Oscar's name till we notify any kin he may have had."

"Like in the war." Ruth flipped to a clean page in her pad and hovered her pencil above it. "Fast as you like," she said. "I'm a whizz at Pitman."

"It has been determined that the painter Nora Britton, originally thought to have died from an accidental fall, was murdered. She was given poisoned cookies to eat while working on a mural in the sanctuary of Christ Church Grange Park. As part of their investigation, police detectives interviewed a suspect in his apartment on Queen Street West on the evening of Tuesday, October 18. During that interview, the man picked up a revolver and shot Detective Sergeant Harry O'Brian — B-R-I-A-N — in the leg. Mr. O'Brian and

Detective Sergeant Paul Shenstone returned fire. The suspect died of his injuries at the scene."

"'…at the scene.'" Ruth looked up from her squiggles. "How do you like that? Nora Britton murdered! Did Oscar do it?"

"Further inquiries need to be made. You can draw your own conclusions from his aggressive behaviour."

"Nora and Oscar — both artists in a not very artistic city of five hundred thousand. So I guess he knew her. How well?"

"They were seen exchanging endearments in an ice cream parlour."

"Sounds like a lover's quarrel. What was the poison?"

"Scientists are still working on that. I can maybe give you more in a day or so — but do you have enough for your scoop?"

"Sure, Paul — a swell scoop. Say, did Oscar admit to having bust Wellington up?"

"Not in so many words, but I'm in no doubt. What made you think he did it?"

"Kicking with boots on," said Ruth. "When I read in this morning's paper Oscar had served in the Foreign Legion, I figured he'd been trained in savate. That's a style of unarmed combat they favour. Besides, I could only make a good story of it if Wellington's punisher were you or Oscar. You were the two men I saw outraged by the rigged fight last Thursday. Now, thanks to you, I don't just have a good story, but a great one."

I wondered if I'd let the idea that Oscar was a kicker distract me. Had I been too busy up in that apartment watching his feet to look for the gun?

"Gee, Paul, I'm sorry to sound so happy when your friend's just been shot." Ruth took my hand across the table, holding it quietly and tight.

Five minutes later she went back to her office to write up her story. I stood watching the cab I'd hailed for her pull away and get smaller and smaller until it disappeared behind other eastbound traffic on Queen Street. Then I went back up to Oscar's apartment to find Rudy and Ned.

One look at the pile of treasures my teammates had assembled in the middle of the living room floor was enough to tell me we'd need a squad car to get them back to headquarters. The glass fish tank alone had practically the dimensions of a coffin, that of a large child at least, and I counted more than a dozen rungs in the rolled up rope ladder. The other items were smaller — Craig's 8 millimetre Lebel revolver, an artist's portfolio, a manila envelope, and a circular tin with a picture of the King and Queen Mary on the lid. Ned told me the latter contained four chocolate cookies, which he had without too much difficulty restrained himself from eating. He thought if they were from the batch Nora had sampled eight nights ago they might be somewhat hard and dry.

"Why would he keep such incriminating evidence?" Ned asked me. "You knew the man, Paul. Do you think he wanted to get caught?"

"Doubt it," I said. "In my experience he thought pretty well of himself. Perhaps he was confident he could avoid suspicion, so there was no need to sacrifice the trophies of his crime."

I picked up Oscar's portfolio and found inside a number of pencil sketches of a fish with a white stomach, a spotty back, and a disconcertingly unfishlike little oval mouth. In some poses the creature was puffed up into a sphere with spines projecting all over. Its uninflated proportions, still portly, were shown in other drawings. The manila envelope contained a receipted invoice for the paint job Mr. Panzer had done on Craig's Model T and Craig's bank book. The most recent balance would cover the cost of a funeral with several thousands to spare.

"Any sign of a will?" I asked.

"I didn't see one," said Rudy, now seated and resting after his labours.

"I've been over the whole apartment," said Ned. "Not that it's very big — but I've looked in every corner where papers might be kept. I didn't find a will, or any letters that would indicate whether he had living family."

"I have his address book," Rudy put in. "There may be relatives in there, but none with the name Craig."

"Look for a Gussie or Gus with a New York City address," I said. "She's a friend at least."

Rudy turned up an Augusta Buchanan on West 10th Street, which he told me would be in Greenwich Village. I don't know how he knew; he said he'd never been to New York.

That night I sent Miss Buchanan a telegram asking if she knew who might be Oscar Craig's next of kin. Next morning, Wednesday, Rudy and Ned started contacting other people Oscar had entered in his book. By noon it was looking as if half of them were art collectors or people who'd commissioned Oscar to paint their portraits and half were women he'd paid attention to and then dumped.

I thought it must have been an ugly break in the pattern to have Nora reject him before he rejected her. But perhaps her offence in his eyes had been worse than that. Myrtle Hutchinson had reported seeing Nora Britton kiss the man in the green car passionately on October 5, days after she had decided to return to Herman. What looked passionate to the rector's wife might have been a good deal less. All the same, a Judas kiss in Oscar's eyes perhaps when — later the same day? — she told him of her decision. I wondered what Nora had meant by that kiss. I couldn't believe it had been intended to deceive or torment Oscar. That would have been clean out of character with the Nora Britton I had fashioned in my head over the days — not yet a week — I'd been obsessed by the mystery of her death. I preferred to think she had meant to convey that she still found Oscar attractive, was not angry with him, and didn't want to show any coolness towards him until she had a chance to sit him down and explain that the reason for leaving him was only a rediscovery of her love for her husband, a love based on the grace of Herman's character in adversity as well as on the soul expressed in his art. In short, she had kissed Oscar in a spirit of consideration rather than betrayal.

It wasn't until I went for a sandwich from Uneeda Lunch that I remembered to pick up Ruth's paper. Her story was there all right, with her name on it, plump on the front page under the headline, "Muralist Murdered: Gunplay on Queen West." Ruth promised to bring her readers more details as they became available.

I hadn't got to any other parts of the *Dispatch* when Gussie phoned from the Stuyvesant Theatre on Broadway before a Wednesday matinee. She wanted to know how Oscar had died; she hung up when I told her. I called the theatre back, even at the risk of having to pay for the call myself, and someone persuaded her to return to the phone. I got it through her head that whether or not she believed my partner and I had shot in self-defence, we needed to find an heir. She calmed down and told me Oscar had a brother, Peter, an architect in Montreal. They hadn't been on speaking terms for years, Oscar had told her. And unless Peter could be convinced of their cash value, he was likely to throw out any artworks of Oscar's that came his way.

Gussie's tone was hard and bitter, the voice of a girl that knew the score. I wondered how much she did know, having just spent a weekend with Oscar.

"It must come as a shock," I said, "hearing Oscar's suspected of murder."

There followed a long moment when static was the only thing coming into my ear over the five-hundred mile line from New York. I waited it out. At last Gussie's need to talk got the better of her.

"I knew he'd killed a lot of men," she said. "And slept with a lot of women, but to kill a woman … Oscar got dealt manly good looks, irresistible to fans of the strongman. That was me at one time."

"Was there a kind of woman he might have resented?" I asked.

"He ever tell you the story of the deserter and the nurse?"

"It was in a newspaper interview I read."

"This kid was only lightly wounded, but terrified of being sent back to the trenches. He tried to injure himself further, which might have got him in trouble. But a nurse's pity made things a lot worse. Oscar despised compassionate women. He mentioned that more than once last weekend. Was Nora one of those?"

"Possibly," I said. "Sounds like a cockeyed reason to kill someone. Anything else seem to be on Oscar's mind?"

"He talked about wanting to do something original before he died, to contribute something new to the world. It bothered him that George Bellows had painted boxing matches before he did. He didn't care if what he did were never recognized. Knowing what he'd done would be enough for him."

I didn't say anything to that.

"Say, Paul, I really liked it when you and Oscar stood up to those baboons that wanted to throw me out of the speakeasy last Friday. Do you think there'll be a funeral in Toronto?"

"That'll be up to Peter Craig," I said.

"If there is, I might … Oh-oh, five minutes to curtain. Gotta go."

Later that afternoon I got confirmation of Oscar's originality in the form of a phone call from Professor Ramsay Keller, fish expert at the university. He'd identified tetrodotoxin in the vomit on Nora Britton's knapsack. It was the first time he'd ever heard of the poison being used as a murder weapon. I told him I'd sent four cookies presumably containing more of the same to Professor Dalton Linacre, who would doubtless be passing them on.

On hanging up the phone, I knocked on the door of Detective Inspector Sanderson's glass-walled office and was waved into his pipe-smoke filled asphyxiation chamber. He had been pestered all day by requests from newspapers and radio stations for details of the Britton murder, and hadn't been able to add anything to what they'd already read in the *Dispatch*. He scowled at me under his connecting black eyebrows as if it were all my fault. I reported on my conversations with Gussie and Professor Keller, hoping he'd be so grateful that he'd authorize a call to Aurora.

"What investigative purpose would that serve?"

"I'd like to brief Nora Britton's family."

Sanderson gave his lower lip a thoughtful pinch. "Leave it a day. Maybe they'll call first and spare us the cost."

And so to my surprise it turned out. I'd just got off the phone to Peter Craig at the Canadian Arena Company in Montreal, a long distance charge Sanderson could not refuse.

Peter Craig was saddened but not shocked that his brother had died a violent death. He had expected, though, it would have resulted from a brawl or possibly the attack of a jealous husband. He had trouble accepting that Oscar had started a gunfight with police — and more trouble yet with the idea that Oscar had poisoned a fellow artist. I heard from the architect none of the spite against Oscar that Gussie had prepared me for. He said it was true the two brothers hadn't spoken in years, but that the coldness was all on Oscar's side. Peter had been glad to read in the press that Oscar had made a major sale to the Whistler Gallery in New York. Work tied Peter Craig to Montreal for the foreseeable future, but after the post-mortem on Oscar he would send for his brother's remains and possessions. He particularly wanted an expert to inventory the art from Oscar's apartment and classroom studio at Central Technical School. Perhaps at a future moment, when grief for Oscar's victims was less raw, some sort of public exhibition could be arranged.

I was just wondering how that suggestion would sit with Nora's family when Effie Britton phoned. She was actually in Toronto, having taken a day off teaching to have a new brace fitted. She wanted to tell me that Herman, without needing to be asked, had offered to send Nora's ashes to Aurora so that her parents could give them Christian burial.

"I don't imagine he'll be attending," I said.

"No. I wouldn't mind, but it would be torture for him and everyone else."

I told her what we now knew about Nora's death. There was no longer any need to withhold Oscar's name. It didn't mean anything to her.

"How awful, though," she said, with a catch in her throat. "I thought that — although I live in a small town and don't go to parties with artists — well, I thought I understood Nora's world a little." Effie paused. "Nora took a fellow artist as a lover, and he killed her. Can you make sense of that?"

I couldn't, of course, but I did my best.

"He resented Nora for wanting to break with him and return to Herman, but resented her more for doing it considerately."

"That's perverse. In Nora's world, isn't taking lovers and changing lovers expected?"

"Oscar Craig wasn't just an artist, Effie, but a fighter — a belligerent long after most of us had given it up. And a self-appointed execution squad."

Effie took some time to mull that over.

"Just as well he wasn't taken alive," she said at last. "The trial would have rubbed nerves raw, and the strain wouldn't have ended with a guilty verdict. My parents disagree about the propriety of capital punishment."

Chapter 20

The person I was waiting to hear from was Ruth, and I had to wait until the detectives on night duty arrived and only Rudy Crate and I were left over from the day.

I asked the Englishman if he really had no home to go home to. He said he was sleeping on the chesterfield of friends of a cousin — at no expense so long as he was out of the flat by seven thirty each morning and didn't return till ten thirty at night. Not an ideal arrangement long term, he granted.

"Here's a thought, Paul," he said. "With all the notoriety, Craig's landlord may have trouble finding a new tenant for the murderer's flat. Do you think he'd let it to me at a discount?"

I was saved from answering by Ruth's entrance, in a slate grey business suit with a longer skirt than I'd ever seen her wear. The crime reporter had replaced the fashion page contributor. Parsons had gone home to an early supper; she installed herself at his desk and asked me for all the "now it can be told" stuff — information released or acquired since last night. She wrote as fast as I talked.

"Well and good, Paul, thanks," she said when I'd finished. "But what I really need is dope you didn't give other journalists. For example, in which ice cream parlour were Oscar and Nora seen canoodling?"

"Polar Treat, opposite Christ Church."

Ruth made a note. "I don't know if you heard," she said, "but I was just talking to the rector, and apparently they're going to hold a third competition for the mural design. Nothing against Nora, but some parishioners were disturbed by the depiction of modern weapons of war on the church wall. Swords would have been acceptable, but out of tune with the Great War uniforms. Rather than have an understudy step in to make modifications, they're going back to the beginning. Sir Joseph Deane hasn't decided yet if he's willing to involve himself."

In my mind's eye, I saw the waters closing over the winner of the second competition as they had over the first. The image made me all the keener to celebrate Ruth's triumphant rise. She had once asked me to escort her across the Don River to Pork Chops Lariviere's gambling club. Tonight I did it. We took Oscar's photo and found witnesses to his dust-up with Jack Wellington. No one else suspected Oscar, and for jurisdictional reasons the fight formed no part of my department's investigation. This would be Ruth's exclusive.

People sometimes won money at My Blue Heaven, money they actually carried out the door. Pork Chops must have figured that the spectacle of a winner from time to time gave the suckers hope. One lean-jawed bird, for example, a man of thirty in a shabby suit, was just getting up from the blackjack table with a fistful of bills, distributing ten-dollar tips to waiters and the hat check girl. He looked familiar, but more so once he'd crushed his fedora down over his forehead. I could suddenly see his clean-shaven mug with two-days stubble and his thin mouth with a toothpick hanging out of the corner.

I moved in and grabbed Lloyd Hanson by the upper right arm just as he was heading out the door to the parking lot where his Ford touring car waited.

"I guess you must be on your way downtown to get a lawyer for Iva and arrange some bail. Mind if I hitch a ride?"

While I held Lloyd to his conjugal responsibilities, Ruth took a taxi back to the city to write her story. She promised to see me Saturday.

Ruth's story — where was it? Next morning, Thursday, I went through the *Daily Dispatch* from end to end without finding a whisper of it. I turned the pages again, slowly. Among the editorials lurked a muddle-headed rant against the city's Jewish community. Jews were condemned both for being acquisitive and for fomenting Bolshevism. They were damned both for crowding into slums and for infiltrating genteel neighbourhoods. I wished Ruth could have found a better newspaper to make her mark in, but I didn't immediately connect the racism to Ruth's absence. I phoned the newspaper offices to speak to her. I was told she no longer worked for the *Daily Dispatch*. No further information was offered. I couldn't even find out whose idea the parting of the ways had been.

I tried to reach her at home. Before I paid a call on Jack Wellington, Ruth had told me she lived with her parents on Dunvegan Road. But Bell Telephone had no listing for Stone on that street, either within the Toronto city limits or further north where Dunvegan extended into the suburbs. I couldn't find the name in the *City Directory* either. I'd have to wait to hear from her.

While I was waiting, other journalists phoned. Inspector Sanderson tired of rehashing the details of the case and passed the public relations job to me. I no longer had any reason to hold anything back. Eric Hutchinson phoned as well. The Christ Church rector wanted to remind me that, although he'd been wrong about possible murderers, he'd been the first to question the accident theory of Nora Britton's death.

"I saw her on that scaffold," he said. "She was sure-footed as a ballerina. And as lovely."

I heard the wistful yearning in his voice. I could sympathize. He'd been lucky enough to know her, whereas I'd only been able to see Nora Britton through others' eyes — her own and those of her circle. But perhaps I was the lucky one. My remove was already starting to help me over my infatuation with the dead woman. I'd done what I could for her. Now it was time to think of Ruth, and I found that not hard at all.

I'd have welcomed any excuse to stay late at City Hall in case she phoned. No excuse presenting itself, I left promptly at the end of my shift and went to see Harry. I found him at home, jiggling his daughter June on the knee of his good leg. I asked if she'd been born in June. No, he said, July — but that was no name for a girl.

Although June and her mother were unbeatable company, boredom was starting to gnaw away at Harry's nerves. For his entertainment while housebound, a kindly neighbour had loaned him a radio. It was a revelation to Harry how many organ concerts were broadcast, and — in the absence of a church service or a movie to accompany it — how grindingly unrewarding organ music could be. He'd promised the family and Inspector Sanderson, an unexpected visitor the previous evening, to stick out the week at home. But come Monday he'd be back raising hell in the detective office. I was to consider myself warned.

"Well, Harry," I said, "you got the day off you told me you wanted."

"Yeah, in triplicate — more than enough."

I asked him quietly if he wanted to talk about Oscar. He said no — not now, at least. He'd known when he joined the force that one day he might have to shoot to kill. And known that someone might shoot him. Today all he was thinking about was getting back in the saddle. When the hospital had got the bullet out of his leg, the head sawbones asked Harry if he wanted to keep it. No, Harry had said; he wouldn't have room on his mantel with all the gold medals he planned to win at next year's Olympic Games in Amsterdam.

Next morning, Friday, was Acting Detective Ned Cruickshank's first back at his regular post in Station Number

One. He phoned me early, asking what was going on in our office at City Hall. I wondered if you could be homesick for a place that wasn't — but should have been — your home. I didn't know how many of my older colleagues would have to die off before Ned could be promoted to the rank of detective sergeant. All I knew was that, in terms of diligence, he was already worth any three of the men over sixty.

Ned asked me if I'd like to come for supper tomorrow, Saturday. His mother was making the meatloaf I always had three helpings of. I asked Ned to convey my regrets. I was still hoping I had a date. Ned was discreet, but if he'd asked me who she was I'd have said the doll with the explosive red hair and the legs to make a Ziegfeld girl rethink her career.

She phoned a long hour later, her voice unusually tentative.

"Paul?"

"Hello, beautiful. How are tricks?" Those were my words, but I felt far from that bouncy.

"I thought you might be wondering about me."

"And how! I couldn't find your name in the phone book or the directory."

"That's because you were looking for Stone, not Steinberg."

"Huh — oh. I didn't know." I didn't know because she hadn't told me. Should she have? Not unless she wanted me to look up her phone number — not unless it mattered. "Not that it matters," I said.

"I wish that were true."

"Did they fire you because they found out?"

"No, Paul. I quit because I saw that editorial before it was printed. You once suggested my career would benefit if I used a man's name. In fact, I'd already changed my name once. That hurt my father, but he loves and forgave. I was willing to work under a regime of tacit bigotry. But for anti-Semites not even to be able to recognize the people they hate — to show me, whom they take for one of them, their libels — it's just too stupid."

"What'll you do, Ruth? Do you think you might write for the *Examiner*? This morning they published a denunciation of the *Dispatch* editorial. They said such race hatred was grossly unfair, and what's more unrepresentative of Toronto."

"Maybe it is, maybe not. I'm trying to get my normally impulsive little noggin to do some mulling over before I jump into anything big." Her tone brightened. "I've got an exhibition picked out for us tomorrow."

Saturday it was lightly raining for the fourth day in a row. Normally that would have meant wet hair or a hat, but for the occasion I broke out my umbrella. Around one thirty I rode the Queen car downtown and walked north on Yonge. The exhibition — I forget whether it called itself "Portraits and Landscapes" or "Faces and Places" — was being held in the Arts and Letters Club on Elm Street. A three-storey building dating from late in the last century welcomed me in through an impressively arched centre entrance.

Ruth was waiting for me in the foyer and passing the time in conversation with an art critic from *Saturday Night* magazine. This gentleman, who sported a polka-dot bowtie and a white goatee, insisted on accompanying us around the show. On learning I was a detective, he waved a slender hand towards a painting of birch trees with blue water in the background, identified in the label as Canoe Lake.

"Perhaps Mr. Shenstone could solve the mystery of this artist's death. Tom Thomson was an expert woodsman and guide, as at home on the water as on land, and yet he drowned on this lake ten years ago. Was he murdered? We still don't know."

"Paul did solve the mystery of Nora Britton's death," Ruth put in.

"Ah, yes," said the critic, gesturing and leading the way. "*Sunny Lake*, just over here."

It seemed Sir Joseph had found his opportunity to exhibit the full-length nude self-portrait. It looked very well among the unpopulated scenes of mountains and icebergs hanging on the same wall. We stood a long moment in front of the canvas.

"Strange," said Ruth. "While I was writing about her I was thinking of her as a victim, but of course that's not at all how she saw herself. Do you think it occurred to her, Paul, that a man that changed women as often as he changed shirts would be jealous enough to kill her?"

"I don't think it was jealousy so much as vanity."

Hand on hip, Nora stared over our right shoulders at the next subject she planned to capture in paint. She appeared to have her mind on matters far above identifying who wished her ill — a subject of no more interest to our critic companion.

"Notice how there are no shadows in her art," he said. "However brilliant the day, you can never tell where the sun is."

"Any paintings in this exhibition by Oscar Craig?" I asked.

"Gracious no. He's not quite in this league. Maybe in a few years he will be. Oh, I'm afraid I'm going to have to excuse myself: I've just noticed Mr. Lismer is here."

Ruth and I exchanged a look.

"I don't think Cyril's quite caught up with the week's events," she said.

"Is it too soon for me to take you to tea?"

"Let's stay a bit longer."

We did, and I was glad of it. The last painting I found was a portrait of Sir Joseph Deane in his yellow cardigan, a roll of important-looking designs in his right hand, standing in front of the blank white wall of Christ Church Grange Park, the still empty and unscaffolded back wall of the chancel where the memorial mural was to be painted. Deane was not flattered by a low viewpoint, which would have made him seem taller than his five feet two or three inches. Rather he appeared dwarfed by the space to be decorated. And yet, without obsequiousness, the artist had made him look heroic. Was it the eyes? They seemed to burn with passion, ambition, love — in a way I'd seen when I'd met the man, but could never have put words to.

And it was all done with thick brushstrokes, which lost their effect when viewed from up close. The canvas was unsigned. The artist identified on the accompanying label was Herman Koch. It was the perfect note to leave on.

To my surprise, Ruth had a car, a smart Chevy coupe. My apartment was only a bed-sitter, but I'd recently acquired a bed that transformed into a sofa for polite entertaining. So I said she could drive me home and have tea at my place. She did. I was encouraged. She was back in short skirts, this skirt part of a very short blue dress with a dropped waist. That encouraged me more. After tea I gave her a kiss. Her slender arms went around my neck as she kissed me back. Then she took my face between her two hands while her amazing green eyes gave me a tender look.

"Paul," she said, "I'm not going to be a tease, and I assure you I'm not a prude. But I want to say something before we go any further. I think you're swell."

"Likewise."

"Were you going to want to see me again?"

"And again and again," I said, my hand resting on her stockinged thigh.

"Because that's not going to be possible."

"What?"

"I've met someone."

"Someone you love?"

"I want to see if I can."

"Why not see if you can love me?"

She dropped her hands and shrugged.

To me the road ahead looked open. I was willing to give us a chance: why wasn't she?

"I'm thirty-five," I said. "Do you think that's too old?"

"I'm just ten years younger. It's not the difference in our ages."

"Our religion?" I was incredulous.

"I'm not religious. Are you?"

"No."

"We're able to make up our own minds about religion, but not about race."

"You're not letting that poison in the *Dispatch* get to you, are you? That's just garbage, Ruth."

"It's not only me I have to think about. My family worries. Their friends in the community worry."

"Could I come home with you and speak to your parents?"

"It would only upset them and would change nothing."

I knew she was tenacious. My only pretext for hope was that she didn't love this other man yet.

"Who is it?"

"Will it help if I tell you?"

"Is he in love with you?"

"Starting to be, I think. It's Michael Leavitt, son of the ice cream parlour man."

"The medical student," I said. "Seems like a nice kid."

"He had to have higher marks to get admitted to the faculty of medicine than a Gentile would. Once he graduates, he won't be able to find a hospital placement. Except perhaps at Mount Sinai, and there's no surgery there yet."

"Ruth, I had nothing to do with any of that." Any more, I thought but didn't say, than Herman Koch had had to do with killing our boys in Flanders. "Are you thinking I should have done more to prevent it?"

"God no!" She pushed her hair back from her face and put extra emphasis into each word, as if afraid of being misunderstood. "I'm not trying to punish you, Paul. The reverse. I wanted a juicy crime story; you gave me one. It wasn't your fault I couldn't use it. You deserve nothing but good from me."

I wondered as I looked at her young face, so determinedly sweet, if this wasn't worse than punishment. Ruth wasn't going to date me ever again, but she was ready to reward my news tips with her trim little body.

I'd gone to bed with women when neither one of us intended we should stay together all our lives. But I'd never accepted sex as frank and futureless payment for a favour.

Ruth, impatient by nature, tired of waiting for me to say something. She dropped her voice, without the least trace of coquetry. "I'll take my stockings off, shall I?"

"I guess I'm the prude, Ruth. But don't worry. You did me a good turn by dragging me to that art exhibition. I'd say we're quits."

She took this well — better than perhaps I'd hoped. We talked about painting for a few more minutes, and I walked her to her car. We said goodbye forever with pecks on the cheek.

This is where the story ends, except perhaps for a mention of my visit on Sunday to Herman's studio in the old Central Prison chapel. I found the artist in good health and working on an autumn landscape, his brown corduroy suit spattered with yellow and orange paint. I gave him back Nora Britton's letter and the artistic supplies left on the scaffold when she had fallen; I told him I was sorry I'd persisted so long in suspecting him of her murder. He said not to mention it. He was grateful to the Toronto police for having put down that deranged poisoner. Then I confessed I had another reason for coming.

"Mr. Koch, I have a little money I set aside for entertaining girls. As there are none on my horizon just now, I was wondering if $150 would buy me one of your scenes of the Ontario north country."

Author's Note

Winner's Loss is a novel set in 1927. The reader may be curious as to how much is history and how much fiction.

Some names of actual people are used, but all characters with speaking parts are imaginary, as are the houses and apartments they inhabit. Imagined also are Christ Church Grange Park and Pork Chops Lariviere's gambling den My Blue Heaven (although in the 1920s similar clubs were located just outside Toronto to avoid the attention of the city police). Other locales — including the Coliseum, Central Technical School, and the Arts and Letters Club — are real. They existed at the time the novel is set and remain in place to this day. The historic Walker House Hotel, on the other hand, was demolished in 1976.

The newspapers *Daily Dispatch* and *Toronto Examiner* are fictitious. Nevertheless, the anti-Semitic editorial published in the former and the subsequent denunciation that appeared in the latter did have their historical parallels in the *Toronto Evening Telegram* (defunct) and the *Toronto Daily Star* (extant) respectively.

Another element of the made-up plot was inspired by historical events. The sculptor Emanuel Hahn was born in Germany in 1881, moved to Canada with his parents in 1888, and was naturalized in 1903. In 1925, he won a blindly-judged competition to design a war memorial for the city of Winnipeg. When his German birth was revealed, he was denied the contract and a second competition was organized, again with designs submitted anonymously. This time the winner was Hahn's Canadian-born wife, Elizabeth Wyn Wood, an accomplished sculptor in her own right. Disclosure of Wood's marriage to Hahn resulted in the rejection also of her winning design. Readers will recognize a rough parallel to the course of the mural competitions in the novel.

Finally, I have used two exact quotations from the Winnipeg controversy (as reported in the *Manitoba Free Press* of February 25, 1926). While by no means everyone shared his view, a representative of the city's Board of Trade had this to say about new Canadians such as Emanuel Hahn: "Naturalization of an individual does not make him a Canadian in the true sense of the word. He may be naturalized, but he does not come in on an equal footing in any sense." The same man went on to say that having Hahn build the monument would be "like asking the relatives of a murdered man to accept a memorial or tomb constructed by the cousin of the man who committed the murder." In *Winner's Loss*, the Christ Church rector attributes both these quotes to one of his parishioners.

Acknowledgements

The manuscript of *Winner's Loss* benefited from reviews by Carol Jackson, Lesley Mann, and Nelson Patterson. In researching the art department of Central Technical School, I was fortunate to have the assistance of CTS alumni Fernanda Pisani and Lorne Strachan as well as of art teacher Dustin Garnet and former Vice-Principal Robert Longworth. Thank you all.

I am grateful also to the fine people at Iguana Books. Greg Ioannou, Mary Ann Blair, and Jen Albert have been a pleasure to work with.

The painting on the cover, *"Gesture" and Elizabeth* by Gordon Davies, is reproduced by permission of the National Gallery. The subject of this portrait is Canadian sculptor Elizabeth Wyn Wood.